ALSO BY D. H. GUTZMAN

OTHER WORKS BY D.H. GUTZMAN

AGITATO

THE DARK SIDE OF LONDON

DEBAUCHED GENIUS

THE CLOWN OF GOD

TWO NOBLE KINSMEN

Coming up in the near future:

THE SINS OF CELLINI

THE SECRET LIFE OF NIKOLAI GOGOL

DRACULA AND MR. HYDE

THE MASTER SINGER is dedicated to Sandy Lewis, and also once again to my secret Goddess.

This book and all its contents are the property of D. H. Gutzman and was published in 2023

D.H. Gutzman may be reached at
dalegutzman @gmail.com

THE MASTER SINGER

A NOVEL OF OPERA, LOVE AND NAZIS

D. H. GUTZMAN

PART I

GATHERING STORM

"But what a strange new world of feeling
awoke in me when I heard you!"

Tannhäuser

"The worst is not so long as we can say
'This is the worst!'"

King Lear

CHAPTER 1

1923

    LINDERHOF, BAVARIA
    HUNDING'S HUT

IT WAS all because of that stupid equality thing! That hopelessly idiotic concept that all men are equal. Of course, it is not true, and had never been true. The rich had always wanted to be rich and powerful and, equally important, elite. And those who were not, struggled always, by any means possible, to attain some measure of those things. The rich and powerful fed them scraps, just enough to keep them hoping and doing the necessary work.

Whenever a revolution in any country overthrows the oppressors and declares everyone equal, some immediately become more equal than others. Some own automobiles, others still walk, or crawl. Some dictate rules from fancy, wood-paneled offices, while others follow the rules in hovels. Some think actual labor of any kind highly overrated, while others slave in factories or worse. And all of this does not even consider different levels of talent, skill or intelligence. And the art of any culture, often created by those at the bottom of the social ladder, only takes on value when it is recognized, prized and preserved by those at the top. The foolish notion that in a "free and equal" society, everyone has the opportunity to "pull themselves up by their own bootstraps," presupposes that everyone has boots and straps and two legs.

No, there never was true democracy of equality. But in times of peace, there might at least be harmony.

There was perfect harmony that fine summer day in 1923, in the green Graswang Valley and surrounding forests of Bavaria. The whisper of the wind through the trees, the bubble of the brooks, the songs of the sparrows, and even the crunch of the hiking boots on the gravel and stones of the hillside created a unified, harmonious whole. And the pure, clarion tone of the boy's singing voice blended in as well. It belonged.

The boy wearing the boots was sixteen-year-old Hans Becker. His virginal tenor voice, already at that age, quite astounding, was still admittedly undisciplined. Even Hans himself, who knew it was a very good voice, had no idea just how good. Mutte and Papa praised it, but good, loving parents do that. Nor did sixteen-year-old Hans have any notion that his voice would become both the best and worst thing about him. It would give and take. Well, perhaps not quite the worst thing about him, depending upon how one looked at things.

Hans had been much too young to serve in what some were now calling "the Great War," but he had been old enough to recoil in horror at what returned from it, and to experience the mourning for those that never returned. Boys only a few years his senior, often lame, blind, or limbless, no matter what they had been promised, now faced a future of inequality in the building of the "new Germany," their once beautiful bodies and minds decimated, their homes destroyed, and their family dinners replaced by bread lines.

Thus far, the upper classes and the comfortable "middle classes" had escaped the reality. At most, their grocery lists had to be amended, as their favorite mustard was no longer available. "What? No fresh strudel today?"

Hans came from a not inordinately wealthy, but certainly a comfortable, family. He was the perfect specimen of the ideal German youth, the hope for the Master Race of the future. A new, stronger Germany in every way. Not overly tall, but of good, sturdy body, he was blondhaired and blue eyed. That he got from his mother. His strong jaw and slightly turned up nose, gave him a confident look that would be the pride of any Aryan family. But there was one fly in the ointment.

You see, this blue-eyed, blond-haired, future heldentenor was a Jew!

His grandfather had emigrated to Germany from Ukraine during one of the many pogroms of the mid-1800's. He was an artisan, a cabinet and furniture maker, and he built a new life for himself and his family in Munich. There, he felt, his children and grandchildren would be safe. To be on the safe side, he changed his name and re-invented his history. "Better for business," he told his new Jewish friends. For many years, he still wore a star of David around his neck, and he observed Shabbat, but as time went on, even these fell by the wayside, as he and his family acclimated to life in Germany. After all, certain concessions must be made if one is to fit into a society where everyone is equal. Mustn't make your new friends and customers uncomfortable.

The sixteen-year-old hiker's father, Jacob, son of the immigrant Jew, had fit in so well that he married a beautiful, blond-haired, German girl named Gretchen, and the result of their union was the boy with the golden voice. There had been another boy, an older child, who died when a wagon tipped over on him in the street. It was no wonder that Gretchen had overly protected and pampered Hans, raising him in a rarified atmosphere of art and music. She had filled the boy's head with stories of German myths and the almost mythic life of mad King Ludwig II of Bavaria and his fairy-tale castles. And of course, the music of Richard Wagner, the very soul of the German people.

Hans had seen the wonders of the Bavarian Alps before. His parents had brought him there on summer holidays, but this was his first "big boy," solo adventure. Up here, in the cool, clean air of mad Ludwig's castles and the surrounding countryside, it seemed as if the war had never happened. This was reality. The war was illusion. This was the land where valleys had been created by the footprints of the gods. Wotan and his warrior hoard had stomped the very earth into existence, and smeared the sky with dazzling rainbows. They had given men and women sex and love and dreams of glory. And all of this was interpreted through the musical wonder that was Richard Wagner.

The whole, aching evolution of mankind, with all of its virtues and flaws, was defined for us by Richard Wagner.

Hans' father, Jacob, had resisted the "Wagnermania" at first, given the composer's vicious, anti-Semitic ideas and his writings about them, but even he had reluctantly admitted that the music itself was revolutionary and unlike anything ever composed before. It swept the listener up in feelings so intense they hurt. "The only Jews, according to Wagner, are bad Jews, money hungry, crippled, filthy creatures.

Nibelung." Still, grudgingly, he accepted his son's love of Wagner. He did insist however, over glasses of tea served Russian style, that the boy also appreciate Tchaikovsky, Mussorgsky, Prokofiev, and others, and the operas of Puccini, Verdi, and of course Mozart. Gretchen, who had been a cabaret singer and pianist before meeting Jacob, would play for hours, while Hans sang all the great pieces. So the boy was nourished on a diversity of art and music, but with Wagner always commanding a special place in his head and heart.

Jacob sent Hans to study with Mirah Hirschbein before his voice had even changed. She was a leading music teacher at the university in Munich, but she quickly passed the talented boy on to Professor Werner Glam, head of the department. Hans did have, it seemed, a remarkable voice. To Hans, who lived only for art, all of this seemed like a beautiful dream, the only reality he had ever really known.

The summer of his sixteenth year, Hans was on his own, visiting hamlets and towns in Bavaria, and making the almost sacred trek to the castles of King Ludwig II to relish their connection to the music of Richard Wagner. He had already toured Neuschwanstein castle and now he was approaching a special place in the forest above the palace of Linderhof. This place was quite remote and less visited by summer tourists.

The green of the forest closed over him, and the dappled light played across his youthful form. The sounds of nature here were particularly intense, and the calls of the birds reminded Hans of the bird who sings to Siegfried. How glorious! But the sounds also seemed encapsulated in a bubble of some kind, as if Hans and the whole area were in a grand snow globe. The boy's clear voice, singing snatches of "Tristan" and "Siegfried" grew less resonant until time and the air itself stood still.

His loose, white shirt grew filmy with sweat, and his tanned, muscular thighs bulged out of his hiking shorts, as he climbed uphill over the broken branches and twisted brush from a recent thunderstorm. Here, the gods played rough. At last he came upon the clearing with the hut. It was quite large, more like a lodge than a cabin, built around a gigantic ash tree. A perfect replica of the set design for Wagner's opera, "Die Walküre." Hans held his breath. It was as if he were actually enclosed in the opera itself. He was part of "Der Ring des Nibelungen." He was Siegfried! This hut and the nearby "Venus Grotto" were the main destinations of Hans' summertime journey.

He approached the hut, singing out "Ho yo, ho yo!" and looking for some kind of attendant, but the place seemed deserted. To his amazement, Hans found the great wooden door unlocked, so he went in. Of course, on a small desk near the door there rested a stack of brochures and a box for contributions, but other than that, everything seemed as it should be. Light from high windows and from between the wooden slats of the walls sliced across the otherwise dark space. Everything centered around the great ash tree: wooden benches, couches, even hammocks in the tree itself, and furs and drinking horns and musical instruments and a plethora of antlers. The ash tree itself was fifteen feet in circumference, with limbs that stretched out over the hut like tentacles winding around and into the ceiling beams themselves. The whole space smelled of ancient wood and smoke, and somehow of Wagner and Sigmund and Sieglinde and Hunding. It smelled of the old gods. Not the Christian or Jewish God, but the pagan gods who preceded them, the passionate, bestial gods.

And the link to this other world for Hans, of course, was the music. The music he now heard in his head. He set down his knapsack and reverently entered the sacred space, stepping through razor sharp slashes of light and dark. He raised one trembling hand and placed it on the trunk of the great ash tree. Somewhere up in the rafters a lone bird warbled. Hans stood very still so the floorboards would not creak. It was the most religious moment of the boy's young life.

"He would bring boys here to fuck them, you know!" The sound cut through the sacred silence like a saber.

"Huh? Oh!" Hans jumped, suddenly afraid he was trespassing.

The youthful baritone voice continued. "Or to be more accurate, he'd bring boys here to fuck him!"

Understandably, Hans was immensely confused. "Ah, do you work here? Are you the attendant?" he asked, his tenor voice atremble.

"No, like you, I am a worshipper." A six-foot tall, lean and hard, angular figure appeared from the shadows. About the same age as Hans, the boy was dressed in expensive trousers tucked into even more expensive riding boots. He wore a brown, tweed jacket with patches on the elbows, over a loose white shirt. In direct contrast to Hans, this boy had hair of black silk that tumbled over his high forehead and partly hid dark, flashing eyes that were both alluring and terrible at the same time. The nose was slim and regal, the lips full, almost lush, the chin strong and commanding. His manner spoke of money.

Hans' first reaction was, "He must be a prince." The figure moved with the languid ease and assurance of an athlete, or perhaps the school bully. Hans gulped but held his ground. "I come here to worship the world of Richard

Wagner that King Ludwig made possible," almost quoting the travel brochure. This tall boy with the dark hair intimidated him terribly.

"Ha!" the tall boy laughed. "I come here for the decadence."

"The decadence?" Such an odd word, implying both excessive sin and a life of leisure at the same time.

The shadow shifted. "The utter, complete decadence. You've seen Neuschwanstein, I presume. The fairy-tale castle. And Linderhof, the gaudy monstrosity in the valley. The world can no longer tolerate such narcissistic self-indulgence. A nation's wealth wasted on artifice and ornament, while its people starve."

"Art is never a waste. Art is what keeps us civilized," Hans snapped back. He was smaller than the dark-haired boy, but in his own way, just as feisty. "The new fairy-tale palaces are towering bank buildings, just as narcissistic and self-indulgent, but not as beautiful."

"Ha! So true!" The highly polished brown leather riding boots actually squeaked as they moved closer to Hans, and the blond teen finally saw the piercing black eyes. He felt like Faust meeting Mephistopheles. There was an almost cruel smile on the lush lips.

"You say art keeps us civilized. Look at Germany. Look at Europe. Are we civilized? Our civilized culture is a bombed out, gas-riddled, quivering corpse of a world. What good is your art, when people have no eyes to see, no ears to hear, no hands to touch?"

Hans was so young, so naïve, and now so dismayed. His shoulders slumped and he hung his head. He couldn't argue with the limbless limbo in which Germany found itself after the war.

"You are quite beautiful, you know. Quite perfect," the

tall boy said. "Almost good enough to eat." This understandably made Hans even more uncomfortable. The dark-haired boy moved closer. So close, in fact, Hans could smell the sweat from his body and the mint from his breath. "I come her to bask in the decadence. Imagine having a fucking, fairy-tale hut built just for sex!"

"That's a lie," Hans hissed, looking up into those devilish eyes. "It's an homage to Wagner's 'Ring Cycle,' an exact copy of the stage set from 'Die Walküre!'"

"That may be, my boy," the taller, sixteen-year old said to the shorter blond one, "but that didn't stop the crazy king from bringing lackeys, valets, grooms and guardsmen galore up here for sex orgies. It's kind of romantic, actually. They'd lie around here naked or wrapped in furs after copulating and sing patriotic, German songs. Beats a quick blow job in the school toilets." He held out a leather canteen to Hans. "Take, drink!" he intoned, followed by a little laugh.

For some reason, Hans obeyed. He put the canteen to his lips and drank. It was liquor. Some kind of strong liquor. He snorted and coughed and the dark boy chuckled. "I never touch it myself. It's a magic love potion I save to seduce strangers." He held out a hand. "My name is Rolf. Rolf Kainz."

"Hans Becker. You should have warned me," he said, handing back the leather canteen.

"What, and spoil the surprise attack? Expose my secret weapon?" Hans had never seen such white teeth as this boy had.

"Kainz? King Ludwig had an actor friend named Kainz!"

"A lover, you mean. A fuck boy. An infatuation! A distant relative, perhaps, and certain predilections have been handed down through the family!" Hans was silent. "Are you blushing, Hans? I can't see you clearly in this semi-darkness."

Hans slumped onto one of the fur-covered couches. "I know your type from school. All bluster and bombast, strutting around in your riding boots, reeking of money, attacking the world because, inside, you don't feel a part of it." If there was to be a fight, so be it. He would probably be beaten silly by this tall, lean brute, this upstart who had ruined the music in Hans' head.

But Rolf only laughed more openly than ever and flopped down next to Hans. "So, the little blond pony becomes a war horse! But you're correct. About me, I mean. What you said. I'm all show and no substance. I do and say things just to shock. Inside, I am the wasteful product of German gentry."

They both sat in silence, sulking perhaps. Then Rolf drank from the leather canteen.

"I thought you said you never drank from there... from the magic love potion."

Rolf burped. "I lied. I lie a lot. Whenever it suits me. But I didn't lie about coming here for the decadence. I find this place incredibly sexy."

"What an odd reaction."

"Why?" Rolf handed the canteen back to Hans.

"Because to me, it's almost a temple. Religious!" Hans drank and felt Rolf's eyes drilling into him.

"Oh, Hans, you're the kind of kid who never took part in circle-jerks at school, and who was more at home in the choir loft than on the tennis court."

"Exactly!" Hans snapped back, defensively. He'd had to defend his masculinity, or lack of it, before... often! "Besides, we didn't have tennis at my school."

"How about circle-jerks?" Hans clammed up. "Well, Hans, what did you do then?"

Almost petulantly. "I sang in the choir. I sang opera."

"Very well, go on, then, Pretty Boy, sing for me. Sing something for me." Rolf's arm was around Hans' shoulder. "I'll tell you if you're any good."

Hans tried to shrug off the arm. "How would you know if I am any good?" he muttered.

"I'll know. Go on. Sing for me."

Hans had always been a rather solitary boy. He found it easy to dig into his own imaginary world where he could be a mighty, German warrior. He loved to playact. He was forever rescuing damsels in distress, or forming eternal bonds of devotion with other handsome knights. Now, on the fur-covered couch with a stranger, Hans closed his eyes and transported himself. He launched with little hesitation into Tristan's third act near-death aria. Of all the roles, of all the moments to tackle spontaneously, this was ridiculously difficult. His voice, still much too immature for the piece which even trained opera singers shy away from, was already a remarkable instrument. It was filled with clarity and vocal brilliance. And his feeling and understanding of nuance in the aria was breathtaking. Anyone listening would weep!

Hans sang of love that is greater than life or death. Of love as the only thing that ultimately gives life purpose and meaning. He sang of things far too mature for a boy to understand. And when he finished, the last notes hung in the air of Hunding's Hut, to be replaced eventually by the lonely solo notes of the bird in the rafters.

For minutes, neither boy spoke. Rolf stared at the boy singer. Finally, "You're good. Gottuerdammt, but you are good! Remarkable! A fucking, boy wonder!"

He reached out and with one fine, slender, privileged hand and cupped Hans' cheek. Hans felt the fingers on his face. They burned. He jerked back and pulled away.

"Well, I can see that this is not going to go anyplace! Waste of very expensive liquor."

Hans suddenly grew livid. "Where exactly was 'this' supposed to go?"

"Up to the moon, not down into the mud. You sing of love. Of passion. But do you feel it? Have you ever lived it?"

"A higher love. A noble love. Not a blow job in the boys' toilet!" Hans rose and almost ran into the darkness of the hut.

Rolf felt suitably chastised. "Well, you can't blame me for trying," he mumbled. And then, to recover some self-esteem, "I do read books you know! I'm not just a walking Schwanz!"

"You'd never know it!" Hans snapped back.

"I'm not a dolt! I know Shakespeare and Schiller, and Goethe and the Greeks. And music, too. Beethoven, Bach, Brahms and all that!" He was actually yelling now, his voice bouncing off the walls. He turned and stomped toward the exit, but stopped just short of the large, wooden door. After a moment, he crossed back to Hans. "Look, here's my card. If you are ever in Berlin and want to hang out with a dolt, call me! I'll introduce you to decadence!" He leaned in and kissed Hans hard upon the mouth. Hans sank into the fullness of the other boy's lips. It was stupid and sinful and lush and lovely, and dirty and cleansing. "Goodbye, Hans Becker. I hope to see you in Berlin." And he was gone.

Hans stood absolutely still for a very long time, with only a bird for company. "What in the name of Gott was that?"

CHAPTER 2

1924
BERLIN
TIERGARTENSTRASSE

"You bite the hand that feeds you!" Professor Peter Kainz admonished his son, glaring over his wire-rimmed reading glasses.

Rolf withheld the scrappy answer on the tip of his tongue. He was far too good a son for that. He stood at semi-attention in his father's inner sanctum of an office, where even the professor's wife Helga entered only when invited. The office was cleaned with the precision given to a surgery, and God help anyone who replaced an item in the wrong position. The professor was not necessarily this fastidious about everything, but his office was the place where he wrote and read and contemplated humanity. To tamper with it was to tamper with his mind.

To the eyes of anyone else, the room was a disaster, cluttered with manuscripts and books, some stacked high, others scattered across tables, open and marked with slips of colored paper. A family photograph of the professor, his wife and their two children sat on another table along with an impressive pile of phonograph records minus their jackets. The view from the large bay window presented a wide street of other well-appointed mansions and a beautifully tended park. The facades of the homes lining Tiergartenstrasse announced the status of their dwellers. The Kainz's owned a second house in Switzerland, and the current political situation in Germany made the Alpine retreat look more and more attractive.

Still, it was almost impossible to imagine abandoning the Berlin house which had been in the family for generations. Modern Berlin had in some ways grown up around this house and the others in the old neighborhood. But the city had so changed since the war that it was almost unrecognizable. Not just the tall buildings with art deco facades, and the trolleys and trains and subways, and the autos which had transformed from burping, boxy, horseless carriages into sleek sedans with running boards, but the people themselves. The rhythm of the place had changed, the pace now almost frantic. People rushed to a new kind of jerky jazz pulse, and everyone seemed hyped-up on coffee and cocaine. The drivers of those sleek new autos forever leaned on their horns, relishing the cacophony of the modern age.

In the Kainz mansion, tradition was observed, and old rituals were strictly adhered to by family and staff. The cooks, the gardener, the upstairs and downstairs maids, the professor's private secretary, all followed a comfortable, unchanging pattern, a patter that at times drove Rolf crazy. The boy often felt trapped in a surreal prison when he entered his own house. He even modulated the volume and snap of his own speech. Ergo, he now stood silently before his father, who was speaking of "biting the hand that feeds one."

Rolf was appropriately garbed for the parental audience. He wore a respectable pair of grey flannel trousers, which still managed to nicely hug his attractive buttocks, a lilac-colored shirt and a grey, sleeveless, pull-over sweater, with large, brightly-colored block prints, which reminded one of the new art movement. The professor, who was not a curmudgeon, approved of stylish clothing. However, he did frown on tinted dress shirts. There was something unsettling about them.

Studying his own stiff white cuff, the professor noticed a tiny spot of ink on it and frowned. "As I said, you bite the hand that feeds you. You and your new friends feel free to attack the very establishment that gives you license to do so. You do realize, do you not, that it is only your very life of relative ease that allows you to be intellectually and socially radical. The average working man has no time to be either radical or decadent. Decadence is the privilege of leisure."

He always spoke as if giving a lecture, even when he ordered cheese or wine. He even spoke that way to his wife. It was, Rolf thought, as if the man had rehearsed when to peer over the rim of those damned glasses, and when, to make a point, to remove them completely. Now he folded the eyeglasses, gave a great sigh and looked with disappointed eyes at his son.

"What is it this time?" Rolf finally asked, not wanting this late morning meeting to last until sunset.

"This time, you and your rough trade friends were apprehended singing unseemly songs to elderly parishioners as they exited the Sunday church service."

Rolf put a hand to his mouth to stifle a laugh. "Unseemly

songs, Papa? They were positively filthy. We sang of cocks and cunts. But you, yourself, in many a lecture, have recognized the artistic merit of erotica." Rolf had a huge grin on his face, he couldn't help it. "You have brought up your son in a liberal manner."

His father slapped the desk hard, sending something Nietzschean flying. "But you don't have to shove it down other people's throats! You are blessed with the intelligence to see things from many perspectives, and I have encouraged that in you. But you don't have to continually blitz those with less fortunate minds and positions. You are cruelly irresponsible, Rolf!" He sensed ominously that his handsome seventeen-year-old son had the potential for great good or great evil.

The professor rose. He himself was a handsome man, with a great shock of black hair not unlike his son's, but peppered with bits of grey. He had a formal dignity about him which his son lacked, or perhaps had not yet acquired.

"We face difficult times," the lecture voice continued, "The war brought down courts and kaisers and imperial glory worldwide. Those of us in the upper classes have a responsibility to those less fortunate. I know you know I know that. But smashing store windows or mocking simple religious beliefs will get us nowhere. There are at least five different political movements in Germany today, all scrambling for power and advocating anarchy as a tool."

"Sometimes things need to be shaken, like a good cocktail, Papa. Tell me, are the cobweb-covered skeletons who attend Mamma's precious salons going to save us? Do the rich have any goals except to line their own pockets?"

The professor shrugged. "The steel mills are productive again. The economy is on the rise, thanks to efficient management and savvy business leaders."

Rolf nodded aggressively. "Yes, and the sweat of the workers who don't even make a living wage. There is a revolution of some kind coming, Papa, perhaps not like the Soviets, but just as powerful. But until then, at seventeen, I shall Lindy and Charleston my way through life." He performed a few quick, frantic dance steps, almost defiantly.

The professor put one well-manicured hand on his son's shoulder to calm him down. "Dance, do dance all you want, but destroy as little as possible. I forget sometimes that you are seventeen. Try not to embarrass us too much, eh, Son?"

There was a knock at the door, and the downstairs maid stuck her head in the room. "Telephone call, sir."

"I'll take it in here," the professor said, reaching for the candlestick phone on his desk.

"No, sir, it's for young Master Kainz."

Rolf took one step toward the phone on the desk and then stopped. "I'll take it in the hall." Before he left the room, he said, "I am sorry, Papa if I embarrass you."

"Hello? Hello, Rolf Kainz?" The voice sounded tinny and very distant.

"Ja, hello, who is this?"

"Hans Becker."

Rolf tapped the toe of his two-toned shoe impatiently against the leg of the hall table, on which, along with the telephone, stood a silver-framed photograph of the happy boy yachting somewhere with his parents and little sister. "Who? Who is this, please?"

"Hans Becker."

"Look, if this is about the bicycle, I told the police I never even touched the Gottuerdammt…"

"You gave me your card last summer." The voice became less sure of itself.

"I give my cards out like cigarettes!" The impatience grew.

"You told me to call you if I ever came to Berlin. Well, here I am come to study music, and I am calling. I'm awfully sorry to disturb you, it's just that I don't know anyone in the city and I thought..."

"Wait a moment!" Rolf's toe stopped worrying the table leg. "The blond, Bavarian, boy singer! I remember you."

The voice brightened. "You do? That's a relief. Believe me, Berlin is not like Munich, and I'm feeling rather lost at the moment, and a bit lonely, and I thought..."

"And you want Auntie Rolf to take you under her wing?" Rolf's natural exuberance and spark had returned.

"Well, my father, as a parting gift, gave me two tickets to the Komische Oper Berlin's new production of "The Pearls of Cleopatra."

They are for this evening. He said I might like to invite a nice young lady, only there is no nice young lady and..."

"And you'd like me to be your date!"

"Well, I'd like you to go with me, if you are free."

Rolf laughed. "I may be cheap, but I am never free. It will cost you a kiss."

"Well, uh, I'll meet you outside the theater then at seven. You'll be the only person I know in Berlin other than Frau Greenberg, my teacher."

"Well, if you'd rather, you could ask her instead of me."

"Guter Gott, no! She smells so of talcum powder and cologne; she'd clear the theater. Besides, I gather the operetta is quite naughty."

Rolf did a little dance step on the highly polished floor. "Well, all right then, blond Bavarian boy, I'll see you at seven, and don't forget the kiss!"

Helga Kainz had entered the hallway just as Rolf hung

up, hearing only part of his last sentence. She smiled. "You boys and your girlfriends nowadays, Lord how you talk. So differently from my day. This really is a new age."

Rolf kissed his mother on the cheek. "You have no idea, Mamma, you have no idea."

CHAPTER 3

1924
BERLIN
THE KOMISCHE OPER

Whereas Munich moved to the sound of violins and piano, Berlin pulsed with percussion. Jarring rhythms perpetually pounding one to a faster pace. "Push, push, pull, stomp!" Hans, who had always been sensitive to sound, was concussed by the cacophony. Some great internal force had been released by the war and it's sickening, pathetic finish, and that force spread across the city in great shock waves. Everything huffed, puffed, pounded and rattled in a panic to rebuild itself out of its ruins. The dust left behind hung in the air and clung to the clothing along with unwanted memories.

Hans wore his only best suit, he had a second pair of pants for daily use, and a short, fat, maroon and purple, flowered necktie. He carried his cloth cap in his hand. He was sure he would be stood-up and only half-troubled by that. He was used to being alone, which was different from being lonely.

The great lighted marquee overhead read, "The Pearls of Cleopatra. A new operetta by Oscar Straus." There was a special buzz in the air because Straus combined the traditional operetta formula with jarring, new, jazz-age rhythms and melodies. He also didn't stint on social satire. Egypt, in the new show, was a thinly disguised Berlin.

If Germany was a poor, destitute, lost nation after the war, it certainly didn't show on this night in Berlin. Top hats and canes, silk- lined capes and beaded evening gowns, feathered fans and damned near everyone in gloves, stepping gaily from the latest loudly honky vehicles. Hans didn't feel too much out of place, as there were people of the middle class in attendance as well, most clutching tickets for the cheaper seats in the balconies or the gods as they were known. Jacob Becker, who loved his son very much and fully supported his dreams of a musical career, had splurged on two of the very best seats in the stalls.

And then, like Venus rising from the foam, Rolf appeared. Heads turned, of course. To innocent young Hans, he was Lohengrin and Parsifal and even Don Giovanni, all rolled into one. Since that brief fateful meeting at Hunding's Hut, Rolf had lived and grown in Hans' imagination, and here he was in the flesh. Like a swan-knight, he sailed through the crowd, smiling and nodding to strangers left and right. And then he caught sight of Hans, and he lit up like a Christmas tree.

"I wasn't sure I'd remember what you looked like. Only that you were blond and terribly Nordic," he shouted, carelessly shoving dowagers and their dates aside. He was dressed in a pink shirt, no jacket, wide-legged trousers held up by purple suspenders, and an open, grey waistcoat adorned with a green carnation. And on the wild sea of black hair floated a straw boater.

"Ha! I'd forgotten how beautiful you are," Rolf literally sang, drawing the attention of those around them, as he threw himself into Hans' arms and planted a kiss upon his cheek. It would have been smack upon his mouth, but at the last second Hans averted his face. Still the lad from Munich felt an undeniable elation at the attentions from his new, old acquaintance. Rolf ceremoniously pinned a carnation to Hans' lapel.

"I hear this show is a stitch! They lampoon everything and everyone in this ridiculous country." His bright eyes travelled up and down Hans, taking in as much as he could of him amid the crowd. With almost frightening energy and enthusiasm, he hooked his arm into that of his new companion and almost dragged Hans into the crowded lobby, where he insisted they have a glass of champagne to celebrate their "re-uniting."

Hans couldn't take his eyes off Rolf, whose eyes took in everything and everyone around them. And others took them in as well. They were, after all, only seventeen, and their excitement was infectious.

"I'm so glad you agreed to meet me. I was so alone," Hans gushed, champagne tickling his nose.

"You, my dear, will never be alone again!" Whatever that meant. Hand on his back, Rolf steered them to their seats. You'd think he was the host, not the guest.

The composer and librettist did not disappoint. The operetta was a confection of satirical delight. The audience members howled with laughter, and none more so than the two seventeen-year-old boys. There was much camping it up and even a bit of cross-dressing amid the catchy melodies and sparkling dance routines.

More than a few times during the performance, Rolf pressed his leg against that of the stunning, innocent, blond boy, and at this or that particularly naughty bit of business, he placed his hand casually on Hans' thigh and squeezed. Rolf had to admit, he found himself somewhat mesmerized by this virginal, country lad, and Hans was overwhelmed by the entire event, including the saucy chivalry of his new companion. Hans found Rolf to be so strong, so sure of himself, that his very nature, not to mention his head turning beauty, seduced the boy from Munich. His body had remembered the thrill of Hunding's Hut accurately. It was not just fantasy. Surely Rolf must be the most popular boy in school. All the girls must adore him. And tonight, he was out with Hans Becker!

During the long interval, they sipped more champagne and chatted.

"I'm starting university, but I don't know if it will last," Rolf said, craning his neck to take in everything and everyone. "It all seems so useless and stuffy to me. Scheisse, I should have brought cocaine! Never mind, we'll get some later. Tell me about your life." His dark eyes settled into Hans.

To be honest, Hans was never quite sure if when he spoke Rolf was actually listening. His eyes drilled into him for a few moments and then flitted away toward this or that soldier, or young gentleman... seldom a female.

"Does everyone here know you?" Hans asked at one frustrating moment.

"Huh? No, not at all. I wish! I am just an admirer of beauty. The world is a garden with fragrant blossoms just waiting to be plucked." On the word "plucked" he flicked Hans' carnation with a finger. Rolf shook his head with delight. "You are so fucking naïve, Hans, so totally unaware of how many people here around you are eating you with their eyes. How you compliment me!"

Hans was naïve, but not stupid. "Am I a new friend, then, or just a cufflink?" he asked.

Rolf swiftly and smoothly placed a hand on Hans' cheek. "Oh, a friend. A very special friend, I hope. A David and Jonathan friend. And... and... and there's the bell for act two!"

There was a singular disturbance which disrupted an otherwise perfect performance. During one particularly scathing bit of satire aimed at the dozens of mostly disorganized revolutionary political parties, one of the beloved and versatile performers of her time, Jewish actress Fritzi Massary was in the midst of masterfully pulling off a bit of comic stage business, when a man seated on the opposite side of the auditorium, dressed in a brown, militia uniform, stood up and shouted at the stage.

"Oscar Straus is a dirty Jew! All of you filthy Juden should be washed off the stage with a big fire hose!"

The action on the stage halted. The audience was stunned and embarrassed. Then a well-dressed older gentleman seated near Rolf and Hans stood up. "And you and all of your brown-shirt homosexuals only have tiny, little hoses, so you can't do it!"

The audience erupted in applause and cheers, and by then, ushers had appeared to escort the SA militia man from the auditorium.

"Mein Gott, isn't this wonderful fun?" Rolf squeezed Hans' thigh. Hans had heard his father called derogatory names from time to time in Munich, but only rarely and always by idiotic louts. But to insult the great Oscar Straus and the members of his highly respected company was something quite troubling. So troubling to Hans, he hardly noticed Rolf's hand.

As they were leaving the theater, still exhilarated by the fine performance, Rolf hugged his new friend even closer. "And now my timid tenor, it is my turn. Now, I will take you someplace that will make tonight's naughty operetta seem like Sunday School!"

CHAPTER 4

1924
BERLIN
THE ELDORADO CLUB

THERE WERE a number of different Eldorado Clubs in Berlin during this period. The one on the corner of Kantstrabe 24, Charlottenberg, was owned by Ludwig Konsetschni and advertised itself as "the meeting point of the international sophisticated world." It was a factory-like warehouse building of several stories which might be totally overlooked were it not for the thirty-foot high marquee featuring an entertainer of dubious gender holding a feathered fan. The roaring twenties jazz and German cabaret music poured through the entrance onto the street from late night until early morning. Nobody much showed up before midnight or went home before sunrise, and morals were always left at the door.

In the 1920's, Berlin was advertised as "the gay center of the world," and indeed it was in both senses of the word.

The Eldorado drew authors, actors, artists of all kinds, celebrities and tourists, hetero and homosexual. Because of the licentious liberties of its drag performers and their floorshows, and because it allowed same-sex couple dancing in a country where, under paragraph 175 of the criminal code, sexual relations between men were banned, entry to the Eldorado Club was by membership only. Memberships could be purchased at the door.

Rolf simply flashed his "membership coin" at the doorman, and the two seventeen-year-old boys passed into something straight out of, depending on your viewpoint, Adam's Paradise or Dante's Hell! It was the music that first hit Hans Becker, of course. The nail-pounding drive of the jazz animated the muscle jerking bodies on the dance floor. All detail was lost in a lavender haze of shadowy silhouettes.

Bored, fat men sipping beer, perched on platforms near the high ceiling of the room, swung the glare of large, carbon-arc spotlights across the floor, catching this or that customer in a moment of madness. On a brightly lit but smallish stage at the far end of the room, a middle-aged man, heavily painted to look younger, danced and sang into a microphone that made his voice sound like tin, the latest American sensation, a tune called, "It Had to Be You," accompanied by a five-piece band.

Floating through this Bosch-like world of cigarette, cigar and something much more exotic smoke, were creatures unlike anything Hans had ever seen before. Glorious, six-foot tall feathered angels of neither and every sex. Some resembled but were not women, with sparkling eye shadow and earrings heavy enough to stretch the lobe. Others had beards and moustaches but were otherwise totally feminine. And there were women, Hans thought, totally got up like men in top hat and tails, puffing on thick, dangerous-smelling cigarettes.

Of the couples on the dance floor, in the center of rings of tables bearing small lamps with red shades, few were of opposite genders. Here, women danced with women and men danced with men, often using the occasion for rather heavy petting. The dancing alternated between slow and sensual and spasmodically frenetic.

A statuesque drag queen called "the Countess" floated across the room and greeted Rolf like an old friend with a lingering kiss during which her lips never quite touched his, so as not to smear her fire-red mouth, and then repeated the gesture with Hans, inquiring where Rolf had picked up such delicious young meat.

"I found him selling his ass in the street," Rolf responded gaily, giving Hans a hug.

"Oh, no, no, no!" the Countess replied. "This one is a treasure, an Apollonian Ice God!" She ushered them through the room, swaying to the music and slightly drunk with drink, toward a long table at which were gathered a passel of bright, young, gay things. They greeted Rolf and his companion with cheers and eyed them both shamelessly. A cute cocky, kid of twenty in green spoke up. "Where do you find them, Rolf, and whatever draws them to you? You are such a totally narcissistic, nasty boy." The kid took Hans' hand and pumped it warmly. "Welcome, I didn't mean to refer to you as an object."

"It's the tremendous size of Rolf's schwanz, don't you know," offered another, and Hans blushed in spite of himself.

"Well, we all know that, because we've all had it!" from still another.

"I guess you get around, huh?" Hans asked Rolf trying to get his footing amid all of this good-natured joshing.

"A bit, ja!" Rolf laughed. "Don't mind these animals, they are just putting you on."

"Welcome to the 'we've all had Rolf' table!" Mugs were raised.

"Well, in that case, I guess I don't belong here," Hans replied, but they dragged him down onto the bench.

"I've never had Rolf, either. In fact, I'm not even one of the boys," stated a round-faced, bespectacled, young man with thinning hair.

"Well I have definitely not 'had him,'" Hans stated, trying to fit in with the atmosphere.

"Yet!" Rolf announced, seating himself in a chair at the head of the table. There was a gentle, but still naughty smile on his face.

"Yet!" Hans acquiesced, and everyone cheered again.

The boy in green stood up and lifted his mug. "A toast, gentlemen. I believe we may be in the presence of a virgin."

Rolf leaned in to whisper to Hans, making sure his lips grazed the others' ear, "Don't let them rile you. This is all in good fun." The others went back to their various conversations. Rolf stood Hans up and eased the boy out of his suit jacket, hanging it on a wooden peg. Then, sitting again on the bow-backed chair, he drew Hans onto his lap. "Sorry, Hans, but there is just nowhere to sit." Between songs, the room rang with chatter. Laughter and chatter. Holding Hans on his lap like a ventriloquist's dummy, Rolf raised one hand and ordered two beers. Hans became intoxicated by the feel of Rolf's warm breath on the back of his neck and the rising arousal in the lap on which he perched.

"This will soon become quite unbearable for both of us,

you know," Hans remarked, "and apparently, what your friends say about size is first-hand knowledge."

"You're right, it is becoming painful," Rolf admitted and he plunked Hans back down onto the bench beside the round-faced, bespectacled Helmut. Fresh pitchers of beer and hot pretzels arrived. Suddenly, Rolf took Hans by the hand and raising it, kissed the boy's fingertips.

"I'm sorry. I'm sorry for all this teasing." He whispered, great warmth coming from his eyes. Hans had never had another boy treat him like this. He gulped down half a mug of beer. "You don't need to know the serpent-tongued divas across from you, Hans, they are better forgotten, but the gentleman to your left is worth knowing."

"And being straight, I am, ergo, safe," Helmut said with a pursed- lipped smile that made him look cherubic. "I submit myself to these animals as a form of self-flagellation. And I use this den of iniquity to make social, not sexual, connections."

On stage, a real girl, well she looked like a real girl, with cocoa- colored skin was doing strange contortions with her limbs to the beat of jungle music. Her considerable efforts went mostly ignored.

Rolf introduced Hans formally to the man to his left. "This is Helmut Schreiber, a talented magician who..."

"NO! No, no, no!" the round face interrupted, holding up a hand in protest. "I am no longer Helmut Schreiber, measly student of film production. I am, now and forever, Germany's master magician, 'The Great Kalanag.'" Suddenly, from seemingly bare hands, a plethora of playing cards tumbled down onto the table. Hans giggled with delight.

"Kalanag here has just been accepted into the elite

Magic Circle," someone from the other side of the table offered.

Helmut smiled slyly. "Within two years, I shall become the head of the Magic Circle." He patted Hans on the shoulder in a friendly manner. Hans found himself quite charmed by the ambitious magician. Charm would remain Kalanag's gift and his secret weapon in the difficult years to come.

"Show Hans something," Rolf urged. Kalanag shook his head shyly, but scooped up the spilled deck of cards from the table. He now had the full attention of the group as he flipped through the deck.

"Tell me to stop at any time," he said to Hans.

"Stop," commanded an eager Hans, almost at once.

"Take the next card and look at it. Do not show it to me! Good. Now place the card back in the deck."

"Now, he'll find your card in the deck," said the boy in green.

Kalanag shook his head. "Ach, no, that would be a child's trick. Hans' tell us please, what was your card?"

"The ten of hearts."

"Good. Very good. But I cannot find your card in the deck, because you see, your card is no longer in the deck!" He fanned out the cards on the table to reveal that the ten of hearts and only the ten of hearts was absent. "The ten of hearts has flown elsewhere. Perhaps to your heart!"

Hans and Rolf looked at each other and grinned.

"Ja, ja, I am serious," the magician continued. "The ten of hearts has already flown to your heart. Why not check your shirt pocket?"

Hans gasped as he found the missing card in his breast pocket. Everyone at the table cheered and applauded. Helmut Schreiber, now Kalanag, stood up and took a slight bow. A strand of his thinning hair tumbled over his brow, and he self-consciously brushed it away. He sat and took a sip of beer.

Just then, with a crashing drum roll, all attention was directed toward the stage. A tremendous ovation greeted a slender, blond, young man of about nineteen who appeared totally naked except for a top hat on his head and a black mesh jock strap over his genitals.

Rolf leaned in and quickly kissed Hans on the cheek. "You're going to want to watch this act. It has its own kind of magic!"

In fact, from the silence that fell over the club, everyone wanted to watch this act. The boy's pale, slender, totally hairless body lacked muscular definition, making him look even younger than he was. He tipped his top hat and began to sing:

"I'VE GOT A SPECIAL PROBLEM, AS ALL OF YOU CAN SEE.

IT ISN'T ONE OF MODESTY, BUT OF MILLINERY!"

He waved the hat around as if passing it for money.

"I WENT TO BE A MODEL FOR AN ARTIST OF RENOWN.

HE MET ME AT THE DOOR IN NOTHING BUT A DRESSING GOWN.

HE SAID, 'I'LL PAINT YOU IN THE NUDE.' HE STRIPPED AND THAT

WAS THAT.

HE SAID 'NOW YOU' AND I OBLIGED, BUT WOULDN'T REMOVE

MY HAT!"

While he sang this verse, he held his hat discreetly over his groin and slipped out of the jock strap. Next, waving the jock strap gingerly in the air, and keeping his genitals hidden behind the hat, he led the audience in the chorus of the song, which they all seemed to know.

"TAKE OFF YOUR HAT, TAKE OFF YOUR HAT,
IT'S AWFULLY RUDE WHEN IN THE NUDE TO KEEP IT ON LIKE THAT.
YOU'VE HUNG YOUR TROUSERS ON A PEG
AND UNDONE YOUR CRAVAT...
NOW COME ON, PANSY, SHAKE A LEG,
AND DOFF THE GODDAMNED HAT!"

The singer obligingly shook first one leg and then the other, obviously jiggling his bits behind the hat. At the end of the chorus, the young man tossed the jockstrap into the audience where a group of middle-aged militia in brown uniforms fought over it. For the second verse, the singer turned his back, revealing his naked ass, and looked over his shoulder.

"I WENT TO JOIN A GANG OF HEARTY FELLOWS FOR A SWIM,
THEY STOOD THERE BARE-ARSED ON THE BANKS AND ONE
BY ONE DOVE IN.
I RAISED MY ARMS AND ARCHED MY BACK AND SWAN DOVE
WITH A SPLAT!
BUT WHEN I ROSE UP FROM THE FOAM, I STILL HAD ON MY HAT!"

The audience once more took over for the chorus, while the singer broke into a kind of goose-step dance, holding the hat over his crotch.

The third verse was the show stopper! The boy singer faced front, and then removed his hands from the top hat over his crotch. The chapeau remarkably stayed in place, held there, supposedly by the boy's erection. The crowd went wild!

"How does he do that do you think?" Rolf asked.

"You should have asked him when you had him," one of the guys at the table replied. Even Hans pursed his lips and studied the magic of the naked boy with the twitching top hat on his genitals.

"I WENT TO A GYMNASIUM TO GET SOME EXERCISE.

I HUNG AROUND THE SAUNA WITH A LOT OF BEEFY GUYS.

A VERY HEALTHY NORDIC TYPE SAID, 'HERE'S SOME TIT FOR TAT!'

I GAVE HIM ALL THE TIT I COULD, BUT TAT STAYED 'NEATH MY HAT!"

He turned his back again, but this time bent over and spread his legs, revealing the rear of his scrotum. He waved the hat around like a tambourine, and the audience clapped in time and sang:

"TAKE OFF YOUR HAT, TAKE OFF YOUR HAT!

IT'S AWFULLY RUDE WHEN IN THE NUDE TO KEEP IT ON LIKE THAT!"

And then the singer, facing the audience, crotch covered, very demurely sang:

"WHAT'S THAT YOU SEE THERE IN THE STEAM

SO PROUD AND TALL AND FAT?

IT'S NOT THE THING YOU THINK IT IS...

IT'S JUST MY GODDAMNED HAT!"

The audience pounded the tables in approval, but there was still the coda to come. The band slowed down the tempo, as the boy gingerly hopped from the stage, and in only the traveling spotlight, sat on the lap of a well-dressed elderly man in the audience. The boy teased the gentleman's thinning, grey hair.

The Master Singer

"BUT IF YOU BUY ME DRINKS SOME NIGHT
AND COME UP TO MY FLAT
AND IF YOU HAVE DEUTSCH MARKS ENOUGH,
I MAY REMOVE MY HAT!"

Seated on the man's lap, naked legs crossed, in a final gesture, he raised the hat into the air. Almost the entire audience stood up to see what they could see, but the spotlight went out, leaving them in the dark. Oh, well, there was always tomorrow night!

When the lights returned, the young man had wrapped a white tablecloth around his waist, and was bowing and holding out the hat for tips, which flowed like the Rhine.

"And when you entertained him, Rolf, did you give him a tip?" Karl, one of the guys at the table asked.

"He gave him more than a tip!" another of the boys jested.

Rolf looked at Hans looking at him. "Well, I have been coming here for an awfully long time," he said in weak defense, shoving a bit of pretzel into his new friend's gaping mouth.

"Look who else is here," Kalanag remarked when things had settled down a bit and the dance band had taken over. A big, beefy man in a brown uniform had just dropped some money into the boy singer's hat and then roughly kissed him on the mouth, holding him by his blond hair. "Herr Ernst Röhm himself, the master protester of Munich!"

"I thought he was still in jail for that Munich Beer Hall Putsch with his crazy buddy Adolf Hitler?"

Kalanag laughed. "Ja, both he and nutsy Adolf were convicted of treason, but Ernsty pulled some strings and got probation, while Hitler got four years. Of course, he only had to serve nine months, and I heard he spent his time writing a book."

"Some say Röhm and Hitler are boyfriends," Karl said.

"You'd better hide under the table, Rolf. If the big brown bear of the SA catches you, he'll eat you!" said the boy in green.

"He already has," Rolf snapped back, but starting to get embarrassed in front of Hans.

Hans had been holding Rolf's hand, but now he pulled it away. "Him too?" he asked, staring with repulsion at the huge boar of an SA officer.

"For God's sake, Hans, you sound like my father. It was one night in the club toilet. He promised me a brilliant future in politics, if I let him suck me."

"Don't be hard on Rolf, Hans. He can't help it if he is gorgeous and everyone wants him," Karl said.

Rolf shrugged so innocently, even Hans had to laugh. "And who am I to refuse? But I would never have a man like Röhm for a boyfriend. He looks too much like a Christmas pig."

Everyone except Kalanag laughed riotously again. The magician seemed to possess a crystal ball. "They're ones to watch, Ernst Röhm and his artist friend, little Adolf. They just might indeed be stars we should be hitching our wagons to."

The evening wore on. Someone produced a cocaine-and-something blend and Rolf insisted on rubbing some of it on Hans' upper and lower gums. Hans, who had never experience an evening like this, was far more aware of his new friend's finger in his mouth than of the narcotic.

Rolf proved to be the most potent drug. Every time the dark-haired boy touched him, Hans felt a strange heat shoot through his body, a heat he had only before felt when listening to "Tristan and Isolde," odd as that may be. Was this that magical feeling other boys described when being touched by a pretty girl? Was that drink from the leather canteen in Hunding's Hut truly a love potion out of "Tristan and Isolde?" But how could Hans love Rolf? He wasn't sure he even liked him. He was far too showy and full of himself. And Hans didn't know anything about him. No, the feeling was certainly not something akin to love. It was the drink and the drugs, or perhaps Hans was coming down with the flu!

The room spun gently and delightfully, and Rolf leaned in and with his hot breath whispered to Hans, "Take off your hat... take off your hat." They snuggled closer and closer, and Rolf led him to the dance floor where they danced the Charleston, and then they stood before the bandstand and immensely enjoyed a black singer from America. And when he found himself slow dancing with Rolf, with the young man's hand on his ass and his mouth buried in his neck, Hans felt the way he had never felt with anyone before, and was sure it must be the flu.

Sometime in the early hours of the morning, as daylight crept down from the end of the wide boulevard giving everything a ghostly glow, the two boys stumbled out of the Eldorado Club, Rolf's arm draped around Hans' neck. It must have rained, for the pavement had a certain eerie glow to it, or perhaps it was just the way things looked when you were in that wonderful, youthful, wasted condition. With every few steps they took, Rolf would order, "Halt!" Hans would obey, and the two boys would sink into a long, rapturous kiss. Progress was slow, and the kisses many.

After about two dozen of these progress-impeding lip locks, Hans put his hands on Rolf's chest. "Wait a minute. Where are we going?"

"To your place of course." Rolf kissed and kissed again.

"But it's late. No, it's early, and I have to get some sleep. I feel like Scheisse!"

Rolf smiled dreamily and sniffed Hans' neck. "I'll tuck you in, and then climb in after you."

Hans shook his head vigorously and almost toppled over. "No, no, no, no, you will not! I will not be another one of your one-night conquests!" He waved a drunken finger at the other boy.

Rolf frowned. "Why not? I like you."

Hans pouted, a flash of anger in his eyes. "I don't want to end up as one of the guys at your table, or as the butt of some future jokes!" He was fairly certain he knew what he was saying.

Rolf's hand closed gently around the back of Hans' neck. "You're not. You're special, and I have a hell of a painful hard-on for you."

Hans pushed Rolf away, and they both staggered and almost fell over. "You are too drunk to have a hard-on, and every boy you want is special!" He was proud of himself for standing up to this endearing lout. Then why were there tears in his eyes?

Rolf twisted up his handsome face in thought. His hair tumbled over his eyes. "You're totally wrong, I can have a hard-on when I am drunk, and I can prove it. And not every boy I want is special. Most are not."

They stood there in a kind of staggering stand-off. Then Rolf's shoulders slumped, and he began to look kind of forlorn and pathetic.

Rather like a rejected puppy. Hans felt a bit guilty.

"Look, Rolf, this is all new to me. I feel like I'm in some fantastical, romantic masque or something. Yes, I'm still a virgin, and until tonight I honestly never considered sex with a boy. Well, maybe I did, but I didn't really realize it. I know it's stupid and old fashioned, but I want to save some things for somebody I love!" God, did he sound like a dolt!

"Gott, do you sound like a dolt!" Rolf stood there swaying and considering. He nodded as if he understood completely. He nodded harder, his black forelock dancing. "How about a quick blowjob in the alley?"

Hans was so angry, he growled. "What the fuck is wrong with you, Rolf Kainz? I really, really like you, but you are a selfish, thoughtless animal!"

Rolf blinked several times. "Is that a no, then?"

Hans balled his fists. "Go find somebody else to blow you!" Both boys stood there in defiant silence as a light rain started.

"What a waste!" Rolf hissed, lashing out at himself as much as at Hans.

"Thank you, very much," Hans replied, his heart bursting.

It began to pour. Rolf thrust his hands into his trouser pockets, spun around and began to stagger off, leaving a trembling Hans to stand there feeling more alone than he ever had in his life. "Alone, but not lonely," he lectured himself. "Well, maybe a little lonely, too!"

The dark-haired boy got halfway down the block before he stopped, silhouetted by the morning glow and drenched with rain. He turned, tilted his head, squinted his eyes, and slowly staggered back.

Hans stood statue still, rain mixing with the tears on his face. Rolf stepped right up to him, only inches away.

"Well, then, would it be all right if I saw you tomorrow, Hans?"

"Yes," Hans answered sotto voce.

"Do you want to call me in the morning?"

"It is morning." A beat.

"Do you want to call me in the afternoon?" Rolf asked.

"Yes, I'd like that."

"I'm sorry for what I said. It wasn't a waste. It was the best. Now, you had better go. I need to stay in the rain and punish myself some more."

They hung there in the downpour, not together but almost.

"May I kiss you once more?" Rolf asked.

"Yes." They kissed.

"If you are not a homosexual, Hans, I would seriously consider considering it." He turned and disappeared into the now cascading rain, a surprising spring to his stagger.

For the second time in their two meetings, Hans asked himself, "What in the name of Gott was that?"

CHAPTER 5

1924
>BERLIN
>THE INSTITUTE OF SEX

AND SO, it began! They didn't have sex. They dined together, went to films at the big, Berlin, movie palaces, attended plays, concerts and lectures, danced until dawn, and immersed themselves in each other.

They sat together in cafes, or in Hans' one-and-a-half room apartment, and read aloud to each other, classical novels and comic books, poetry and pornography. Hans sang for Rolf, and they kissed, possibly more than any young male couple had ever kissed. They held and hugged and touched each other through their clothing and fell in love, but they didn't, as yet, have sex.

For the first time in his wild, young life, Rolf curbed his carousing, and for the first time in his life, he felt something deep in an intimate relationship. Perhaps both boys were growing up. Hans became more and more certain that Rolf was the "right one," but he still clung to his Wagnerian dream of perfect love decreed by destiny. But is such a thing real? And to be realistic, is there ever a future for anyone's first, foolish love? Hans wanted, he needed, to do forbidden things, sexual things, and felt he would die if he held back any longer. Rolf, of course was constantly like a mad dog on a leash, and at least four times a day, Hans had to fight the poor boy off. Hans explained to Rolf, "I promised my parents I would be good."

"But what is good? Isn't having sex with the one you love, good?"

"It's the conflict, Rolf between inclination and obligation. Life is filled with that." But they both knew It was time for things to progress.

And one evening, about six weeks since their chaste affair had begun, they found themselves once again at the Eldorado Club. There, they sat at a table for two, the future of Germany, one blond, one dark, the Apollonian and the Dionysian. It was too early in the evening for the den of devils to be in full swing, but still, there was a sizable crowd, some of whom stopped off at their table to lament Rolf's recent absence. Hans became excited when the band launched into "The Drinking Song" from Romberg's new operetta "The Student Prince."

Everyone knew it already and joined in singing, Hans as well. He sang so confidently and with so much enthusiasm that the voices around him quieted, and soon, he was singing solo. His remarkable tenor voice rang out. Someone handed him a beer mug, and he raised it, his eyes lost in the magic of the world of music. They cheered him when the song finished, and the Countess asked him if he might some evening sing something special for the club.

"Oh, I couldn't," Hans demurred.

"Of course, he will," said Rolf. "He's going to be a great opera singer. Countess, this is my boyfriend, Hans Becker." It was strange how pleasant it was for Hans to hear that spoken out loud.

"You were here with him before," the Countess said in silky tones, "and I hope you bring him back to sing for us." But she could not linger, for she had special business on this night. Taking the hand of a swooning, young customer, she allowed herself to be helped up onto the stage, where her dress of silver sequins blinded everyone. To the sound of a thunderous drum roll, she approached the big, round microphone.

"Meine Damen and Herren, your attention, please. Tonight, a bit of class for our cheesy cabaret. A special guest, whose friendship goes all the way back to 1902, the days of the salon on Friedrichstrasse. I was just a child then, of course. He is a world-famous doctor who, every day in the courtroom as well as the medical clinic, fights for our equality. The champion of same-sex love and the fight to repeal the hateful Bill 175. The creator and curator of the Scientific-Humanitarian Committee, Clinic, Library and Museum. A doctor highly respected around the world and endorsed by Kraft-Ebbing, Thomas Mann, Sigmund Freud, Frank Wedekind, Herman Hesse... and the boys." There were cheers at the mention of these names. "And a darling, affectionately known in our community as 'Auntie Magnesia,' take off your hats for Dr. Magnus Hirschfeld."

The round, meek-looking gentleman, who received a standing ovation, looked more like a burgomaster than a reformer. He wore rimless glasses, had a bushy, unkempt moustache, a cherry nose, apple- dumpling cheeks, and a small prune of a mouth. His eyes sparkled merrily, and he had a kind of Father Christmas appeal about him. Rumors were that he was once very slender and handsome, but when a lover left him, he consoled himself with bon bons. He coughed into the microphone, dabbed at his forehead with a handkerchief, and when he spoke, his voice was soft, smooth and even.

"Thank you, Vielen Danke, Tausend Danke! First of all, I have seen the lovely show here, so for my sake, keep your hats on, please!"

Hans, who for so much of his life had been a loner, felt part of the "in crowd" at last. It was like he'd found a new family. He impulsively leaned over and kissed Rolf on the cheek.

"Did I do something good?" Rolf asked, raising one black slash of an eyebrow.

"You are something good," Hans replied, and kissed him again, this time on the mouth.

On stage, the sexologist continued. "Tonight, I want to ask for your help. Back in 1903... mein Gott, I am getting old... back in 1903, we developed the world's first same-sex questionnaire in an attempt to document the activities of what I then called 'The Third Sex.' The astounding results demonstrated that there were far more of us than we thought. Far more, my friends. And it is not you or I who are unnatural, it is the law!" On this he got a rousing cheer and much applause.

"It is not you or I or those like us who suffer disorders, but those who, because of their own prejudices and fears, waste life's precious time in hate!" He cleared his throat and someone handed him a glass of water.

"Our petition before the Reichstag to repeal Bill 175, criminalizing homosexuality, failed. We are still, technically, in the eyes of the law and many people, criminals. But the fight goes on. Our institute, the first in the world to offer help, not only to homosexuals, but in matters of marriage counseling, abortion, sexual abuse, anxiety, parental rejection, women's rights and what I would call 'unusual sexual proclivities,' needs your input to build a thorough data base for research." He held up a paper. "The answers on these questionnaires will expand our knowledge and increase the help we are able to give. All information will, of course, be kept confidential. Please take up a form and fill it out. And, as always, I am at your service night and day." The small, round man fairly glowed.

"How about tonight, Auntie Magnesia?" someone affectionately shouted.

Hirschfeld blushed. "I am afraid tonight my dance card is filled. But I make you a toast." The Countess handed him a snifter of brandy. "It is time we stopped bearing the guilt for our situation. To the day when our variety of love is accepted as a normal part of human sexuality. Prosit!" Everyone, including Rolf and Hans, who had tears in his eyes, cheered, raised their glasses and drank, and the band struck up "Yes, We Have No Bananas."

"May we go visit the museum?" Hans asked Rolf, squeezing his hand.

"May we? Mais, oui! Tomorrow if you like. It just might resolve some of our issues."

Hans looked blank. "What issues?"

"Well, my raging, unsatisfied dick for one!"

The next day, hand in hand, the two boys climbed the steps of the imposing and intimidating building that was the "Institute for Sexual Science." They had had stood across the street in Tiergarten, not hand-in-hand, for a long time. This was Berlin, the most liberal and progressive city in the modern world, and the boys were seventeen.

"Do we really want to do this?" Hans asked, having second and third thoughts.

"Do what? We are going to see a museum. Where's the harm? Besides, we might learn something about ourselves."

"About my sexual fear, you mean," Hans said.

However, as they stood there, they saw several male couples, arm in arm, or hand in hand, enter or leave the building, as well as women couples and solo males and females. Rolf, with his usual aggressive nature, grabbed Hans by the hand and dragged him across the street.

There were more women than men, seated or standing in the entrance hall, which resembled a train station, with a grand curved staircase at one end. There were benches and chairs lining the walls for "clients" and more in isolated alcoves, for those who wished anonymity. Most everyone looked a bit nervous. A surprisingly large staff, some with clipboards, approached those waiting and ushered some of them up the wide staircase. The atmosphere was part medical facility, part university.

"If you are wondering what is all going on here, allow me to enlighten you," a voice behind the boys said. They spun around to face the cheery face of the good doctor himself. "Upstairs, the clinic provides counseling and medical treatment for physical and psychological sexual disorders, including but not limited to: transitional surgery, abortions, cases of physical or sexual abuse when the patient does not want to go to the police, treatment of sexual diseases, and we also take on cases of women's and homosexuals' legal rights." He smiled, looking from one teenage boy face to the other. "Our museum has been visited by thousands of visitors from all over the world, including numerous religious and school groups." He pointed to the two large rooms to the right and left of the lobby.

"Look, Hans, it's dear, old Oscar Wilde," said Rolf pointing to a large portrait of the author hanging over the entrance to one of the museum wings.

"And look," shouted Hans pointing to another framed portrait, hanging over the entrance to the other wing, "It's King Ludwig II of Bavaria. Just think, he made Richard Wagner possible."

Dr. Hirschfeld nodded. "And Richard Wagner made Ludwig possible. His music and his dream gave Ludwig a reason to live."

Rather shyly, but eager to share, Hans said,"You know, Dr. Hirschfeld, it was at Hunding's Hut on Ludwig's estate where Rolf and I met."

The doctor chuckled. "How perfectly romantic. And are the two of you an… item then?"

Rolf elbowed Hans. "Well, we're trying to be, but we haven't gotten very far in some areas."

A red-faced Hans confessed to Hirschfeld, "I'm very new to all of this, and I am not certain what I am or what I want at this point. I mean, I love Rolf, but I am a bit sexually afraid."

Hirschfeld was absolutely charmed by both boys. "So, you'll experiment. You'll discover who and what you are. And your wild friend here, infamous at the Eldorado Club, will just have to be patient."

"But it's so hard, Doctor," Rolf moaned.

Hirschfeld's eyes sparkled. "An Ill-chosen phrase. Remember, as a child, at Christmas or Chanukah, how the anticipation was half the fun? Enjoy the moment. But now, if you'll excuse me, I have patients to attend to. Wander through the museum, see what you learn. Much of it is from my own private collection. Not bad for an old Jewish doctor, eh?"

Neither boy had ever seen such things. Every normal and abnormal sexual activity and eccentricity was on display. Giant dildos of elephant ivory, prized because they warmed to body temperature almost instantly, rough leather phalluses, and carved stone penises and vaginas. Collections of cock rings and genital cages, scrotum stretchers, nipple clamps and jars of stimulants. Leather whips and crops, birch rods, shackles and bindings, masks and costumes of leather and feather, ticklers and teasers and toilets.

And there were books, on sex and of sex. De Sade, Apollinaire, Wilde, Beardsley, sonnets of Shakespeare and Michelangelo, essays by Freud, and more. Shocking illustrations, sketches, statues and paintings by Rops, Saint-Andre, Boucher, Rodin, Picasso and even some erotic works of Rembrandt.

But there was more. Hand clapped over his mouth, Hans approached Hirschfeld's famous wall of photographs. Naked men, women, boys and girls, genders and genitals of every variety. Those with both sexes in one body, and those with seemingly no-sex at all. There were photos of the acts of intercourse, sodomy, fellatio, masturbation, pedophilia, infantilism, sadism, masochism, and even romantic love.

Both teenage boys stood there before the wall of photographs with red faces and erections. Finally, with a half-embarrassed laugh, Rolf said, "Who knows, perhaps with enough hard labor, we'll be up on that wall one day."

Visitors moved slowly and quietly, almost reverently, through the displays, whispering about African and Asian genital piercings and photos of men and women copulating with dogs and horses. "It's a bit like being in church," Rolf whispered, "only more fun."

Somewhere amid the aisles of display cases, at some

time during their excursion, it happened. "I want to have sex with you," Hans whispered, gripping Rolf's arm. "I have wanted to have sex with you since that first day at Hunding's Hut, but I was too frightened. I'm ready now. I love you!"

"I love you too, Hans. I am in love with you. I never said that to anyone before." Hans lifted his head to kiss his tall, dark lover, standing before a display case filled with anal beads and plugs.

They stood there, sweaty and only semi-conscious of their surroundings. Finally, Rolf said, "Now, could we please leave this lovely museum and go back to your room and fuck?"

CHAPTER 6

1924
 BERLIN
 THE APARTMENT

It did not go as anticipated. Was this to be a tale about the happiness we are all promised and yet few are granted? Let's see.

They returned to Hans' small, comfortable apartment, bursting with both love and lust, as only the young can do. Once there, they both stood awkwardly and silently, staring at each other in a new way. There can be great fear attached to the knowledge that you are about to give your body and soul to someone else. Great vulnerability. They kissed, but suddenly even the kisses were different, carrying with them a certain weight, a certain responsibility. But then, like a river beating against a damn with a widening crack in it, the kisses became more feverish and demanding. This was new and mysterious even for Rolf, who had in his young life known much sex but little love. He found himself frightened at the depth of his feelings for Hans. He suddenly felt protective and responsible for him, but at the same time driven by a lust such as he had never known.

For Hans, amid the excitement and fear, there was an overwhelming need to give himself completely to this person. Both boys began to undress. Rolf fairly threw off his clothing until he stood naked and proudly erect, like a warrior god. He knew full well that he was really something!

Hans behaved like the blushing virgin bride. Slow, hesitant, meticulous. He more undraped than stripped, until he, too, stood naked, pale and beautiful in the afternoon light pouring through the window.

Pale and beautiful and circumcised!

Rolf stood frozen in confusion, then terror, then terrible anger. His face grew dark red, and he balled his fists. "Jew?" was the first word out of his mouth.

"What?' Hans asked, confused now as well. He saw his lover's face twist into something dark and ugly. "What's wrong, Rolf?"

"Jew," Rolf repeated. "You are a Jew!" Tears filled his eyes and rolled down his cheeks.

Hans, not really comprehending the problem, muttered, "Half-Jew. I'm sorry, does that matter?"

The tears dripped from Rolf's jaw as his twisted face betrayed his inner struggle. He ran a hand through his raven-black hair and stared at Hans with an incomprehensible expression. He looked around the room like a trapped animal. Then in an explosive move, he hurled a pewter water jug into the large floor-length mirror, shattering it.

Hans put his hands over his mouth in horror. What had just happened?

"Does it matter? DOES IT MATTER?" Rolf spit. "How can I love you?" He fumbled with his discarded underwear, trying to step into it. "You deceived and betrayed me!"

Huge round tears now ran down Hans' cheeks as well, like delicate crystals falling from a broken necklace. "Rolf, I love you. I've secretly loved you from the start. I never thought about being a Jew. I mean, I thought about it from time to time, but not much. There are famous Jews all over Germany who are accepted and revered, like Dr. Hirschfeld. What need it matter to us?" The boy shook so badly, he found it difficult to stand.

Rolf stood there panting, shoulders tense, head bent, like a bull about to charge. "Don't you understand? Don't you see where this country is going? What would people think if I got into business or politics?"

"Well, they wouldn't be crazy about you being a homosexual, either!" Hans snapped back, his own anger now rising above his deep hurt. "Besides, what we do in our bedroom is our business!"

In blind fury, Rolf hurled his underwear at Hans who deftly caught it. "And what about you, Mr. Opera Singer? What about your dream of singing someday at Wagner's Bayreuth? They only accept pure German performers. You'll be stuck at the Komische Oper your whole life!" He fairly spit the words in a disgusted, sarcastic way, wanting to hurt.

Hans was crying hysterically. "I can hide the fact that I am half-Jew. My mother is pure-bred German. Even my father suggested that I pass myself off. I am neither proud nor ashamed of what I am, but either way, I can't help it. Just as you can't help being a narcissistic, narrow-minded bully!"

Rolf hopped from foot to foot, attempting to get into his trousers without his underwear. "It's ridiculous. Impossible!

You let me fall in love for the first time in my life, holding this terrible secret in your heart! Deceiving me! Where's my shoe?"

"Under the chair. STOP HOPPING AROUND, ROLF, AND LOOK AT ME!" It was the first time he had ever really shouted at Rolf. "I am the same person, Rolf! The same person you've been kissing and holding for weeks. I am ready to give myself to you, body and soul. I held back until I was certain. I want to spend my life with you. It won't be easy. We are both young, and have dreams and goals that may get in the way. We will certainly be apart from time to time, but that's all right. My love can endure that."

Rolf shook his pretty head and the tears flew. "Oh, Hans, those foolish operatic notions of yours..."

"Perhaps, Rolf, but they are my reality. Look at me, Rolf. Except for a few inches of missing foreskin, I am the same person you have grown to love, and I want you so badly, I ache!"

Like a vaudeville comic's routine, Rolf's suspenders snapped, and his trousers, into which he had only half-way climbed, tumbled around his ankles. "It's impossible. Impossible and dangerous for both of us, I tell you!"

Hans stood there naked, holding Rolf's underpants. "Sweet danger..." he said simply, and Rolf stumbled and fell into his arms. They tumbled onto the bed, twisted in Rolf's trousers. They slobbered and licked foolish kid-kisses on each-others' bodies, heedless of what their own better sense was telling them. They had literally fallen in love, in every sense of the word.

Rolf took Hans roughly, almost as if to punish the blond boy for stealing his mind and his heart, but also to completely possess him forever. And Hans relished the

Wagnerian pain of two becoming one. The music he heard in his head was from "Tristan and Isolde," and Hans understood for the first time how it was the most erotic piece of music ever written. It grew in waves toward orgasm, pulsing and pounding, reaching higher and higher, then, pulling back slightly only to rise even higher. And when it crashed in a shattering orgasm, pain and pleasure melted together into one. And Hans believed they would be one forever!

In the election of 1925, Hindenburg was elected President of the Reich. There was a resurgence of commemorations of war heroes, and political victories included a bill passed the previous year that, "No Jew could join the highly respected 'Stahlhelm,' the 'Steel Helmets,' a right-wing veterans group. It was a small but significant first step. Such groups were rising all over Germany, including Adolf Hitler's "Sturmabteilung," the SA Brownshirts, first formed in Munich in 1921.

Hans and Rolf spent most of the next few months in bed, making love, eating, reading poetry and literature, chatting, lazing, laughing, cuddling and occasionally sleeping, uncaring of the world outside. Rolf loved to hear Hans sing and demanded daily concerts of classical and popular songs.

Eventually, they ventured forth, Hans to his music lessons and a part-time job he accepted singing at the Eldorado Club, where he was enormously popular, and Rolf to university classes, majoring, to his father's delight, in History and Philosophy. But still, they cherished most their time together, and for the most part kept the world at bay. They did both take time to visit their parents, Hans to Munich and Rolf just across Berlin, but it only made them yearn all the more to be together again in Hans' tiny apartment.

"You see, Hans, your love for a better Germany, expressed through music and art, is not so very different from my political goals. Wagner's dream of glory is quite in keeping with goals for democratic social equality." If one closed one's eyes just a bit, one could almost forget that one of these two beautiful young men in bed together was a Jew.

CHAPTER 7

1860, 1925
UKRAINE, BERLIN
FAMILY

SOLOMON WEISMAN HAD BEEN A MODERATELY religious Jew, celebrating Shabbat each week, and honoring the Jewish holidays with his family in their moderately sized Ukrainian shtetl. He was moderate in most things; moderately successful in his carpentry business, moderately strict and moderately lenient with his children, and moderately critical of the Tsar and of the Russian approved Lord who controlled Solomon's land. He touched his forelock respectfully when required to, and mumbled along when anthems were sung. He was always carefully moderate in his remarks at the local tavern, where he spent an hour each evening unwinding after dinner.

He was not moderate about his gambling, his swearing, and like many Ukrainians, his drinking. No bottle of vodka remained un-emptied by evening's end. His wife Rachel understood and carried this burden, knowing that her husband was a good and loving man. They were good, God-fearing people, and so, of course, they were punished by God with hardships. The pogroms were part of that punishment. They didn't fully understand these Russian/Ukrainian raids, but when they came, property and people were laid to waste. Solomon's eldest son, a hot headed, defiant teen, was cut down by a Cossack saber. Solomon knelt in the dust, cradling his boy's bleeding head in his lap and asking God what the boy had done to deserve this. Jews were expendable, and the wealthy Ukrainians, as well as the Russian rich, often offered handsome rewards for their removal.

When he had had enough, and lacked the brute strength to endure more of God's punishment in this location, Solomon, Rachel and their two remaining children, Sarah and Jacob, climbed aboard a two-horse wagon heaped high with samples of Solomon's carpentry work, and set out for a new life. They travelled west. The old family clock along with some samples of Solomon's work, was lost in a raging river, and there was a huge setback when one of the horses died, but eventually, they made their way to Germany. Solomon, a practical, thorough man, decided that Bavaria would be their promised land, and that Munich looked especially attractive.

Munich, the ancient town of beer halls and beautiful parks, palaces and old-world tradition was peaceful and sweet, with the personality of a giant cuckoo-clock. Here, Solomon opened a furniture showroom, featuring not only his own work, but acquired pieces as well. Having an eye for, and a love of, fine art, he began to deal in that as well. He prospered, and he and his family lived in a comfortable apartment above the showroom. Solomon and Rachel often chose the best pieces for their own apartment, so Jacob was exposed early to fine art. Rachel played the piano and both Russian and German music filled their home.

But Jacob was a new person in a new land, and he adapted quickly. He almost tore the family apart when, as a young man, he fell in love with a blond-haired, German, café singer. He was thrown out of the house, but only for a month, as a son was more important to Solomon than tradition. Besides, were they not German now themselves? It was beautiful young Gretchen's piano playing and singing that won them over. For years, they had an idyllic life.

When the world fell into disrepair, due to feuding royal cousins, power-mad politicians, land-grabbing barons and an assassination, Jacob was drafted and like a good, young German went off to war, much to the dismay of his little boy, Hans, their only child since a tragic accident had taken the life of his sibling.

Their Ukrainian Jewish name of Weisman had been buried with Solomon, who passed away while his son was fighting on the Siegfried Line, and the family was now called Becker, after Gretchen's family. It was a blessing in disguise that Jacob was wounded in the leg and sent home before the final German disaster. To have to walk with a cane and a limp was a small sacrifice, compared to the many returning grotesqueries and the endless heartache over those who never returned.

Amazingly, the family business became a gold mine after the war, with moderately wealthy families forced to part with treasures, and very wealthy ones scooping them up. Jacob began to delve into really fine art, and buyers appeared from all over Germany. Hans entered his teens surrounded by beautiful music, exceptional art, mythic tales, and oodles of protective love.

It was this artistic dream world in which Hans had lived, and which he now shared with Rolf between kisses. A world of brave knights on impossible quests, hunts for the Grail, legendary giants, fine ladies who were almost goddesses, and even dragons. There had to be dragons.

Rolf could also sense Hans' deep love for his family, and he envied him that. Rolf, too, had grown up in a world of art, but an elitist, privileged one. His famous professor father showed his love by lecturing his son, and his highly strung, socially conscious mother, constantly forced him into awkward, artificial social situations. They cared deeply for their son, but showed their love in a distant, almost cold manner. Where one placed one's spoon was ever so much more important than displaying sloppy affection. Goodnight kisses were something only read about as a child. In fact, Rolf could not recall his father ever kissing him, and his mother simply pointed to the place on her cheek where he might kiss her. Nannies raised Rolf and his little sister, Heidi. But even before the unusual little boy properly knew what sex was, Rolf had his little tin soldiers coupling and billeting intimately.

It had always been a deeply seated part of him. He would watch with great curiosity when, in summer, the gardener or the grounds men worked without their shirts. He was especially fascinated in the area where their abdominal muscles melted beneath the fabric of their trousers.

He learned much more about these things at boarding school, where he became immensely popular. Perhaps a gift from his parents, Rolf developed a talent for being terribly charming while not really feeling any empathy for others.

Others were often objects to him, a means to an end. Meeting Hans changed all of that, and for the first time, Rolf found himself more concerned for someone else than for himself. This wonderful new purpose in life led to Rolf taking a rather dangerous risk a year later. Sweet danger!

CHAPTER 8

1926

    BERLIN
    MUSIC LESSONS

FRAU GRETA GREENBERG could have been so much more than she was. She was enough, and highly regarded by those scholars in the field of classical music, but she could have been world famous. Somehow, fame was of no interest to her, and the efforts required to reach it repulsed her. She loved music too much to bargain with it. She had played for Toscanini and Furtwängler, and she was known by those in the know as one of the best voice teachers in Europe. She lived in a memory-cluttered, well-appointed but unostentatious apartment on the top floor of a huge hundred-year-old building in a rather rundown section of Berlin. The other tenants included several war veterans, two hookers, a stenographer, a bookseller, a widow, Frau Hoffman, Herr Gutman, who played the clarinet in a jazz club, and several others she didn't know.

Quite frankly, she preferred the ramshackle of this quiet, old neighborhood to the rumbling shocks of the bustling, modern Berlin, with its blazing, art-deco buildings and its underground trains. In just a few years, it seemed the streets had filled to overflowing with motor cars, all honking their ugly sounding horns at the same time.

Greta Greenberg, with the flaming red hair of a much younger woman, was the voice teacher of Hans Becker. She wore too much make-up, smelled of too much perfume, and had a scandalous story attached to every one of the four fur coats hanging in her closet. Her lessons were not cheap, but also not exorbitant, and if she believed in you, money did not matter. In fact, she floated several talented but destitute singers.

She had first heard Hans sing when he was fourteen, the summer she had purchased an Emil Nolde landscape from Jacob Becker. She told Jacob that if the boy was still serious about a music career in a few years, he should be sent to her in Berlin. From time to time, she posted vocal pieces for him to work on. He did so, reverently.

"You're late," she barked, seated with her back to him at the piano, in a voice that always seemed a bit thick and gravely. She heard the door slam. "Don't slam the door, it's only a door, not the enemy." He took off his cap and bowed his head to his teacher. "That's twice in three weeks. That never happened before. You used to be hungry for music and always early. You must be in love!" Hans' mouth dropped open. "You know what your buddy Wagner says about love in 'The Ring;' to have power, you must renounce love!"

"Sorry," Hans mumbled, setting his satchel on a chair and taking out the Mahler piece on which he had been working. "I missed the trolley."

The truth was that he and Rolf had been making love... again.

Frau Greenberg shook her head. "It is fine and fitting for an artist to write and sing and paint about love. Preferably lost love. But being involved in love messes things up." She droned on with only mock seriousness, punctuating her thoughts with chords on the piano. "For you, with your potential, music and only music must be your love."

"Ja, Frau Greenberg." Hans smiled with the taste of Rolf still on his tongue. "I shall sing rapturously of love and never pollute my body."

"Putz!" she snapped, popping a mint into her mouth but not offering him one. Treats were only awarded for excellence in performance. "You have already wasted ten minutes of your time. Warm up!" She played a note, and Hans matched her, his voice, as always, remarkably clear and beautiful. "Your voice is lazy. You spend too much time in bed. You need exercise." Hans performed her unique set of exercises including making a whole series of animal-like sounds.

"When you sing at that damned club where you work, don't strain your voice trying to sing over them. Make them listen to you."

"But Frau Greenberg, I need a much stronger voice to someday sing at Bayreuth."

She snorted. She actually snorted. "You see, such a dummy you are. The acoustics at Bayreuth are unlike any other opera house in the world. Most of the big voices find they have to pull back and sing more quietly. Wagner created his hall for singers, with a sunken orchestra pit, and walls specially shaped for the human voice. At Bayreuth, it is the operas themselves which will exhaust and destroy you. Who can sing for four hours straight? Don't stay in bed so much... exercise!"

Hans couldn't help but think of Rolf, still back in bed in what was now their apartment, and the exercises in which they engaged there. He cleared his voice and launched into one of Mahler's "Songs of the Earth." Madame corrected his every fault, arms waving and bracelets clattering. She clicked her teeth and shook her head at every mistake, not letting on that she knew what magnificent talent he had in him. Hans felt he couldn't do anything right and vowed to never again have sex before a lesson. But he knew that was a foolish vow as Rolf wanted sex all the time.

After the lesson, as always, they had tea. Frau Greenberg kept a samovar steaming at all times. She had an unusual gleam in her eye and a smug twist to her mouth. Something was up. Hans could feel it.

"I have news for you. I have secured for you an audition with the Berlin State Opera. Erich Kleiber is presenting the premiere of a radical new work composed by the Austrian Alban Berg. It is shocking, modern and atonal, and based upon a play by Georg Büchner, just the thing for an eager, young pup like yourself."

Hans sat there like an idiot, a bit of strudel hanging from his open mouth. "Close your mouth and put down the tea cup before you break it. Many current opera singers will not be able, or not want, to handle Berg's score, but you will shine. Now, you hear me, you had better nail the audition, my reputation is at stake." She allowed herself to smile warmly when she said this, a rare thing indeed.

"Ouch! Not much pressure," replied Hans, setting down the rattling cup and saucer.

"If you want to sing opera, your life will be nothing but pressure from now on. I don't know if you will ever sing at

Bayreuth. For two months each summer, well-established opera stars from all over Germany are happy to sing in the Bayreuth chorus. But, you are quite young to have such a promising voice, and with the proper dedication, you could make your old voice teacher here quite proud of you."

Hans was crying now. He cried much too easily. "How can I ever thank you Frau Greenberg?"

"Don't fuck it up. Now pour some more tea."

Hans, was of course, insanely anxious to share his good news with Rolf, who was not at their apartment when the singer returned. The blond boy paced the bedroom, sat on the edge of the bed, thought about telephoning his parents, paced the bedroom some more and looked out the window a dozen times at the street below. He watched the line of starving veterans begging on the street, many of them maimed, and could have kicked himself for being so high on hope while others suffered. But he couldn't help being on cloud nine.

Then he saw his boyfriend coming down the street, shifting the weight of two huge parcels in his arms. Rolf balanced the bulkiest package on one hip so he could toss some coins to a few of the veterans, then he turned into the building, and Hans heard the familiar clump of feet on the stairs, and a "Guten Tag, Herr Rotter," shouted by Rolf to a downstairs neighbor. Soon, the door swung open and there he was.

"Rolf, what in God's name..."

"A gift for you!" Rolf beamed, lugging his burden to a table. Unwrapped, it turned out to be a brand-new Victrola phonograph, a big boxy thing with a crank and built in speakers. The second parcel was a stack of records.

"Rolf, I love you," shouted Hans flinging himself around the others' neck, "But why? What for?"

"So, I don't have to listen to you sing all the time." Hans threw Rolf onto the bed, where they remained for some time.

Later, they celebrated Hans' audition news by dining at Zur Letzten Instanz, touted as the oldest restaurant in the city, at the same location since 1621. It had just had its latest renovation and resembled an old-world, beer hall and garden. The cozy inside sported rough, wooden tables amid old-fashioned, hanging lanterns and shuttered, bottle glass windows. The service was friendly and the food exceptional. They ate accompanied by accordion and zither music, and it was all quite romantic. After eating, they scoured Berlin record stores for anything by Alban Berg. And later... in bed, with romantic music playing, Hans remarked, "Is it really such a big deal, this little hunk of pecker skin?" He toyed with and flicked Rolf's foreskin.

Rolf slapped his hand away. "It's your cock I'm worried about. Every day, there seem to be more and more restrictions against Jews."

Hans grabbed his lover's penis again and tugged on it. "But you forget, I have fake, German papers!"

"Lousy, fake, German papers. They would never hold up under a close inspection."

"But my darling," Hans whispered, kissing the other boy's member, "my mother is a full-blooded German. When I was born, my parents fought over whether to call a priest for a baptism, or a mohel to cut me."

"They should have called the priest. You'd be better off today. And you'd better leave my thing alone before you have to take care of it."

"I am about to take care of it. Everything will be fine, Rolf. This wave of anti-Semitism will blow over just like the others. We still live in a democracy. The political parties just need someone to blame for these hard times. And speaking of hard times, my goodness!"

Rolf rolled his body over on top of Hans. "And anyway, liebchen, I like the Mahler much better than that dissonant noise by Berg."

"Well, you're going to have to get use to that atonal 'noise' if I pass the audition, because I am making you come to every performance."

Rolf put his hands over his ears in mock protest. "I shall go mad, I tell you. I shall go mad!"

CHAPTER 9

1926

    BERLIN, ALEXANDERPLATZ
    AUDITION

THE AUDITION WAS HELD on a Tuesday at a large, modern office building near "The Red Castle," the police headquarters on Alexanderplatz, Mitte, Berlin, the city center. Hans, dressed in a suit that made him look older than his eighteen years, with his blond hair pomaded and slicked back off his forehead, carried the soft leather satchel containing his music into the art-deco elevator and got off on the sixth floor. He showed his appointment card to a bored-looking, female receptionist with a severe bob hairdo, and took a seat in one of eleven empty, modernist chairs that lined the green hallway. The corridor had large glass bowls of ceiling lights every ten feet, and reminded Hans for some reason of a prison. He was nervous beyond belief, and Rolf, who was almost as nervous for him, had been unable to calm him. "I can't go," he had announced more than once, and yet, here he was.

He wanted to run. He also needed to pee. The receptionist who never even smiled, placed a phone call, and then powdered her nose. How could anyone be expected to audition under these barbaric conditions?

A door down the hall opened, and Hans heard the tap, tap, tap of shoe leather on the cold, stone floor before he saw the loose-limbed, slender-hipped, young man in shirt sleeves and suspenders who came to fetch him. The intense look behind round-rimmed spectacles and the long forelock of floppy, brown hair dangling over his forehead, made him look like a communist agitator. With hunched shoulders and a long, extended neck, he hovered over Hans, who at last stood at attention.

"Hans Becker?" the reed-thin inquisitor snapped in a thin voice.

"Ja! I'm Hans Becker." For God's sake, he was the only one in the fucking hallway!

"Follow me, please." The coat-hanger thin body spun around and went clicking down the hall, followed by a stumbling Hans, who had to return to the chairs to fetch his satchel. His nerves were getting the better of him. One, two, three, six green doors down.

The room was hollow and empty except for an upright piano, a long, folding table with several folding chairs behind it, and along the far wall, mirrors and a ballet barre.

Before he even saw the man, Hans was shocked by the sight of an ashtray on the table, overflowing with cigarette butts, and the stench of tobacco in the air. Just the right atmosphere for a vocal audition.

The table also contained several coffee cups, a water glass filled with pencils, a dozen piled up musical scores, some scattered sheet music and two yellow legal pads. And then there was the famous conductor!

Erich Kleiber was a sensitive looking man in his mid-thirties, whose fair, wispy hair was already thinning. He was a "wunderkind" who had come up through the ranks in the music world: Darmstadt, Dusseldorf, Mannheim, and the previous year, he had been appointed the Musical Director of the Berlin State Opera! As well as having astounding success with the works of Beethoven, Bach, Mozart, Wagner and the other traditional giants, Kleiber also encouraged and conducted works by radical, young composers.

He gave Hans a brief, tight-lipped smile and a nod of his head, stood, slipped off his jacket and hung it on the back of a chair, sat again, took a sip from the coffee cup, and then shuffled through a stack of three by five cards.

"Heinrich..." he began.

"Hans Becker," corrected the lean, fluid fellow who now sat at the upright piano and shoved a stick of chewing gum into his mouth.

This was all unbearable. Hans thought he would faint. He must get out of this room, jump out the sixth-floor window if necessary.

"Ach, ja. Forgive me Herr Becker, I am a bit discombobulated today.

Thank you, Fritz. Hans Becker, of course." He fished the correct card out of the pile. "Welcome, Herr Becker, you come highly recommended by dear Frau Greenberg. The gentleman at the keyboard is Fritz, our accompanist. Please give him your music. What are you going to perform for us today?"

Hans cleared his throat. He'd kill for a glass of water, or a piece of gum, or anything to lubricate his throat. When he spoke, it was in an artificial voice that sounded totally alien to him.

"Today, I will be performing a song from 'Das Lied Von Der Erde' by Gustav Mahler, in A minor for tenor voice." Fuck, the words came out all a jumble. He fished from his satchel a stack of music which he proceeded to unfold for Fritz at the piano.

The lanky, young pianist looked at the piano transcription of the difficult piece before him and whistled. "Who is auditioning today, you or me?"

Kleiber, with a grin on his face, looked down at the table so as not to embarrass Hans. "Indulge us, Fritz, will you, and muddle through it the best you can?"

A trembling Hans blinked nervously and looked from pianist to conductor. Had he done something wrong? Something to ruin the rest of his life?

Maestro Kleiber raised a reassuring hand. "It is nothing, Herr Becker, just that young singers... you are how old?" he glanced down at the audition card.

"Eighteen, Maestro."

"It's just that young singers seldom choose such demanding pieces for their auditions."

An embarrassed Hans looked down at the cocky, wispy, gum- chewing pianist, who grinned broadly. He tried to regain some dignity by explaining, "It's Mahler's own transcription for piano, and Frau Greenberg plays it very well."

At the table, Herr Kleiber seemed to be enjoying the moment. "I'm sure she does. Fritz will have to do the best he can. But I must warn you, young man, do not try to win me over with Mahler's emotion and sentimentality. I am a cold and exacting musician, and I shall look for technical proficiency. Fritz, on the other hand, is a push-over for poetic indulgence."

Fritz chewed and gave a lopsided grin. "Would you like a glass of water before climbing the mountain, Herr Becker?" He nodded toward the pitcher and glass sitting on the table.

"Danke, that would be very much appreciated." Hans poured and drank with shaking hands and trembling lips.

"I must also warn you, Herr Becker," the maestro said, "that with a stack of auditions like this to get through, I seldom listen to the entire piece. Please do not be offended if I stop you mid-way through your audition. I am judging your voice, not the piece of music. I can sometimes tell if the singer meets my needs in just a few phrases."

"Sometimes sooner," added Fritz.

"Manners, Fritz. All right, Hans Becker, let's hear how you and Fritz tackle Gustav Mahler."

Fritz played beautifully, supporting and urging Hans beautifully. Hans used the powerful first part of "The Drunk Man in Spring" to show off his Siegfried-like, powerhouse tenor. Later in the song, when the narrator of the Chinese-based poem hears a bird, Hans showed what he could do with light, delicate tones.

"IF LIFE IS ONLY A DREAM
THEN WHY LABOR AND WHY
   STRUGGLE SO?
I DRINK UNTIL I AM FULL
I DO IT ALL THE BLESSED DAY.
AND WHEN I HAVE DRUNK MY FILL,
I STUMBLE HOME TO MY DOOR.
I SLEEP DEEPLY AND WONDERFULLY
AND WHEN FINALLY I WAKE,
WHAT DO I HEAR?

A BIRD SINGING IN A TREE!
I ASK HIM 'IS IT SPRING ALREADY?
OR AM I STILL ASLEEP?'"

The song continued and Erich Kleiber did not stop him. And when Hans finished, and the last note of the piano had died in the hollow room, the conductor had tears in his eyes. So did Fritz. The room was still and silent for what seemed to Hans like an eternity. When Hans could stand the stillness no longer, he turned to Fritz and said, "Thank you. You played that beautifully." He collected his music, bowed his head and clicked his heels toward the conductor, and certain he was an utter failure, turned to leave the room.

Herr Kleiber cleared his throat, and Hans halted. "Young man. The Staatsoper of Berlin goes back to the court opera of Friedrich II. It was rechristened the Deutsche Oper Berlin in 1919, after the collapse of the monarchy. It is the most highly regarded opera company in Germany, precisely because it does not adhere to the ideas of the grandiloquent opera houses of the past. It is concerned with the substance of the art, not its ornamentation."

Hans felt crushed, even though he had not entirely understood Herr Kleiber's meaning. He bowed his head once more and moved toward the door, his trembling hands clutching his leather satchel.

"Herr, Becker! Where are you going? Don't you wish to sing with us at the Berlin State Opera?"

"I... eh... oh! I... ja. Ja, of course!" The room was spinning for Hans. He couldn't breathe.

Herr Kleiber flicked his fingers through one of the scores on the table. "This piece, 'Wozzeck,' is not piece of cake. It is an avant-garde experiment in atonality. It does not follow the techniques of major-minor tonality at all. Do you think you can handle something like that?

"Ja voll, I'm certain I can." He was not even certain of the words coming out of his mouth.

"And the subject matter concerns sadism in the military and the government, and the subjugation of the common man. It is certain to cause controversy. Can you handle that?" There was a certain hungry fire in Kleiber when he spoke of this.

"Ja! With enthusiasm, sir."

Kleiber sat back, relaxing in his chair. "You have a remarkable voice for one so young. You showed too much emotion, as I suspected. You must be in love. If you self-indulge in it too much, you deprive the audience from feeling it. It becomes masturbation instead of a sexual coupling. Do you sight read?"

"Ja, of course."

"Then, Herr Becker, you are hired."

Hans nervously fished in his coat pocket, and crossing the room, presented his identification documents. "My papers, Herr Kleiber."

The conductor waved them away. "I don't care about that. I only care if you can sing... and you can."

As Hans walked down the green hallway in a daze, he heard quick, hard footsteps behind him on the stone floor. It was Fritz, one hand thrust into his trouser pocket.

"Are you?" Fritz asked, one eyebrow arched, and a quirky little smile on his lips.

Hans stopped and turned to the lanky, young pianist. "Am I what?"

"Maestro Kleiber said that from your singing, you must be in love. So, are you? And if you are not, do you want to go for coffee?"

Hans tilted his head slightly, and then shrugged his shoulders. "I am," he said simply, "and I am not sure going out with you would be appropriate."

"Scheisse!" Fritz responded, scuffing the stone floor with one foot.

"Oh well, we'll be working together every day for the whole season, so there will be plenty of chances to put the make on you. Perhaps, until then, we could at least be friends?" He held out his hand.

Hans saw the young man's eager kindness. "Ja, let's be friends. I could use some good friends." They shook hands. "What do I do now, about the job I mean?"

"You'll be sent materials and a rehearsal schedule from Herr Buchman, the chorus director. You saw the overflowing ashtray... that was his. He stepped out of the room for a phone call before you arrived. He's going to melt like a piece of chocolate in the sun when he hears you sing. He's a sour, sweet, old thing whom we call 'Auntie Lou.' And there will be a contract to sign."

There they stood, two young men chatting about music like two kids in a candy shop.

"Have you heard, of course you have, the Bayreuth Fesitval is running again since 1924." Hans puffed out his chest. "I'm going to sing there some day!"

"I don't doubt it," Fritz laughed. "Well, when you do, make sure to get me a job as a rehearsal pianist. I specialize in Wagner. And also in American Tin Pan Alley!"

"I have great hope, Fritz for the future of our country. In spite of sky-high prices and unemployment, there is a new energy in Germany."

Suddenly, to their mutual chagrin, they realized that they were still shaking, or holding, hands. "Sorry," said Hans, taking a step backward, "I'd better go."

Fritz pouted and thrust both hands into the pockets of his wide-legged trousers. "Yes, you'd better. I'll be seeing you soon." He spun around and actually tap-danced down the hall.

When Hans reached the elevator, he had to lean against the wall to clear his head. His sudden good fortune was almost too much for him. Outside, the fall air swept in and enveloped him, and in his euphoria, he was almost hit by a trolley.

"Hey!" a voice shouted out to him from across the busy street. "Hey!"

Hans, still lost in his audition, stopped, turned and narrowly avoided being hit by a honking auto. There on the opposite curb stood Rolf, holding a large bouquet of roses.

"Rolf, what are you doing here?"

"Waiting for you to finish your audition. Here, these are for you." He thrust out his hand with the roses, looking like a fancy traffic warden.

"Oh, mein Gott, Rolf, you are so fucking sweet!" Hans embraced his lover. "I got in, Rolf, I was hired. I'm going to be an opera singer."

"I knew it," Rolf beamed. "That's why the roses!"

Hans frowned and grabbed Rolf's ear. "And if I hadn't gotten in?"

"Then they would have been consolation." He gave one of his devilish smiles.

"Oh, how I love you. I want to kiss you right here on the street."

"Feel free! This is the jazz age, Baby!" So, they did. And although people noticed, no one really much minded. Eight years later, they would have been arrested on the spot, or perhaps shot right there on the street.

CHAPTER 10

1926-27
  BERLIN
  THE STATE OPERA
  SA HEADQUARTERS

THESE WERE happy years for the two young men, perhaps their happiest. They lived like bohemians in their little apartment. Rolf studied history, and philosophy, perhaps to become a teacher like his father, although he had a natural aversion to that and wanted to explore politics. But mater and pater seemed quite pleased with him, only wishing they could see him more often, a sentiment they had not expressed when he had been a wild, young colt at boarding school. On the occasions when he tore himself away from Hans and did return across town to their home, he had civil conversations with them about art and literature, the latest technological advancements, and philosophy, but not politics. They were kind enough, and it wasn't their fault they were stuffy and wealthy, but they did seem blind to the fact that the old Germany was dead, and there was great impending change in the wind.

While Hans performed with the dance band at the club and studied voice for his upcoming opera gig, Rolf began to delve into the intricacies of the various political parties vying for power in Germany. More and more, Rolf became worried about Hans' status as a Jew. Juden were being foolishly blamed for many of the country's woes. Anti-Semitism ran high not only in Germany, but in other European countries as well. Rolf was shocked that many intelligent people believed Jews to be vampires, not in the literal sense, but that they were sucking the blood from the state with their corrupt business practices and conniving cabals. There was no actual proof to corroborate or counter these claims of course, but more and more people felt that Jews were not true Germans. Four out of five of the quickly growing new political parties hated the Jews on principle, and the fifth just didn't admit it.

If Jews were indeed corrupt, how could Hans Becker be a Jew? He was the dearest, sweetest thing Rolf had ever known, and was cherished beyond measure. Rolf wanted nothing less than to love and protect Hans forever. How could he be a part of what was being called an "infected, sub-human race?"

Hans, meanwhile, was in heaven. His talents had been quickly spotted by Lucius Buchman, called "Auntie Lou" by everyone except Maestro Kleiber, and the eager young tenor was given the position of "understudy for Marcel Noe" in the small but vital role of "the Madman." The friendship between Hans and Fritz grew almost immediately, and the two young men chatted away for hours at a time about opera and music in general. Fritz was quite open about his infatuation with the blond tenor, and not just because of his talent.

Together, over salami and cheese, they paged through the pages of

gay magazines, of which there were over twenty in Berlin at the time, laughing at the cartoons and pretending to swoon over the endowments of the men in the photographs. Hans would often steal the old issues from the opera green room and take them home to Rolf. The boys invited Fritz to join them at the Eldorado Club, although the young pianist stayed a bit formal and distant from Rolf.

The two lovers partied hard during this period, dancing their asses off in the jerky style that emulated the robot and enslaved workers in Fritz Lang's new film "Metropolis," which hadn't even been released yet, but had taken the city by storm. Females wore silver metallic dresses and men metallic shirts and jackets, and they jerked themselves into frenzies to throbbing, percussive, maddeningly heavy sounds.

Hans floated on wings of music and love. And wouldn't you know it, Marcel Noe was hit hard by influenza, and young Hans Becker got his first chance to sing a role on the legit opera stage. Rolf was given a house seat for the event and, of course, declared to anyone willing to listen, that Hans was the best thing in the production.

Rolf hated the piece in general. It was more noise to him than music, and the subject matter of sadism and murder was rather disgusting. The betrayal of the common-law wife with a guardsman, the experiments performed on poor Wozzeck, and the eventual madness and murder did not sit well with Rolf. Still, Hans was damned good, and Rolf even got his parents to come see his "friend." Professor Kainz thought the piece "interesting" both artistically and politically. Rolf's mother was properly and politely offended by it. These two views pretty much reflected the opinions of the critics.

Just before the performance, on the night of Hans' first appearance as "the Madman," something quite special happened. Rolf appeared backstage and, cornering Hans in a dressing room, presented him with a small box containing a gold ring for his lover's little finger. Han's swore he would "never remove it," but of course had to immediately for the performance. "I'll never take it off, except for the stage," corrected Hans, kissing Rolf a hundred times. "We are bound by this ring in life and death." Rolf, brushing away a tear, chuckled at Hans' overly romantic zeal. How could one not want to devote one's life to this sweet, innocent angel?

After Rolf had gone to his seat, Fritz rushed up in a fit of pre-show anxiety, hugged his friend, and whispered "toi, toi, toi!" He accompanied the traditional, opera, backstage good luck wish with a quick kiss on the tenor's mouth. They locked eyes, and it was a tense moment. "You'll be great," Fritz babbled, "Just remember your blocking and keep your eyes on the Maestro, without stumbling into the pit. I'll be down there at the piano for you. Sing your arse off!" He hugged Hans once again and flitted off shouting, "I love you," over his shoulder.

Erich Kleiber was so impressed by the young tenor's performance, he hired him for the following production and the one after that, each time giving the boy more to do. And when the season closed, he offered Hans a chance to tour to Vienna and beyond with a planned concert tour. He would be singing several famous opera solos as well as some duets and ensemble numbers. Hans was breathlessly excited at the opportunity. Rolf, understandably, somewhat less so.

"It's three months during the summer, and I'd write you

every day, and telephone once a week, no matter the cost. I wouldn't even have considered this if I could have gotten tickets for Bayreuth for us, but it's sold out, and I've applied for next year."

Rolf smiled and nodded but was silent.

"You know you are my life to me," Hans said, tears in his eyes.

"As you are to me. I can see you want this badly. It's inevitable that our lives should move in different directions…"

"NEVER!" Hans blurted, clinging to his lover. "Do you hear me, Rolf? We may be parted for a while from time to time, but it is our destiny to be together always."

Rolf smiled, tears running down his own cheeks. "You sound like an opera aria! Of course, you must go. I shall visit you and make good use of the rest of the time." But Rolf knew there was something terribly important he had to do for the talented young man he loved.

The temporary headquarters of the Berlin branch of the National Socialist German Workers' Party, or the Nazi Party as it came to be called, was a squat, round building that looked to Rolf like a giant machine gun pillbox from the war. The headquarters were temporary because the ban on the party of the past nearly two years, resulting from the Munich Putsch, had just been lifted. This new headquarters building was adorned with and draped in huge red flags bearing the swastika, and plastered with colorful, creative, political posters, many which depicted cartoons of Communist or Jewish monsters crushing the heads of trampled German workers. The large number of these small splinter party groups like the Nazis, that battled each other for power, still made them all politically ineffective against the rule of Military General Paul von Hindenburg, President of Democratic Weimar Germany, and his cronies.

More interesting to Rolf than the flags and posters, was the gaggle of handsome boys and young men in high brown socks, brown shorts, and brown shirts adorned with red armbands, who over-zealously guarded the property. Rolf thought them absolutely cute. The young boys had shining, peach-colored skin, and the young men had a kind of rough, thuggish appeal, bolstered by boots and thick leather belts. "I feel like I'm back at the opera," Rolf muttered out loud.

These threatening young men, who leaned in menacingly but did not bar his way, were just the opposite of the hollow-eyed, beaten, German men who had limped home from the last war. No pocked and pitted poison gas faces here. This was the new, young Germany. At least that was the intended illusion. These were the Siegfrieds Hans sang about.

Rolf whistled a bit of one of the leitmotifs from "The Ring" as he strode through the heavy metal Valhalla-like doors guarded by two overly-attentive, young thugs. Rolf couldn't resist giving the more handsome one a wink.

The interior was an impressive, spacious, high-ceilinged vault of a room, in which every sound, including Rolf's whistle, was amplified. There were large murals on the walls depicting flag waving heroes from various eras charging into battle. The whole Nazi movement seemed to have a flag fetish. Rolf felt a tinge of respect. This was no longer a lunatic fringe group that met in rathskellers and toasted their radical ideas with mugs of beer. No, the rag-tag militia movement had turned into a well-organized, political party that now boasted over one hundred thousand members.

A slick-haired, smooth fore-headed, bespectacled, young man with an official bearing strode up to Rolf with boots clicking and inquired with a velvet-smooth voice, "May I help you, sir?"

"How very like a bank," thought Rolf, for some reason removing his hat. "I'm here to see Ernst Röhm."

The smooth forehead frowned. "Do you have an appointment, sir?"

Rolf's naughty side emerged. "If a passing acquaintance in a gentlemen's toilet in a nightclub of dubious reputation is an appointment, then yes, I have one."

The man's nose twitched, his nostrils flared, and his spectacles rose and fell slightly. He did not seem amused. He went over to a very large telephone on a very tiny table, which was the only piece of furniture in the vast hall, and spoke into it, his hand protectively guarding the mouthpiece. Rolf found himself wondering how many of these fit, young heldentenors had already found their way into Ernst Röhm's bed. The word "brotherhood" took on a special meaning at this stage of the SA and almost everyone knew it.

The receptionist looked up from the phone. "Your name?" he inquired, dropping the sir.

"Rolf Kainz."

"Rolf Kainz," the receptionist repeated into the telephone, making it sound somehow dirty or, at the least, distasteful. Then with a displeased look, he almost hissed, "Herr Röhm will see you upstairs in room 215." He hung up the telephone, turned and soon all that remained of him was the sound of his receding boots on the hard floor. Without direction, Rolf wandered the vast halls searching for a staircase to take him to room 215.

The infamous Ernst Röhm had his big, brown boots up on his big brown desk as he leaned back in a squeaking desk chair, whose squeak was not so much the fault of the chair as the bulk of the man seated in it. He was round-faced and beefy with a small, scrub brush moustache, and unlike the fresh, angelic faces of his minions, his cheek did bear a large, ugly scar from the great war. As he was a bit older than Himmler and the other leaders of the new movement who were mostly in their twenties, he had to rely on his close friendship with Adolf Hitler, the rather short, charismatic, blue-eyed writer, to keep him in a position of power. Hitler had just recently made a successful move to take over the Nazi party, so at this point, Röhm could not have been better placed.

The office reflected the modernist view of things, spacious and sleek, with smooth wooden chairs inlaid with dark patterns, several free-standing silver ashtrays, a highly polished wooden bar with more dark wood inlaid designs, and on the walls two large framed paintings- one of muscular, foundry workers pouring hot flames into steel tubs, reminiscent of the Nibelung at work, and another, of naked, bathing, pre-teen boys. On the impressive desk, rested a bronze sculpture of a naked, Atlas-like figure, a fancy, French telephone, a large, square, crystal ashtray, a leather notebook and Rohm's brown SA uniform cap. Perhaps he kept it close in case of a visit from one of his few superiors such as the aforementioned Heinrich Himmler, who currently had Hitler's ear. Or perhaps a visit from one of Hitler's newly-formed SS personal bodyguard police. Not to worry, Röhm's SA were soon to become the official police of the Nazi party.

In the crystal ashtray, an expensive cigar smoked away, a thin trail rising into the air of the room. Röhm felt rather secure in spite of the constant turnovers of power within the party. It was all rather like that game at the carnival where heads kept popping up through holes in a board, and one had to bop them down again. Röhm and his thugs were quite good at bopping. Even the Berlin city police were learning to treat Rohm's boys with, if not respect, at least some deference.

He didn't rise to greet Rolf, but spread his booted feet and looked at his visitor through them. "Well, well, well, look who comes to see me, the sexiest schwanz of the Eldorado Club."

"Ernst," Rolf said, nodding his head politely. He used the man's first name to show that he was not a boot-licking lackey, but also to try to establish a friendly, more intimate rapport. Inside, Rolf's stomach rumbled and his chest felt tight. "You've done quite well for yourself, Ernst, becoming a somewhat feared and well-respected fellow around town." He tried to sound casual, to bring the Eldorado Club-type banter into this severe office.

Ernst smiled. His teeth were a bit stained from tobacco. He took a puff on the great cigar. "You haven't seen anything yet. Just wait a year or two. Sit, sit, it's good to have you here. And what about you, my young stallion? Sucked any interesting cock lately? Oh, wait, I'd forgotten, word around is that you've found love and become a housefrau. Frau Kainz is it now?" he laughed boisterously.

Rolf knew in advance he'd have to eat a certain amount of crow from Röhm. The man was a notorious bully, and most of his relationship with Rolf had consisted of Rolf trying to avoid the thug's groping hands at parties and clubs. And then there had been that one brief, drunken, ten-minute encounter in the Eldorado toilet.

"It's true, I've settled down, Ernst, and so should you. A man in your position can't afford scandal. You should fall in love."

Röhm barked a laugh, climbed to his feet and crossed to

the bar. "The party is my great love. For recreation, I have my stormtroopers and the boys at the club." He poured a healthy swallow of fine whiskey into each of two expensive, cut-crystal glasses. "Yes, my troopers are more than willing to serve. And if you have a taste for something younger, we have started a Nazi Youth Group, all under fourteen and delicious."

Rolf wanted to puke, but he held his composure and took the drink, Röhm's fingers lingering on the younger man's hand. Rolf pulled back slightly in his chair.

"But tell me, Herr Kainz, what is the reason you pay me this visit? I know it is not your uncontrollable desire for me."

The dreaded moment was at hand, and it was not easy for Rolf. "I need a favor. A rather large favor, but something I know you can arrange."

An intrigued Röhm perched on the edge of his desk, one boot swinging casually. "Ja?" he questioned, puffing and sipping, his eyes sparkling with interest.

"I need papers. Identification papers and a passport for a friend. Really good, forged papers."

"Ernst sipped and swallowed. "He is a Jew."

"A half-Jew, and his current papers are ambiguous."

"Suspicious," Röhm corrected.

Rohm's boot swung more aggressively, almost touching Rolf's leg. He puffed on the cigar and blew smoke into the air. "If he were a mere rapist, a thief, a murderer, the request would be a piece of cake, but 'ein Jude!'"

"Like I said. He's half. His mother is a full-blooded German, and he has been raised as a German. He has no Jewish traits. He deserves a chance to serve Germany, believe me."

Röhm slapped his thigh. "Aha! The blond angel from the club that everyone is drooling over. This is your lover.

Forgive me, I have been remiss in visiting lately. There are those in the SA who, while they are happy to engage in exhaustive male/male bonding with others of the brotherhood, look down on the decadent, sissy-boys of Berlin. I have no such prejudices. A cute ass is a cute ass! So, you are in love with 'ein Jude?'"

Rolf couldn't control the tears that welled up in his eyes, tears of anger, of frustration. "He's so very talented, and he wants to sing Wagner, our inspiration."

Röhm's swinging boot just touched Rolf's leg. The boy did not pull back. "Nonetheless, he is the product of a dirty Jew fucking a German woman." He spread his arms, cigar in one hand, tumbler in the other. "The success of our platform rests on three principles: one, eradicate all communist influence in Germany; two, eradicate all Jewish influence in Germany, in business, in the arts, and in social circles, and three, control the government!" He leaned over Rolf, his round face now only inches away. "Do you realize that Hindenburg and his generals have secretly begun to build airplanes, tanks and other weapons in defiance of the Versailles Treaty? Germany is re-arming, and it must do so under the control of the Nazi Party. We require a scapegoat for all of Germany's current woes, and that scapegoat happens to be the Jews."

Rolf lifted his head to meet Röhm's gaze. "But why should an innocent, enormously talented young man suffer for something he has no interest or part in?"

Röhm shrugged. "A casualty of war." He drained his glass and returned to the bar. "I am not insensitive to your request, no matter how foolish or dangerous. Young love knows no reason, and believe you me, your little Jew will need the best, forged papers to survive the coming storm. If he were my lover, I would beg him to get out of the country.

Anti-Jewish sentiment is exploding all over Europe, not just here in Germany." He winked one eye. "There are even secret plans to assassinate a highly placed Jewish Police Commissioner here in Berlin."

Rolf's stomach was in knots. "Can you help me? Will you help me?"

Röhm's face transformed instantly into that of a kindly burgomaster. One could picture him holding two steins of beer, his moustache covered in foam. He walked behind Rolf and placed his hands upon the young man's shoulders, which he began to gently, but firmly, massage.

"I know a fellow who creates masterpieces of forgery. His documents could pass the closest inspections. This, of course, would be a private transaction between you and me, and have nothing to do with my work for the party." Rolf nodded, feeling the fingers dig in.

"Tell me Rolf, when you and your Jew-boy have sex, who is Siegfried and who is Brunhilde? Who thrusts in Balmung, Siegfried's sword?"

Rolf bristled. He wanted to beat the shit out of the fat fuck of a pervert. Röhm could feel the boy's body tense, and it aroused him.

"Or like so many young couples today, do you take turns?" One hand moved down over Rolf's chest to seek his pectoral muscle through his shirt. The other caressed his neck. "You know, in ancient Rome there was nothing considered unseemly about two men fucking, as long as the one fucking was a Roman citizen, and the one getting fucked was a slave, or young man seeking the citizen's patronage."

Rolf chewed his lip and then suddenly blurted out, "Allright, what do you want in return for your help?" He had suspected the price all along, but it was worth it to help Hans.

Röhm released the boy and crossed behind his desk, where he slid a book across to Rolf. "Three things. I want you to read Adolf Hitler's book. I want you to read of his struggles and his journeys. Second, I want you to visit some of our party meetings and talk with some of our members. You will disagree with some of their theories, but you may find others enlightening. No movement is perfect! I want you to chat with me about what you see and hear." Röhm seemed to have grown to twice his size in the last minutes.

"And the third thing?" Rolf asked dreading and knowing the answer.

"I think you know."

A single trail of sweat ran down from Rolf's hairline. Otherwise, he was still. "Shall I remove my clothing now?"

Röhm smiled. "I have a couch. Now is as good as ever, Brunhilde!"

CHAPTER 11

1927
   BERLIN, VIENNA
   THE TOUR

THE SWEET, little apartment bedroom with its aubergine-flowered wallpaper and its old, metal bedframe, its proud, new Victrola phonograph, and clothing and books belonging to both boys strewn everywhere just wouldn't be the same minus one of them. It had been decided that Rolf would stay there amid the T.S. Elliot translations, the framed photos of Lotte Lenya, the Goethe and the Rilke and even some snatches of Dietrich Eckart during Hans' summer Vienna sojourn.

Rolf sat on the bed, hands folded in his lap, feeling a bit lost, as Hans struggled to crush the last of his clothing into the bulging, leather suitcase. "Don't look so glum, darling," Hans said, feeling both guilty and somehow already lonely. "It's only for three months, and you confessed you had to spend some time with your family."

The Master Singer

Rolf pouted very prettily. "With my family, 'some time' is two or three days, not two or three months!" He picked at the knotted, off-white bedspread under which he had secreted a small package. "Have you got everything you need? Do you want my cranberry necktie?'

Hans crossed from his suitcase labor to kiss Rolf on his luscious lips. "Of course I want your cranberry necktie, because it is yours." The two of them sat together on the bed they had been sharing for months.

"Mein Gott, it's going to feel odd wearing pajamas again," Hans said.

Rolf wagged a warning finger. "Better keep that thing of ours well-hidden." Hans laughed and kissed Rolf again. He rose and put something by that American mammy-singer Al Jolson on the phonograph, then he returned to sit next to Rolf once more.

"Don't you think it will be thrilling to have motion pictures with sound? There is already an opera short with a section of "Tannhäuser," and they say it is just like being at a live performance."

Rolf wrinkled his nose. "All they do is play a recording in sync with the images. Big deal!"

Hans playfully punched Rolf. "No, sir, it's going to be much more complicated than that. Fritz told me. He has friends hired by the studio."

Rolf stared at Hans who picked up on his seriousness. "Hans, do you have all your identification papers and documents in order?"

Hans crossed to a folder on the dresser. "Yes, right here in my..." He grew suddenly pale and silent. "Fuck, where are they? I always keep them right here in my... THEY HAVE BEEN STOLEN!"

Rolf smiled a tiny smile. "No, my love, not stolen, only

borrowed. Here." He held up the wrapped package from beneath the bedspread.

"What?" the trembling blond asked, taking the package and unwrapping it. Inside, he found a new brown leather travel folder stuffed with a new passport and travel papers proclaiming Hans to be a pure-bred, German citizen. "What is this, Rolf. How did you get this?"

"Those old forgeries of yours could get you in big trouble. Austria doesn't agree with many of Germany's ideas, and defends its statehood fiercely. So, I've had new papers made for you. Hindenburg himself would be fooled by these. I couldn't have my little, Jewish Siegfried in danger."

Hans inspected the documents. They were perfect. In the back of his mind, he had always been a bit worried about the old forgeries made by a Jewish printer in Munich. He set the documents aside, turned to his lover, took his hands and stared into his eyes.

"Rolf, where did you get these, and how? No lies!"

Rolf chewed his lower lip for a moment. "From Ernst Röhm."

"OF ALL PEOPLE!"

Rolf nodded and smiled. "Of all people. He has connections."

"But now he knows about me."

Rolf nodded. "Now he knows. But Germany is getting dangerous for Juden, and Röhm can't ever say anything without compromising himself." Hans hugged Rolf for a very long time. The needle on the record made a shushing sound and, for a moment, time stood still.

Then Hans pulled back with a scowl. "What did you have to do, Rolf, to get these?"

Rolf blushed. "Believe me, you don't want to know."

"Just the once or..."

"Or... but it's over now. I also promised to read 'Mein Kampf' and chat with him about it. That promises to be worse than the sex."

"How dare he touch the man I love. I'll kill him!"

Rolf put a hand to his chest. "Oh, my, how Wagnerian of you. Look, Toots, my ass survived and you've got your papers. End of story. By the way, you know Hitler visited Bayreuth two years ago. In the guest book, he signed, 'Adolf Hitler, writer.' They say he's become intimate friends with Winifred Wagner, and that she even visited Henry Ford in America to solicit him for money for the Nazis."

Hans pushed Rolf back on the bed. "Rolf, you are trying to distract me from wanting to kill that fat, Nazi pig who molested you, and it's not working."

"I've decided I can't wait three months. I shall travel to Vienna to see you in four weeks, whether you want me or not!"

"Oh, Rolf, I want you. I want you more than anything in the world."

Rolf shook his head. "I come in a close second to opera. But that's okay."

And so, promises and kisses melted into the steam of the locomotive and the waving of goodbye from a train carriage window at the Alexanderplatz station. Rolf grew into a tiny spec and then disappeared.

"Cheer up, Opera Boy," gently teased Fritz, aware of Hans' weighty loneliness. He threw his arm around the tenor. "You should be bubbling over with excitement."

"I am," replied Hans without much conviction. "How can I miss him so much an hour after I left him?"

"Idiot! Are you seriously going to allow being separated from your boyfriend dampen the most wonderful experience of your life? You could be the next Max Lorenz."

"Who?"

"Dummy. He's the young tenor who studied under Melchior's teacher in Berlin and through a singing contest won a contract with the Dresden Opera. Everyone is talking about him. He is now singing with Richard Strauss himself! Think, Hans, that could be you in a year or two! You, Opera Boy, are going to sing opera in Vienna with Erich Kleiber!"

With tears still in his eyes, Hans suddenly grinned. "I know. It's a miracle." Fritz uncorked a small bottle of champagne he had packed in his valise and they toasted their good fortune. Everyone in the small company took to calling Hans "Opera Boy." Hans even signed some of his long, overly-detailed, daily letters to Rolf "Opera Boy", or "Your Opera Boy." Silly letters and poems that only the young in love can write.

Excerpts from some such silly letters:

> "When all the world has burned to ashes
> With crazy dancing in the soot,
> With lazy eyes we read the papers
> While kings and clowns collect the loot.
> When orchestras play agitato
> So, that exhausted, we forget
> We used to live for something higher,
> Than just an ember of sunset.
>
> With you, I remember the moonlight
> With you I begin to trust
> My heart to a thing more important
> Than just some dance steps in the dust.
> With you, I believe in tomorrow.
> With you just a heartbeat away,
> The world is an opulent opera.

With you is where I want to stay.

Ever, Your Opera Boy
P.S. If I keep eating the pastries in Vienna, I will become a fat pig and you will hate me."

Rolf's replies were often leaner:

"So, stop eating the pastries!

Your lean and hungry Rolf"
"Dearest Rolf:
I am allowed to wear the gold ring from you during performances. I think of it as a wedding ring and have begun to gesticulate wildly, so it catches the light.

Your ostentatious lover, Hans

Fritz and Hans roomed together in Vienna, and although it was sometimes a bit awkward with the pianist obviously in love with the tenor, they adjusted, and Fritz was always respectful of his friend's feelings. Together, they loved the city of whipped cream, champagne and operetta. Was there anything edible that wasn't covered in some form of cream, and any music that wasn't frothing with schmaltz?

Fritz smiled tolerantly as Hans read every letter from Rolf out loud several times. The roommates trusted in one another and built one of those special lifelong friendships that defy time and events.

The concerts themselves were high-society affairs held in some of the most sumptuous halls and palaces of the city. Places dripping with crystal and covered in gold. Classic statues of nudes exposed immodestly, some of them engaged in very personal activities, displayed themselves on pedestals. As new and modern and quirky as Berlin was, that was how old and revered and steeped in the past, Vienna was.

Hans almost peed his pants when Maestro Kleiber informed him he would be singing one of Don Ottavio's arias from Mozart's "Don Giovanni." But the biggest thrill and surprise was that he was also to sing his Mahler audition song. "I'm going to sing it in front of people," he stuttered to Fritz, feeling positively dizzy.

"Don't forget to breathe now and then when you sing. The key to being a great accompanist is to learn to breath with the singer. For me to do that, you have to remain alive!"

Hans also sang duets with two up-and-coming divas, one a delight, the other a bitch. One of the duets was the famous Watch Duet from "Die Fledermaus," a real treat. On the whole, the company was close and quite friendly. Frequently, Herr Kleiber himself dined with them, often with his American wife, Ruth Goodrich. Kleiber also took great interest in Hans' development as a singer. With Fritz at the piano, he worked with Hans on his voice, hour after hour, day after day.

"You have a marvelous instrument, everyone including my wife tells you that. But you have yet to become a marvelous performer. To do that, you have to listen to yourself less and listen to others more. On days when you have no practice, come and hear me work with others. Listen to the sound and emotion they produce. Attend the rehearsals of others, not just your own. Pay attention to the lyrical meaning and emotion coming from other singers. The more you absorb from others, the better you will sing. Some people live for their family, some for their business, some for their politics and some for their religion. You must live for your art!" Herr Kleiber dedicated himself to transforming Hans' agility to virtuosity.

Maestro Kleiber tolerated Tilly for her talent. Tilly was a spoiled, self-absorbed soprano, so much so that she failed to notice the mild scorn from the rest of the company, except of course for Rupert, the baritone, who thought she was the cat's pajamas and wanted to get into them. Fritz pointed out to Tilly, whom he re-christened "Silly Tilly," that no opera diva with a name like Tilly would ever be taken seriously, but the poor thing was so attached to and enamored with everything about herself that she refused to change it.

The other leading lady, Marguerite, whom they all called Molly was game for most anything and often sat up late at night with Fritz and Hans in their room playing cards. She was a real flapper and dragged the boys out to dance clubs where she could flirt with men while Fritz and Hans happily danced with each other. Fritz, with his long lean arms and legs and his big hands, out-flapped any other flapper on the floor.

When Hans could keep his dread secret from his friend no longer,

he sat him down on the bed one evening with bottles of beer and Vienna torte. Fritz was in a tank top and boxer shorts, and Hans in a pair of striped pajamas. Hans began his confession.

"Because I love you dearly, Fritz, and you are the second most important person in my life, I cannot bear to keep secrets from you."

Fritz, who by now knew every nuance of Hans' voice and felt the tension in it, took his friend's hands. "What is it, Opera Boy, something serious?"

Hans had tears in his eyes. "Something quite serious, I'm afraid."

"Something about you and Rolf?"

"No, not directly, although I fear it may someday fuck up

our future. When I tell you this, you may choose to no longer room with me. However, I beg you, please keep it to yourself."

"What can be so awful, Hans?"

Hans squeezed his eyes shut. "Ich bin Jude, Fritz. I am a Jew!"

Fritz inhaled and held his breath for a few seconds. Then, "Oh, is that all? Maestro Kleiber suspected as much when Frau Greenberg recommended you. And you sang that Mahler piece, Mahler being a Jew, although he converted to Catholicism for convenience."

Hans opened his eyes, but gripped Fritz's big hands even tighter. "And you don't hate Jews?"

Fritz smiled. "'Rhapsody in Blue' was written by a Jew. How could I ever hate anyone who wrote that? And you know I love you, so how could I hate you?" They hugged and such a big thing became, temporarily at least, such a small thing. Perhaps foolishly, it was forgotten.

Two things made Hans' already perfect existence even more perfect - the enthusiastic response of the audience to the concerts and to his singing, and a visit from Rolf! Rolf arrived unannounced and unexpected. After a performance one evening, he strode backstage dressed in white tie and tails, with his arms filled with flowers and boxes of candy. He looked like an American movie star, and Silly Tilly almost came in her panties. Scattering flowers and chocolates everywhere, he swept Hans up in his arms, and the tenor was delirious with joy.

They went to an artists' café where entertainers of all sorts hung out until morning, Rolf and Hans and Molly and Fritz and two friendly fellows from the orchestra. They wolfed down sausages and dumplings and beer, Rolf and Hans lost in each-others' eyes. "You were the best one," Rolf kept whispering. Fritz, overcoming his slight sense of jealousy, kept things bouncing along with his wit and his gossip.

It was the kind of artists' café where everyone was called upon to entertain, and so, eventually it became Hans' turn. He declined at first, preferring to sit there next to Rolf, but the animated, half-drunken applause and cheering would have romanced any self-respecting performer.

He hopped up onto the small stage and nodded to the band, as Fritz nudged the piano player to take a break and replaced him. Hans cleared his throat and spoke into the big, round microphone.

"Tonight, I would like to sing for you a brand-new song by Franz Lehar, from an operetta to be produced next season. This is the first time most of you will hear it, and I'd like to dedicate it to a very special person in my life."

Never one to be shy in a nightclub or tavern, Rolf waved his napkin in the air. More laughter and applause.

"The song is called, 'Dein Ist Mein Ganzes Herz,' 'You are My Heart's Delight.'"

The usual chatter and clinking of glassware and china, that continued nonstop in such establishments ceased altogether when Fritz began to play, and Hans prepared to sing. Waiters stopped waiting, and the maître d' and hat check girls wandered in, as did the chef from the kitchen. A new Lehar melody did this, along with the talented tenor singing it.

> "You are my heart's delight,
> And where you are, I long to be...
> You make the darkness bright,
> And like a star, you shine on me."

At the table, Rolf stood with tears in his eyes and his

hand over his heart, and Hans sang only for him, with everyone else privileged to listen in. Such schmaltz could only happen in Vienna.

The miracle of Hans' voice was that although it seemed a light tenor, it could, when required, possess a strong, almost baritone quality. This was the kind of voice that might have the stamina to sing Wagner.

When he finished the song, a verse in German and a verse in English, the room remained still and silent. What had he done to them? What magic spell had he woven? And then, a hand somewhere began to pound rhythmically on a tabletop. Others joined in, in a sound that was not unlike a locomotive picking up speed. Soon, the whole room rocked with the pounding, joined now by cheers and whistles, as everyone in the room rose to their feet.

Hans stood frozen, one hand clasped to his mouth. Then, the band behind him struck up a crazy jazz dance number, and Rolf rushed across the room and swept Hans from the stage. Together, they articulated the angular, twisted steps and gestures of the era. Just as the flappers in America had their own particular moves, so the modern generation in the Vienna and Berlin of 1927 had theirs. An oddly geometric frenzy, like one of the modernist art movement paintings brought to life. Others, including Molly and Fritz, quickly joined in, and soon the dancefloor became a kaleidoscope of movement, where at times everyone performed the same step or gesture in unison, and at others the pattern shattered into a thousand shakes and shimmies. It seemed to reflect not only the lives of the two young men in love, but of the world itself.

CHAPTER 12

1927

   VIENNA, BERLIN, MUNICH, NUREMBERG
   BACK AND FORTH

ROLF RETURNED to Berlin after two hectic weeks in Vienna. He loved being with Hans but also felt a bit out of place and useless. Everyone except him seemed to have a purpose.

In Vienna, Jacob Becker and his blond wife, Gretchen, also visited to hear their son sing. How could they miss such an event? They met with their son privately at small, quiet cafés and kept a low profile, even though the "Jewish Problem" was minimal in Austria, and none of them really "looked Jewish," whatever that meant. How proud they were of their boy. Hans promised to spend some time with them in Munich at the end of the tour.

It was in Nuremberg that a rather strange thing happened. The company was rehearsing with only Fritz at the piano, working in a large meeting room at their hotel because of its acoustics, and Maestro Kleiber making some few small adjustments in the program. In the middle of a Rossini quartet, the doors at the rear of the room opened none too quietly and three men entered. They were dressed in the distinctive, brown-shirt, storm trooper uniforms. The two younger men stayed at the door, hands clasped behind their backs, while the older, obvious leader of the trio, strode boldly down a pathway between tables and chairs and plunked himself down before Kleiber and the ensemble. He put one booted foot up on another chair, and leaned back.

The maestro pretended to take no notice of the steel grey man in the brown uniform, and continued to conduct his singers. Fritz continued to play and the singers continued to sing, but there was definite tension in the room.

After the Rossini finished, Kleiber wiped his forehead with a kerchief and announced a ten-minute break. The ensemble exited the room quietly through another door, leaving Fritz and Hans to hang back in case of trouble.

With that gentle smile on his small, sensitive face, Kleiber approached the rather ghostly-looking grey man and extended a hand. "Erich Kleiber. How may I help you?"

The grey man in brown rose slowly and shook Kleiber's hand. He had not removed his brown hat. His face was hawk-like and his nose a sharp beak, obviously adept at sniffing out trouble.

"I am Herr Greuning, secretary of the National Socialist Workers Party here in Nuremberg, and commissioner of the Moral Decency League."

"Ah?" Kleiber said, brightening his smile and acting impressed, although he had never heard of such a league and doubted it even existed. He suspected at once that Herr Greuning was just a local Nazi thug trying to push his weight around and make a name for himself. "And what may I do for you, Herr Greuning?"

The grey hawk cleared his throat somewhat officially, then with a small, political smile, which must have been painful for him, he said, "We would just like to assure the people of Nuremberg that, in national interests, your much anticipated concert here will contain nothing but music by German composers."

"Nothing but German composers..." repeated Kleiber slowly and carefully.

"Exactly! Germany must unite behind its proud heritage and reject all foreign decadent influences."

"Well..." Kleiber took a long pause, "Our program is mostly German."

"Mostly?" The steel-grey eyebrows rose suspiciously. Kleiber observed that the man needed them trimmed.

"Ja, mostly. Who can resist a round of Rossini or a touch of Tchaikovsky, or a bit of Bizet?" The conductor positively glowed when he said this. Seeing the thugs at the door stiffen, Hans and Fritz drew closer to their conductor.

Herr Greuning grew even steelier. "I must insist on behalf of the people of Nuremberg that you remove all works by non-German composers from your program." His voice rose in pitch as well as volume.

"And may I ask who appointed your rag-tag political party to speak for the people of Nuremberg?"

The hawk actually clicked his heels, and the sound carried beautifully through the meeting room. "We have almost one hundred thousand members and can cause quite a disturbance when necessary."

Kleiber frowned. "Is that a threat?"

Greuning drew back his lips to reveal sharp, yellow

teeth. "It is an advisory. It is our duty to speak out for those who cannot."

Kleiber almost spit, "And to think for them, too?"

With much clatter of chairs and slamming of doors, the trio left. Kleiber was livid. He shoved a few chairs himself. "They want German music," he said to Fritz, while digging through a suitcase of scores. "All right, let's give them German music. How about a bit of 'Wozzeck?'" He pulled out and waved some hand-written sheets of composition. "How about some songs from that new team, Brecht and Weill? That will snap the garters on their socks! Who will be brave enough to sing them? Han, will you do us the honor?"

"I'll sing the telephone book if you ask me to!"

Kleiber laughed almost hysterically, as he tossed sheet music into the air like confetti. It was an emotional release. The rest of the company cautiously re-entered the room. Kleiber waved the music in his hand like a weapon. And it was. "Brecht and Weill are taking opera in a totally new direction. I warn you, Hans, it is almost anti-Wagnerian. Whereas Wagner labored to make his operas unified wholes, sometimes weaving one melody through four hours of performance, Brecht and Weill fracture and disjoint the operatic form, with a series of choral pieces made up of individual, often ragged, song. When their 'Dreigroschenoper' opens next year, it's going to cause riots in the streets, mark my word."

Hans grabbed for the music like a hungry child for a heel of bread. "I want to do it! I want to be in it!" he shouted, just as every young, even untrained, actor wants to play Hamlet. The other company members gathered around and Kleiber handed out more music.

"We'll toss in some French pieces, and an American song or two. We'll give them a concert to remember!"

Well, the public adored the evening of "International Classics." It turned out there was never any actual threat. A few clusters of Brownshirts, with their red and black swastika armbands, stomped and chanted outside the concert hall, but it amounted to nothing. Kleiber did warn his beloved company however to beware of a coming storm.

"I am afraid things are going to get worse, much worse for our dear country, and for us artists, too."

Before returning to Berlin and Rolf, Hans took two weeks to visit his family in Munich. Before he even went home, he visited the site of the National Theatre at Max-Joseph-Platz. It was here that the very first performance of "Tristan and Isolde" was given. Also the first performances of "Das Rheingold" and "Die Walküre," as the Bayreuth theater had not yet been built, and an anxious King Ludwig, who had financed, and therefore technically owned the operas, wanted to see them staged. Wagner hated the productions, but the place still held magic for Wagnerites.

Because of the incident in Nuremberg, as well as the recent increasing political strife, Hans also visited Feldherrnhalle and the Bürgerbräukeller where in 1923, Adolf Hitler announced the start of the "People's Revolution," and the takeover of the central district of Munich. Now, almost five years later, after his time in Berlin, the "Munich Hitler Putsch" meant much more to Hans than it had before.

Jacob Becker's Art and Antique Emporium was located right off Neuhauser Strasse in Marienplatz, the city's oldest architectural and commercial hub. The family lived in two floors above the spacious shop.

Hans was welcomed warmly by both Jewish and German friends, on two separate evenings, and the food and music on those evenings was quite different. The young man's home life was actually quite Bavarian, since Jacob had long since renounced most of the Jewish traditions with which he had grown up. The death of his father put the final nail into the coffin. The family seldom practiced Jewish holidays, except in some token way, and they combined together Christmas and Chanukah. Gretchen, Hans' "Mutti," was adept enough to include just enough Jewish flavor amid all the Germania to keep everyone happy. Gretchen had carefully navigated this for the welfare of her husband and son. She, more than the rest of the family, was aware of the rising anti-Semitic sentiment.

For some reason, Jacob seemed least aware of the mounting troubles. Perhaps he did not want to see them. Perhaps it had something to do with his love of Munich and his life there. Or perhaps it had to do with his war service, or his own parents' forced emigration from Ukraine. Perhaps it was all of these.

Evenings for those two weeks, whether Jewish or German flavored, were filled with wonderful food and music. Family friends came to call, and always Hans had to sing with Gretchen or Mirah Hirshbein on the piano. Jacob had a framed poster from the Vienna concert series on his wall.

One afternoon, Hans sat with his father in the store, surrounded by beautiful things, one of them being a magnificent menorah. "Should I learn more about being a Jew, Papa?" Hans asked.

Jacob sighed. "I suppose we both should pay more attention to our heritage, but this is not the best moment in history to have that curiosity, especially with your career goal in mind."

Hans toyed with an exquisite porcelain inkwell. "I am always aware that I am hiding something central about myself, but it is something I neither recognize nor feel. I feel

German. I have always felt German. Why can't I just be a German?"

Jacob chuckled. "I certainly felt German when I fought in the war. I was good enough for them then."

Just then, there was a riotous clamor and a stomping outside the shop. A group of SA brownshirts, who had been forbidden to demonstrate for a few years because of their destructive behavior, were celebrating their new-found freedom. Men and boys, some as young as twelve or thirteen, marched and shouted, sang and spit, forced citizens out of the way, and pounded on the doors and windows of various business establishments. They pasted Heinrich Hoffmann's photographs of Adolf Hitler on storefront windows. One was slapped on the big front window of the Becker's gallery.

Jacob shook his head. "This will get worse, son, before it gets better, and I, like many others, have buried my head in the sand. One of the reasons their membership has grown so astronomically is because they have managed to convince ordinary people that their financial and social misfortune was caused by wealthy Jews who are controlling the country."

"But that's just stupid, Papa!"

"Of course it's stupid. Infantile! But the truth seldom matters to people whose humanity extends only as far as their front stoop! 'What's in it for me?' That is what elects presidents."

The clamorous parade passed, and the street became itself again. Jacob put his arm around his son's shoulder. "You see? Calm once again. But, my boy, if you still intend someday to sing at Bayreuth and to worship the music of Richard Wagner, I strongly suggest you read what he wrote about Jews."

Hans looked around the shop, at all the beautiful paintings on the walls and easels. "Papa, can one separate the art from the artist, the creation from the creator? Can severely flawed men create flawless beauty? And can we love the art and loathe the artist?"

Jacob ran a hand through his head of abundant hair. "That is a question every art lover must answer for him or herself. As humans, we are all flawed, so what do we judge? The art or the artist? The perfection of ballet is created by some of the ugliest feet in the world. Perhaps that is the price for perfection."

On another afternoon, Hans was tending the business to give his mother and father a day off together when the young man was bowled over by the arrival of Munich's most famous resident, Thomas Mann himself. Whenever Hans and his friends had had reason to pass the Mann family mansion on Paschinger Strasse, they had automatically lowered their voices out of respect for the great writer. Some said it was Mann who had made modern Munich famous, or infamous.

The dignified, professorial author puttered around the place for quite a while, while Hans stood anxiously waiting to serve him. Truth be told, he seemed to take more interest in Hans than in the antiques, which both flattered and frightened the young man. Mann had a dignity and bearing about him that was at once both regal and humane, more elegant than masculine. He was extremely gentle, but exuded a kind of superiority of intellect. Hans found himself studying Mann's full, inquisitive eyebrows and his perfectly-groomed, little moustache. He had sensitive, kindly eyes and a not very strong chin. He wore an expensive grey suit with a white, breast-pocket handkerchief spilling out of it as a touch of eccentricity. His shirt was crisp and his tie elegant and perfectly knotted. As he wandered the shop, he struck up a conversation with Hans, asking him about his schooling and interests. Mann had something intelligent to say on every subject, and on every piece of art he discovered in the store. How could one man know so much? Their rather one-sided conversation soon touched on music and Wagner.

"I'm so stupid, I feel like a complete dolt," Hans confessed.

Mann wagged a finger. "Don't talk like that, it's not true. You are young, and inquisitive and you have a passion. Who could ask for more? Except, of course, for beauty, and you have that as well. I wish one of my sons had a true passion for music. It is the most precious of the arts. We authors are forever trapped in words."

As in a dream, they moved through the shop, and at the end of his visit, Mann purchased a most curious item, a framed Aubrey Beardsley drawing entitled, "The Wagnerites," depicting the audience at a Wagner opera. Mann explained to Hans that he adored the satirical decadence of it. He also purchased a lovely, richly-illustrated, five volume set of "The Count of Monte Cristo," explaining to Hans that "everyone needs a little bit of Dumas in his life." And then he was gone, leaving a shell-shocked Hans, who immediately sat down and wrote a detailed account of the visit to Rolf.

Rolf, meanwhile, sat stiffly at an extended lunch with his father, mother and younger sister at their home in Berlin.

"It's so wonderful to have you home with us for a change," Rolf's mother said in that way she had of making her love and approval seem conditional. A little phrase like, "for a change," could dampen any loving compliment. She tipped her spoon perfectly, sending the delicious vegetable soup soundlessly into her mouth. The smile was terse.

"When you are not here, I sometimes don't see your father until dinner." Rolf could understand why. And yet the woman was not without love, and in her own way, she wanted the best for her husband and children. They in turn, were forever trying to discern whether her comments were genuine or attempts to lay guilt trips on them.

Professor Peter Kainz rose each day at seven. He bathed while having a cup of coffee. Then he dressed. Often, it was true, he did not join his wife and daughter for breakfast, preferring to nosh while working in his office. Being a highly respected professor of history and philosophy, he hardly really worked at all. He had only to lecture two hours a week. He had minions to correct papers, and he spent most of his time dabbling in what was called research. He loved to dabble.

In the luxury of his office, and only there, Peter Kainz indulged in one of his only filthy vices, an occasional Overstolz cigarette. It was not a vice to most. All of Berlin, all of Germany, smoked, but to the professor it was decadent and therefor a guilty pleasure.

"I don't know why you don't live at home with us, Rolf," Helga was saying. "We are in the same city, and we hardly see you."

Peter Kainz dabbed his lips with a monogramed napkin. "Boys Rolf's age need a certain amount of freedom," he said, glancing at his son and adding silently with his eyes, "from their mother." Actually, the professor was glad to have his wild, trouble-making son out of his hair. He no longer felt responsible for the boy's antics. "Besides, I'm rather proud of you, Rolf!" he added.

Rolf coughed in his coffee. "Will wonders never cease?"

Hilde, Rolf's fifteen-year-old sister giggled and got a stern look from Mother.

"No, seriously, Son, I am proud of you declaring history as your major at university. A bit of your father rubbed off on you, right? You could do worse. You could do worse."

Rolf figured that this was not a good time to tell his parents that he was seriously considering dropping out of school altogether. So many bright, young men had recently quit school to make a name for themselves out there in the real world. Unable to not say anything negative, Rolf responded, "Yes, although the university is an exclusive, rarified atmosphere that stinks of elitism."

Peter Kainz was not to be put off. "Yes, rarified by nature of intelligence and curiosity. Elite in that it creates leaders."

Rolf frowned, and then asked without sarcasm, "What would happen, Papa, if our leaders came from the other end of society, from the uneducated workers?"

"Chaos, pandemonium, and total collapse. There are leaders in the world, Rolf, and there are followers."

"Yes, but must the leaders always be intellectuals and elite?"

"Ha! I'd hardly call some of the European Royals and their generals these last years intelligent! But they preserve 'class,' and without class, art and leisure for some, society collapses. And somehow elite rulers always emerge. Look at Russia. Do you really think Stalin eats what the common worker eats? Does he drive in the same kind of auto they do? Does he sleep in the same kind of bed or copulate with the same kind of woman? Even Napoleon, who slept in a soldier's camp bed most of his life, and ate and drank with his men, escaped from frozen Russia wrapped in furs, in a comfortable sleigh, while thousands of his men literally froze to death in their steps. There is no such thing as equality."

"This entire discussion has put me off my sorbet,"

complained Helga. Hilde slid it over in front of herself to finish it for her mother.

Rolf took the momentary pause in conversation to bite the bullet. "I want to bring someone here to stay with us for a visit. Someone special."

"Oh, thank God, you've found a suitable young lady at last," Helga beamed, fanning herself with her napkin.

"Not exactly!"

CHAPTER 13

1927
BERLIN

LETTER FROM HANS BECKER to Rolf Kainz
My Dear, Sweet Wildboy;
In two-weeks-time, I shall be back in Berlin and back in our bed, so toss out whoever sleeps there with you now and launder the sheets. Oh, the many, many unspeakable things I want to do to you and with you, and you with me. When I sing, I only sing of you and for you.
You'll never guess who popped into my father's shop in Munich. Thomas Mann. Yes, that Thomas Mann. I know he has at least a dozen children, but I swear he flirted with me, Rolf. He flirted with me! You will swear it was my narcissism. But the proof is, several days later, I received a package from him containing his novella "Death in Venice." Mein Gott, Rolf, have you read it???????? It's all about this older artist who has this obsession for a young boy. Oh, yes, it's filled with a great deal more, allusions to Apollonian and

Dionysian types, and reason and passion, and artists losing and gaining their spontaneity, and so on, but my dearest, above all it is about this artist having the hots for this young, Polish kid! I shall read it to you in bed between kisses. Speaking of kisses, I kissed your ring each night before I sang, and I kiss it still. If it is fake gold and not "The Ring "itself, the finish shall soon wear off, as may your love someday.

You know, you have written exactly one third of the times that I have, and I know you must be tremendously busy doing whatever it is you do. What do you do exactly? You know what idle minds are... the devil's playground. When do your fall classes start? Until then, I shall imprison you both day and night and make you choose between my singing and sex.

Just think, it will soon be 1928, and you and I shall soon be adults.

We are then meant to put away all our toys. Well, not all of them! For the next few months, I intend to smoke and drink with you like a degenerate and crawl back with you by dawn to our bohemian garret, where we shall sleep and fuck all day. Doesn't that sound like a plan, my "Siegfried Man?"

Yours forever, I do love you so,

Hans, the Opera Boy

CHAPTER 14

1928

BERLIN

FRAU GREENBERG'S AND THE KAINZ HOME

HANS PULLED up his collar and tightened the scarf around his neck, as there was a chill in the air. He had a job singing with a dance band at a supper club called "Spätzle" and had to protect his voice. He hated the job, but times were hard, and he needed the money. Rolf always seemed to have enough of Papa's gelt for both of them, but Hans also needed the musical exposure and connections. Fritz telephoned every few weeks with job leads that thus far had not materialized, and prices of everyday things were going through the roof.

However, such things matter little to young men in love, and Hans and Rolf were basically very happy. They saw much theater together including Shakespeare, Moliere, Chekhov, and scads of new German playwrights. They went to concerts and the opera of course, and danced and drank and drank and drank and smoked terribly mysterious things and fell even more in love if that was possible.

On this particular nippy day, while Rolf had disgusting morning classes, Hans went to visit his old voice teacher, Frau Greenberg. He wanted to fill her in on the concert tour and his vocal progress. He thought he might set up some classes with her again. However, when he reached he apartment building, he was shocked to find her name removed from the list of tenants. He rang her bell to no avail, and finally rang the manager.

August Mueller was a small man in many ways. Small inside and out, he had come through the war unscathed due in part to his very pettiness. He was often overlooked. He was not particularly mean or nasty, nor was he excessively pleasant. He opened the door a bit and stuck out a small, oval-shaped face sporting small, half-moon, wire rimmed glasses. His most distinctive feature was an elaborate comb-over which began behind his right ear and swirled down and around his pate almost to the left. He must not have seen the naked shiny back of his head in a mirror. His shirt was open at the neck, and he wore an open waistcoat as well. His heavy eyelids looked Hans up and down and blinked several times.

"Ja? How can I help you?" he asked.

Hans removed his hat. "It's me, Hans Becker. I was a voice student of Frau Greenberg last year."

Mueller blinked again, several times. "She's gone. She doesn't live here anymore." He seemed anxious to close the door.

"Was she ill? Did she die?"

"No, no," the head shook, threatening to dislodge the comb-over. "She was evicted. A big truck came and took her piano, everything. And so, she is gone." This time the door did begin to close, but an irritated Hans stopped it with his hand.

"Where did she go?"

"How the hell should I know? And what do I care? Now, please..."

"I care! She wouldn't just move. She lived here for over thirty years!"

Mueller huffed and puffed. "I told you, she was evicted. Times change. We don't want her kind living in the building no more. The neighbors complained." His nose became red and moist.

A totally naïve Hans responded, "You don't want music teachers? Are they too loud?" He was very confused and agitated.

A red-faced Mueller almost screamed, "Juden! We don't want Juden! It's time to clean them out of our city."

Hans shook his head. This could not be. "But you have lived in the same building with her for years. It never mattered before."

There followed a little struggle with the door. "Well, it matters now! They are vampires, sucking our very blood." He was irrational in his fury.

"Did she do something wrong?" Hans asked

August Mueller was so livid he now almost foamed at the mouth. "What's wrong with you, boy? Don't you understand Deutsch? SHE IS A JEW! We are cleaning the neighborhood. We got rid of the tailor and the crazy doctor who fiddles with people's heads as well. Look," he lost a bit of his fury, "I've got nothing against them personally. Let them live happily elsewhere. But not here! Now, I have to go. I'm missing my radio program." He slammed the door.

When Hans, dissolved in tears, told Rolf, his lover held him in his arms and rocked him. "That's the temperament I now fear, I sense it at the university. But I love you, Hans, and I know not all Jews are bad."

"WOOF!" Hans jerked back. "What do you mean, not all Jews are bad?"

Rolf put his strong hands on Hans' shoulders. "Look, Hans, there are good and bad in all races. In 'Mein Kampf,' Hitler writes that different human races should be kept apart, just as different animal species are kept apart. Some human species are 'culture-creating' while others are 'culture-destroying.'" Rolf's face was shiningly beautiful as he said these things. Hans felt as if his own face were melting off.

But Rolf continued. "According to Hitler, at the top of the culture creating races are the Nordic types. Nordic, Aryan, Germanic. This master race deserves to dominate and control inferior, culture- destroying races."

"Like the Jews..." Hans spit, twisting away.

"Oh, come on Hans. You yourself are at least half master race. You see these ideas personified in the works of your idol, Wagner."

Hans slumped. "And so, Frau Greenberg should be evicted?"

Rolf grabbed him by the shoulders hard. "Of course not! These are philosophical and political propositions, theories to explain things. I would have punched your Herr Mueller in the face. There are always people who misunderstand, or who go too far. It will pass, I promise you. This is 1928, not the Middle Ages."

"And what if Hitler's people win the vote in May?"

"They'll get five percent of the vote at most. But Hans, times are tough and people hurt. We are all going to have to make some concessions. For the time being, at least, it is better that you remain 'pure

German.'" Rolf couldn't stand the hurt-puppy look on Hans' face.

Hans shook his blond head. "To have to live with this through no fault of my own."

"Come, come, my little Hasidic Hun, lots of people have it much worse off than we do. And I've got some good news. I'm taking you to meet Mummy and Daddy! Mater and Pater! What a great time that will be."

Professor Peter Kainz puffed up like a peacock suddenly at the dinner table. "Well, I've taken the plunge!"

"You've become a competitive swimmer?" Rolf asked, raising his eyebrows, and holding up a forkful of schnitzel.

Peter Kainz glowered. "Don't be frivolous, young man! This is most important." To add severity, he removed the cloth napkin from his shirtfront. "I hope our fine young guest won't mind a bit of family business, but I see my son so seldom, and this business concerns the entire family."

Helga Kainz had already arched an eyebrow. Had Peter chosen this moment, with a guest present, to help cushion a blow and prevent a blow-up? "Continue," she said, carefully.

"Are we buying a new automobile?" Hilde asked excitedly. There had been some talk of that.

With mock excitement Rolf said, "Don't be foolish, Hilde. You heard Papa say plunge, so it must involve water!"

Peter tapped the rim of his water glass with a spoon to restore decorum. Hans felt a bit embarrassed.

"Listen, all of you. This affects all of you, except for Master Hans of course, although he may also benefit from my words. I have taken the plunge. The next few months will require measures of extreme austerity. No frivolous spending. I have consolidated all of our holdings and all of our funds and invested them in the stock market!" He looked ever so proud sitting there.

"You didn't..." Helga said, losing her poise a bit.

"I did!" he said, smugly, proud to have acted on his own in a business venture. Professors often do not good businessmen make.

"Surely not all, Peter?" she said with a small frozen smile.

Peter slapped a satisfied hand down on the tabletop. "All, Helga. All our savings and our property, and my retirement package from the university. I needed it all in order for this venture to pay off." He looked terribly excited and pleased with himself, but he could have killed for a cigarette.

Helga allowed an embarrassed sidelong glance at Hans, who sat motionless. "But not my father's..."

"Everything! I needed to use everything. It was the right decision, and I was certainly not alone in making it. Investors far wiser than I have been urging me to make this move for some time. All of our friends, Helga, well, not all, but most of our friends have done the same thing. I would recommend your parents do the same, Hans!"

Rolf had turned quite pale and become as serious as Hans had ever seen him. "Why would you take such a risk, Papa? You have always been a cautious man."

The professor raised one finger and screwed up his face in delight. "But don't you see, it's not a risk. It's only for a few months, a year at most. We invest a huge amount, and then, with the market at its peak, we withdraw with huge profits!"

Rolf's voice remained even, but tense. "But how can you be certain, Papa?"

"Because the group of men I am joining understand the stock market. The proof? The Wall Street Stock Market in America. Average people have become millionaires. This is fact, not rumor. I've seen the figures. They use their savings as collateral to invest more, and when the stocks go up, it's a windfall!" His self-satisfied glee even shocked the servants clearing the plates for the next course.

"And if the stocks go down instead?" Helga asked in a measured voice.

"Ah, but they won't go down. Again, New York is our model. The world is rebuilding, and the stocks go up and up and up. That's why it is essential to invest now… to get in on the ground floor!"

Except for the ticking of the clock, there was a profound silence in the room. Then Helga raised her hand to signal the next course and asked in a very pleasant tone, "Is that the end of your announcement, Peter?"

After dinner Hans sang, with Hilde at the piano. He was reticent to do so, but after all, it was the real reason for his visit. The Kainz family had many friends influential in the arts, and Rolf wanted his parents to arrange an evening to promote Hans. After hearing him sing some Schubert and a new song by a German composer named Robert Stolz, who was currently working in Berlin's "Dream Factory," writing music for the latest thing, sound motion pictures. Helga was so impressed, she announced she would invite the art elite of Berlin to hear Hans. Peter agreed that the boy had a most impressive and unique instrument, and lamented that Rolf never took art seriously. "I believe that you are a wonderful influence on my son, and we will support your efforts with a recital."

"If we still have a piano," Helga remarked wryly.

That evening, back in their own bed, Hans proved several times to Rolf what a wonderful influence he could be.

CHAPTER 15

1928

    BERLIN
    THE ELDORADO CLUB
    THE APARTMENT
    THE KAINZ HOME

THE NAZI PARTY won twelve seats in the Reichstag election. Rolf and Hans were at the Eldorado Club one evening when a fist-fight broke out between Nazi Brownshirt queers and drag queen queers. Imagine anyone queer accusing another queer of giving homosexuality a bad name. Kalanag, the magician, was sitting at a table with the Nazi homos, but came over to have a drink with Rolf and Hans.

"Well, you two are looking fit. The Siegfried helden tenor, and the..." he paused, studying Rolf, "the what? What are you, Rolf?" This was not said unkindly, just a bit mysteriously. "If Hans is Siegfried, who are you in this great saga of current times? Surely not Hagen." He snapped his fingers. "Or, perhaps Hans is Tristan, and you are Isolde who snares

The Master Singer

them both with a love potion." He studied them through those owl glasses of his. He had lost some of his hair, but otherwise he looked the same.

Rolf was not amused. "And you, Herr Kalanag, have made quite a name for yourself in these last years, not only as an awesome stage magician, but as a Brownshirt brownnose!"

Kalanag laughed merrily. His survival tactic was to never reveal his true feelings. He pushed up the sleeves of his jacket and shirt cuffs to show he had nothing in his hands, and then out of thin air, he produced a coin which clattered to the table. It bore an image of Adolf Hitler!

"In the next few years, boys, it will become most important where one places one's bets." He took the coin in one hand, made a fist, and when he opened it again, there were two. "I had the honor of performing for Hitler at a small gathering of his friends - Himmler, Rohm and so on. Just between us, he is quite magical himself." He placed the two coins in Rolf's hand, closed the hand, and when Rolf opened it, four coins spilled out.

"He is small and unassuming, rather like myself. But his eyes, his eyes are piercing, hypnotic and quite dangerous." He swept up the four coins, waved his hands and they all disappeared. "Put your money on the right political candidate boys, or you may lose more than just your wager!"

It would be of interest for some to examine the little table inside the entrance to Hans and Rolf's bedroom. The whole apartment was nothing more really than a bedroom, a bathroom and a hallway. This little table was where they set their keys and mail and often piled their magazines and other reading material. There were always advertisements for this or that new classical or jazz recording and brochures for current film showings. This week, it was the popular sensation, Fritz Lang's "Metropolis," finally playing after months of teasing. And it was every bit as astounding as promised. There were the latest fashion ads from the newest shopping craze, the "Big Berlin Department Stores," like Wertheim's on Leipziger Platz. Floors and floors of everything one could imagine, from crystal ware to funeral caskets.

The mail piled on the table showed these to be intelligent, cultured boys. Well, not entirely. Rolf had an affinity for trashy, homosexual magazines, some covering the club scene, and some uncovering male models. There were dozens and dozens of such magazines available at the local news kiosks.

Then on the overburdened, little table, there were the almost daily letters from Fritz, who telephoned Hans every day but, for some reason, seemed compelled to write as well. He wrote about little nothings, but his gossip about the movie studio where he worked was always fascinating. He had seen Dietrich!

Currently atop the latest pile of mail, there rested a brown, paper package tied with string from Thomas Mann. The enclosed letter to Hans apologized at length for Mann seeking out Hans' Berlin address from the boy's father, but the prize-winning author felt that the young man might be interested in Mann's essay and lecture titled "On the German Republic."

Hans and Rolf got high on cocaine or weed and cheap wine and giggled mercilessly at the essay's extolling a "Dream Germany" where young men lived together in obvious homosexual harmony. Mann even quoted the scandalous Walt Whitman.

"The old goat, Mann, is horny for you Hans, no doubt about it," Rolf teased, tweaking his lover's nipple.

Hans pretended to be offended. "Hush, you degenerate. Mann is a great man, and his vision is noble and pure!"

Rolf grabbed the letter. "Then what is this part about? 'An all-embracing kingdom of phallically sacred, phallically bursting ardor.' That is what the man or Mann writes! I think he wants your phallus to ardorly burst!"

Hans playfully shoved Rolf way, calling him a dirty pervert. Rolf cackled and grabbed his lover, rolling him over on the bed. "You knew that way back at Hunding's Hut!"

Also on the little table, ignored for awhile because of the boys' preoccupations, lay an expensive piece of stationery, bordered in mauve. It was an invitation to a salon to be held by Professor and Frau Kainz, at which the talented young Berlin vocalist, Hans Becker, would be presented in concert, accompanied on the piano by Brunhilde Kainz.

Rolf threw a satisfied head back onto the pillow. "Mamma is a wily old fox and is sure to invite some very influential people, if not for your sake, for her own. Once they hear you, they will all fall in love with you, as I did!"

"Oh, dear, if they shall all love me as you do, I had better hydrate!"

Hans straddled Rolf and tickled him for a bit. "And speaking of you first falling in love with me, as I remember it, at sixteen, you were not particularly interested in higher love or my voice."

Hans spent more than a few afternoons at the Kainz home, rehearsing with Hilde. The young man had tons of vocal scores and spent much of his free time studying and learning various opera roles suggested by Erich Kleiber, things for which his voice was ready.

Hans grew quite fond of Hilde. She seemed a pleasant cross between Rolf and his mother, a bit proper, as a wealthy young lady was taught to be, but still full of life and energy, and with a pinch of Rolf's naughtiness.

Helga hovered. She made a few, but not many, song suggestions, and sensed her limitations. Above all, even with a young friend of her son's, she did not want to ever appear foolish. She did upon occasion attempt to pry from Hans information about Rolf's lifestyle.

"What sort of young ladies does Rolf prefer? He never brings them around to call." There are those who swear that a mother always knows the truth about a son's sexuality.

Hans almost choked on his tea. "Oh, Rolf is almost monastic when it comes to dating girls. He prefers deeper relationships."

That eyebrow went up again. "Oh, really? That wasn't the impression his boarding school headmaster gave us when Rolf was repeatedly expelled. He was called 'hedonistic' in its ugliest sense, not monastic."

Hans nodded sagely. "Well, even St. Paul went from hedonistic to monastic, one might say." Young Hilde winked at Hans, knowingly.

Although he had toured Vienna and other major cities singing with Erich Kleiber, and now sang each week at a posh supper club with a well-known dance band, Hans was terrified to sing before the distinguished guests of the Kainz family. It was as if he had to impress his lover's family and friends.

"You are going to be wonderful, you know that," pampered Rolf, straightening Hans bow tie for the twentieth time.

"Not if you choke me with the fucking tie!" an agitated Hans snapped.

"I can't help it, it is bent!"

"What do you expect, I'm a homosexual."

The Master Singer

Rolf dabbed Hans' sweaty brow with a handkerchief, kissed him, and it was showtime!

He finished with Sir Walther's contest song from "Die Meistersinger

von Nürnberg," one of Wagner's most beautiful melodies. It had only been a forty-minute program, but throughout, the audience seemed stunned by the quality of the young man's voice. Everyone wanted to meet this extraordinary artist, and it was the proudest moment of Rolf's life. He felt almost as if at last he, Rolf Kainz, had contributed something worthwhile, even if it was only to introduce his artist lover.

He had a general loathing for this gang of wealthy snobs, but he did respect their knowledge of art and their connections.

A heavily made-up, florid man in his late seventies, with a shock of white hair, jeweled rings on four fingers and incarnadine lips, making him look rather like a vampire which he may very well have been, took Hans by the hand. He smelled of very expensive perfume, and his tie pin could have paid the little apartment's rent for two years.

"Mein Schatz! Mein magic, little mouse," the man began and his breath smelled of strawberry, although his teeth were tiny like corn kernels, "you simply must allow me to present you socially and artistically. I know absolutely everyone." He went on to list many of them, and Hans, although impressed, became wary of the price tag for such introductions.

Another, kinder, gentler man with a sweet wife attached was more welcomed. "Frau Kainz tells me you have dreams of singing at Bayreuth?"

"A dream, yes sir, but perhaps someday…" Rolf, who lurked protectively brought champagne.

The man smiled. "A dream to become a true Meistersinger, ja?" The smile broadened. "Well, it just so happens that I am good friends with the choral master there, and I'm sure I would be able to arrange an audition!"

And that was it! That night, Hans stood naked at the bed, looking down on an equally naked Rolf, bathed in moonlight.

"Wagner is right. It is at night, by moonlight, that magic happens. Thank you, my love. Thank you for everything."

"I love you," whispered Rolf. "I love you, and I will always love you." He held out his hand, which Hans took.

"There is a melody in my bed, and the melody is you!"

"Oh, my foolish, romantic, Master singer."

PART II

BAYREUTH

"Is it no dream?
　　Glorious rapture!
　　O sweetest, highest,
　　Sharpest, fairest,
　　Blessed joy."

Tristan and Isolde

CHAPTER 16

1929

BAYREUTH, BERLIN
THE AUDITION

THE TWO YOUNG men trudged up the hill from the village of Bayreuth to the rather ominous looking Festspielhaus. The theater was isolated, an artistic edifice that looked on the outside more like a factory or a prison than an opera house, because every mark of money raised had been spent on creating the perfect interior auditorium for the Wagner Ring Cycle. Wagner had planned it that way. Never before had an entire opera house been built for one opera, let alone a sixteen-hour one. One didn't come to Bayreuth so much to see and hear the four-in-one spectacle opera, as to worship at the altar of Richard Wagner, the man-god who changed music forever.

Hans babbled as they walked, and Rolf allowed him to. "It was Wagner, you know, who created the orchestra pit, down partly beneath the stage, unseen by the audience, so their view of the drama would be unimpeded." He had babbled this way all through the train ride, and all the way to the hotel, and Rolf could not have been happier for him. Rolf had wanted to eat before they trekked to see the theater, but nothing doing. Wagner must be worshipped.

Buried deep in Rolf's mind was the knowledge of the terrible anti-Semite Wagner had been, and he was aware of all the ugly things the man had written scourging the Jews. The Nibelung in "the Ring" were often considered a euphemism for Juden, as was the hideous Beckmesser in "Die Meistersinger." But Rolf kept these things in his heart, so as not to dampen his lover's joy. Besides, Hans already knew most of this, and had chosen to bury it.

"The auditorium is designed so that every seat has an excellent view, and the walls are shaped for optimum sound. And you know who is conducting next season, don't you?" It was a rhetorical question and Rolf was about to learn. "Toscanini! The Toscanini. Arturo Toscanini!" Rolf nodded in deference. "I've just got to be singing in the chorus by then. You know, they hire many fine opera soloists just to sing in the chorus, I shouldn't say 'just,' the chorus is very important." Hans kept saying "you know," and although Rolf hadn't known before, he certainly did now.

Finally, in exasperation and exhaustion, Rolf put his hand over Hans' mouth, and they stood there listening to the birds announcing spring.

Letter from Hans Becker to Fritz Horteg:

Dear Fritzy: I hope all is well with you. Your position at the film studio, playing mood music while they shoot the scenes, sounds romantic and exciting. And to think that you also get to work on preparing the new sound films as well. It must terribly be thrilling. Yes, the coffee boy sounds delicious, and I hope there is something good brewing between you. But please, no grounds for dismissal.

You wouldn't believe my audition. I'd telephone you, but there is so much to relate that it has to be set down. On the day, Rolf stayed behind in the village to pick flowers or yodel or whatever, and it would have looked foolish for me to arrive with a big, strapping nanny holding my hand, but "Gott im Himmel," I wanted him there for moral support.

I felt okay leaving him on his own for the day because we had already explored the Festspielhaus and the surrounding property including Wagner's grave twice.

The audition was held in one of the theater's adjacent rehearsal halls. Of the almost two dozen other, eager, terrified auditioners seated on stiff, wooden chairs along one long wall of the large room, I must have been one of the youngest. I took a seat, clutching my satchel, wishing I had peed first, and facing a severe-looking gentleman at a grand, grand piano. This turned out to be Karl Muck, one of the associate conductors of the opera, who had been with the organization since before the war hiatus. Rumor had it he was a stickler for Wagnerian rules and traditions.

The audition itself was being conducted by Hugo Rüdel, the legendary Bayreuth choirmaster, who proudly wore the garland as leader of the finest chorus in the world. He was a small, fastidious, conservative-looking man in his sixties with the ever-popular slicked- back hair and the small brush of a moustache. One might say he appeared "mousy" until he spoke about music, and then he became filled with fire.

"The Bayreuth chorus is unique in the world in that it is made up of the finest solo singers in Germany, Austria and Bavaria. Such excellence is required because of the devilish demands of the Festspielhaus. The stage is designed so that the sound is perfect, but in its perfection, lies an imperfection. The sound from the orchestra, the soloists and the chorus all reach the area in front of the stage at different times. Therefore, in order for the audience to hear a piece as a unified whole, continual adjustments must be made. The soloists are required to sing behind the orchestra tempo, guided by the conductor's eyes, and an upstage chorus cannot hear the soloists or, at times, the orchestra in Wagner's specially designed orchestra pit!" As he spoke, the small man lunged about, waving his arms to demonstrate his words. He was a most fascinating man, and most of us were hypnotized.

"The chorus must learn to intuitively adjust its tempo and volume guided by off-stage signal lights. Sounds impossible, ja?" He laughed like an excited child at Christmas. "Well, it is not, not if you are the best!"

We sat dumb struck. I swear to you Fritzy, this is all true, and I am making nothing up. And that was just the surface of the insanity. I later learned that the conductor at Bayreuth in the pit with an orchestra of over a hundred, often cannot hear the singers and must learn to lip-read!

Rüdel's assistant had already taken our resumes and now, one by one, we were called up to sing. Such voices, Fritz. Voices from Heaven!

I felt totally inadequate. I sat there trembling, and then things got even worse. The door at the far end of the room opened, and in walked Siegfried Wagner, son of the great man himself. He had been running the festival since its return after the war in 1924, and he took a controlling hand in every single aspect of Bayreuth, from staging the productions to designing the scenery, to working with singers and overseeing marketing. He was in fact, the new god of Bayreuth.

You would know him, Fritzy, because, although he is married with four children, he is a notorious homosexual. His escapades are forever being dished about in the clubs and bars.

He is a gentle, clean-shaven, kindly-looking man with short, cropped hair. He was dressed in a pair of white, summer trousers with a matching waistcoat, no jacket, and an open-necked shirt. There was a modest elegance in the way he moved, and we could feel the electricity in the room. Even the Bayreuth choirmaster and staff stiffened just a bit as he quietly sat in a chair on one side to observe.

As expected, everyone sang German songs or arias. Lots of Schubert and Schumann. Often they were cut off midsong and returned to their chairs with a dismissive wave of the hand. And then it was my turn. I handed my music to Herr Muck, and faced Rüdel, Siegfried Wagner, and the terrified lambs who were auditioning, both those about to be slaughtered and those who already had been. So far, not a single word had been spoken by Rüdel since his opening monologue, except for a terse "Danke," and a terser "Nächste!"

"Hans Becker," I announced, my throat filled with sand. "I am going to sing for you Sir Walther's contest aria from "Die Meistersinger von Nürnberg!"

"Stop!" Herr Muck slammed his hands down on the piano top. There was a collective gasp from the auditioners. "You have no business singing that. It is arrogant," Muck continued, glaring at me.

I didn't know what to do, Fritz. I prayed for a hole to open in the floor, so I might drop through. I was in hell. A hell of my own making. I wanted to die. My legs turned to water and I almost collapsed. Whispering traveled the room like the wind through trees.

Herr Rüdel was a bit kinder, but not much. "Perhaps you have something else, a bit less demanding?"

"Eh, yes, of course, let me see..." I muttered, grabbing my satchel and rummaging through it, and of course the whole thing tumbled to the floor, spilling sheet music everywhere. And then...

"Let him sing from 'Meistersinger!'" It was Siegfried Wagner, speaking in a quiet, authoritarian voice. "Let him sing the aria he has chosen."

And that was how I sang one of Wagner's greatest pieces for his own son!

When I finished, Herr Rüdel said "Danke" and "Nächste," nothing more, and the auditions continued. I sat in my chair, clutching my satchel to my chest, sweat running down my face. But when we had all finished and were filing out of the room, having been told we might not hear the results for some months, as I neared the door, Siegfried Wagner approached me. The other hopefuls backed away, but I simply froze. And then, Fritz, he patted me on the ass. Let me write that again. HE PATTED ME ON THE ASS, FRITZY! He patted me, and he said in a very friendly voice, "You have nothing to worry about."

When I told Rolf back at the hotel, he bounced on the bed merrily and chortled like a villain in a melodrama, "You have nothing to worry about my boy," just before he ravished me.

Well, that is all for now, as if that is not enough. All my love to you and your "Dream Factory." Make miracles.

Your friend, Hans

CHAPTER 17

1929

    BERLIN, THE APARTMENT, ALEXANDERPLATZ
    BEWARE OF EVIL DAYS

1929 CHUGGED INTO APRIL. Hans and Rolf returned to Berlin, after making plans to attend the Bayreuth Festival in August. Back home, they went drinking and dancing with Fritz and other friends, jerking and twisting in the dance style that could only be described as spastic. An expert on such things might observe that the dancing had a dangerous, manic intensity bordering at times on hysteria. Rolf, who seemed somewhat more involved in politics than he had been, observed that the art of a time often reflected the inner anguish and turmoil of the people. "Like Hamlet's mirror held up to nature." While Hans studied opera scores and sang with the dance band, Rolf would now sometimes disappear to attend this or that political meeting.

"And what will you do if I get accepted to Bayreuth?" Hans asked him one morning in bed.

"Well, you'll go, of course, and I shall come and applaud as always."

"It would only be for the three summer months next year. Two to prepare and one to perform, like I was on tour."

"Like you were on tour, ja."

"You'll be graduating soon, Rolf. You've got to be thinking about your future, too. Graduate school? Teaching? Writing? What?"

Rolf swung his legs over the side of the bed and sat up, his back to Hans. He lit a Juno cigarette, put the lighter down, held the first deep draw in his mouth for a bit and then let it out. "I have been thinking, I don't want to teach. I think I might go into politics somehow, starting out on the ground floor." He lay back with his head upon Hans' stomach. "But if you do get hired at Bayreuth, you'd best be extra careful. Have you seen the festival brochures and guidebooks for the last few years? They are filled with anti-Semitic articles. The operas themselves are being seen as political propaganda. You seem to close your mind, Hans, to how ugly and vicious Wagner's writing was." He rose from the bed and padded naked to the table near the door. He returned with a libretto from "Die Meistersinger." Cigarette dangling from his lips, he flopped back onto the bed and sat propped against the headboard. He flipped to the last part of the libretto and read;

> "Beware, we threaten evil days,
> If our great German Realm decays,
> If foreigners may rule our land
> The people they won't understand.
> If foreign sham and foreign lies
> Shall ever darken German skies

What true German could ere abide
Had he not German Master Pride?"

"And it goes on. They say the audience stands and sings along with the character Hans Sachs' aria. And while I understand the sentiment, the environment is toxic. Furthermore, have you read some of Wagner's essays about Jews? Considering your secret, I only worry for you."

Hans turned over and bestowed a kiss. "Not to worry, my sweet. While it is true that Bayreuth has become a center of the Nazi movement and a symbol of its rise in power, in the last year, Siegfried Wagner has recently made great changes. He has declared the festival apolitical; no Nazi flags, no propaganda in the brochures, and he even asked Adolf Hitler not to attend, much to the chagrin of Siegfried's wife. The new era at Bayreuth will honor Wagner's art, not his politics."

Hans rolled over further and place one leg over that of his lover. "And Siegfried has announced that he intends to hire singers based on their talent, not their race, color or creed! One of his best singers is the great Friedrich Schorr, a Jew, who sings Wotan in 'The Ring.' Hitler wrote that he was sickened by Schorr, and yet Siegfried hires him to play the ruler of the Gods! That counts for something, Rolf."

Rolf blew several smoke rings. "You are a dreamer, my darling, not a realist."

"So are all artists!"

May first, 1929. Rolf knew where to go because the event had been promoted on handbills and posters all over the city, and it lasted for several, violence-fueled days. He felt a kind of inner excitement that he had never known before, a sense that he was about to witness, perhaps be a part of, something important, monumental. He pulled his cloth cap low on his forehead and thrust his hands deep into his trouser pockets. He waited. Once, he lit and smoked a Regie 4 Austrian cigarette. He lifted his head when he heard a kind of rumbling sound like distant thunder a few blocks away but drawing nearer. The thing might pass right by him!

First came a few, running ahead as lookouts. Like those first few sprinkles of raindrops before the deluge. A woman and two men in everyday workers' clothes, scanning the street, looking high and low, always seeking the shelter of doorways. Rolf supposed they were searching for police snipers. Oh, yes, Rolf knew how the Berlin Police snipers were openly touted, and the noble Berlin Police Force was not above using sneaky, scurrilous tactics to maintain law and order.

The two men and the young woman sprinted from doorway to doorway, seeking cover in the entrances to closed-up shops and locked buildings. Fancy that, mused Rolf, a woman. He envied her. She had a cause worth fighting for, living for, and perhaps even dying for. She was young, sturdy, with nicely-shaped, working-girl legs extending from her cloth coat to her no-nonsense brown shoes. Her face was devoid of make-up, and in spite of rather large, thick spectacles, she was quite beautiful. Rolf fancied he might be in love with her, not the way he loved Hans, but as a great idea or a symbol.

There was no traffic on Alexanderplatz, the streets had been blocked off by the police, and only Rolf and a few other brave curious pedestrians ventured forth. No mothers with baby carriages and no news agent at the kiosk. The woman protestor ran back to the cross street and waved a large red scarf. The two males positioned themselves boldly in the middle of the road. A few more shopkeepers lowered their metal grates, and those who had none lowered their shades and put "Geschlossen" signs on their doors. The sound of thunder was now window-rattling and the storm was imminent.

Rolf felt his heart race. How would it arrive? Dressed in hope or covered in the blood and pain of more suffering?

And then the human storm turned the corner. One, two, ten, fifty, a hundred, a thousand marchers carrying signs and waving red flags. The Communist Party demanding equality for all German workers, for all German people. Was that such an awful goal? Rolf's heart thumped painfully in his chest. They moved toward him, a sea of angry faces, and in front, the angry face of the young woman he had come to admire.

There was singing, too, and amid the anger there was also celebration and hope. And much like it must have been that day in France when they stormed the Bastille, a feeling of pride for people who had never known pride before. Rolf was mesmerized by its ragtag beauty, despite the fact that Germans generally had been taught to despise Communists and Trotsky and Stalin and all that.

"Go back to Russia," someone shouted from an upper floor apartment window, but the sound was lost in the thunder of the marching and chanting and singing. Rolf smiled at the foolish braveness of this mass of humanity. But then, just as they approached him, with Rolf doffing his cap and smiling stupidly, they suddenly stopped and grew deathly silent, almost as if orchestrated.

The entire seething, silent mass of humanity stood there staring right at Rolf! No! Not at him, beyond him, behind him. The young man looked around. A wall! A human wall of uniformed police resistance! Truncheons, Mausers, both semi-automatic pistols and bolt-action rifles, even a machine gun or two, or ten. In front of this barricade of blue stood several plainclothes detectives and officers. Sour-faced, hard men, some of whom bore grotesque, facial scars from the Great War. Twitching, facial hair and red, round noses beneath slouch hats or derbies. Men with badges hanging from cards around their bull-thick necks. A few, the privileged leaders, chomped on cigars. They were Law and Order! And Rolf stood between them and the masses.

He eased himself sideways into the semi-shelter of a sausage shop doorway. He would forever remember the smell of the sausage wafting from under the closed and barred door. Silence and the smell of sausage. And then, one of the bull-necked men with a bull horn put it to his mouth and spoke.

"Achtung! This is an illegal, potentially dangerous demonstration. You must stand down and disperse at once." Wooden barricades had been placed across the road by young, brave, frightened coppers.

The red crowd glowered. The young woman stepped forward and waved her red scarf. Rolf told himself he would gladly perish for her cause, whatever it might be.

She spoke. "This is a peaceful protest demanding equal rights and benefits for all workers! We have a permit. I repeat. We have a permit! The poor and starving of Germany shall be invisible no more!" She had no bullhorn, and her voice was slightly thick and throaty from yelling. A cheer went up behind her.

And then, to Rolf's horror, the roar of cannons. Water cannons! Great gushes of water from firehoses hitting the protestors, knocking them back and down. Washing them away like so much waste. Tumbling bodies, floating and flailing arms and legs, faces spitting and coughing up water mixed with blood. Drenched and gasping for air, their clothing appearing to melt, the front row of protestors, like wounded animals, tried to drag themselves from the deluge. The girl in front, limping and clutching one arm, her soaked red scarf now lifeless and heavy, still foolishly moved forward, followed by crawling, stumbling, shoving masses. The young coppers facing them lifted their truncheons. And as the front line of communists reached the barricades, the police began to beat them down. Inkblots of blood exploded in the air, and Rolf couldn't help but wonder if this hadn't been the fate of Ernst Röhm and Adolf Hitler and their marchers in the Munich Beer Hall Putsch.

Another blast of water, but a push from the protestors in the rear, now stepping over some of their own, and the barricades were flung aside. The thousand-strong marching storm advanced! And then, someone opened fire! "Pop!" "Pop," "Pop," "Pop!" The police later claimed communist snipers were the cause. That they opened fire in retaliation, but the girl in front fell first, a red blossom on her forehead, and Rolf could clearly see that the bullet that hit her came from the police line.

"Pop," "Pop" "Crack" "Pop!" "Rat-a-tat-tat-tat!" Protestors in the front turned and tried to flee the firestorm, but to do so, they had to climb over the still advancing masses behind. Ironically, most of the serious injuries that followed were caused by the protestors' own people trying to escape. The gunfire ceased, and the police began to scrape some of the battered beaten from the pavement and drag them to the waiting Black Marias. Trophies of the victory would be required for confessions.

One red-eyed, foaming-at-the-mouth copper, high on

the violence, sized up Rolf for a possible prize, but moved on to an older, red-faced woman in a scarf and shawl instead. Rolf stood there in the sheltered smell of the sausage shop, mingled with a faint hint of gunpowder and the coppery stench of blood, and for the thousandth time wished that his life had some higher purpose and meaning.

CHAPTER 18

1929

    BAYREUTH, WAHNFRIED
    AT THE TEMPLE

It was August. The art world lamented the tragic death of poet and librettist Hugo Hofmannsthal, who had created "Electra" and other operas with Richard Strauss. Their profoundly important collaborations had been called the final works in the history of romantic opera - the last artistic remnants of a Europe that no longer existed.

Rolf and Hans sat on the grass outside the Festspielhaus during one of the hour-long intermissions of "Tristan and Isolde," having a picnic of wine and cheese and olives and bread.

"It's got to be one of the most beautiful love stories ever written," rhapsodized Hans, lost in the euphoria of the music and the day and the young man seated across from him and the wine and cheese.

"Yes, it's ravishing, I grant you, but the love is a bit of a fraud, don't you think? I mean it's caused by a potion." He raised his glass. 'I don't need a potion to love you, Hans."

Hans waved a piece of bread. "How about that liquor you gave me in Hunding's Hut? For all I know, it could have been some magical witch's brew. You could have possessed me just as Isolde did Tristan, except in the opera they are both victims of the potion.

And besides, in the opera it's a symbol of destiny. It's their destiny to be together always in this world and the next." He pulled some greens from the grass and made a clover-ring for Rolf. "You gave me a ring of gold. I give you a ring of grass." He slipped it on his lover's finger, and Rolf kissed it. Hans lapsed into silence for a bit, then said, "I'm terribly anxious, you know. I should have heard something by now. I'll die if I don't make it."

Rolf took his hand and gently squeezed it. Couples passed, and as if on cue in a play, an impeccably dressed young man appeared before them. They looked up at him with the setting sun behind him turning him into an ominous creature of nature. His black hair was wild and curly, and his features sharp. For a moment, he seemed more raven or wolf than human. Hans feared he was an attendant about to inform them that they may not hold hands in public on the opera grounds, but Rolf just gripped his hand more tightly.

"Herr Hans Becker?" the young man inquired.

"Eh, ja, that's me..." Hans began to rise, but Rolf's hand held him down.

"Siegfried Wagner wonders if you might grant him a few minutes of your time at Wahnfried House after the performance. Your friend is also invited. He looks forward to seeing you." And the shadow disappeared.

"Oh mein Gott! Oh, mein Gott! Rolf! Wahnfried House.

That was Richard Wagner's house. That is where Cosima Wagner, his wife, lives! Why would he want to see me?" Then, Hans slumped onto the grass.

"To tell me they can't use me, that's why." He squeezed his eyes shut.

"Idiot! Do you really think he would invite you just to let you down? Besides, he grabbed your ass and told you you had nothing to worry about. No, he saw you, or knew you were here from the tickets, and out of a thousand patrons, he asked to see you! Perhaps, my darling, your dream is coming true. And you've got cheese on your coat!"

They frantically tried using wine on wet napkins to wipe the cheese stain from Hans' jacket. "He invited you, too, Rolf. He must have been watching us. Perhaps he is watching us now!" They both stopped wiping instantly and sat very still. "If only the opera were over."

"Are the next two acts as long as the first?"

"Longer!"

"If I have any criticism of your hero, Wagner, it's that he could move things along a little faster."

"Oh, Rolf, what if that shadow boy was playing a cruel joke on us? What if he..." Rolf put his hand over Hans' mouth so they could hear the trumpet fanfare calling the audience to act two.

With trepidation, like Hansel and Gretel approaching the witch's house, the two young men came to Wahnfried. As other patrons made their emotionally drained way down the hill through the summer moonlight, Hans and Rolf faced the modernist block building Wagner had designed as his home. Cosima, having turned the home into a kind of museum dedicated to her husband, now lived there like an old queen entombed in a castle turret. Siegfried, Winifred and their four children actually lived in another house nearby, but official Bayreuth business was still conducted at Wahnfried.

Outside the front entrance stood a large bust of King Ludwig II.

Rolf chuckled nervously, "The mad king seems to loom over everything in our lives, doesn't he? Ha! Good old Queen Ludwig, here to protect us." The giant mural carvings on the façade of the house made it look even more ominous and tomb-like.

As they approached the building, the door opened and the shadow boy from the lawn could now be clearly seen. He was indeed sleek and raven-like, quite handsome in a rather pale, wasted, Wertherian way.

"This way, gentlemen," the young man said in a perfect butler voice, and he led them into what could only be called a rather macabre museum, a home left exactly as it was the day Richard Wagner died.

Not a bowl, pen, or scrap of sheet music had been moved, only carefully dusted. The composer's pipe, famous velvet cap, shawl, everything waiting patiently for his return. It was no longer a comfortable living space, but a sacred, memorial altar honoring the composer. Somewhere in another room, his music played.

"Amazing, isn't it? Wonderful and amazing." Siegfried Wagner entered from a doorway at the far end of what had been Wagner's music room. "My mother won't let them move a thing. Adolf Hitler wept inconsolably when he saw this room." Was there a slight touch of sarcasm in his voice? Siegfried was dressed in cream-colored plus fours, yellow stockings and white shoes. Over an open-collared, cream-colored shirt, he wore a sleeveless, pullover sweater decorated with bold diamond shapes. "Of course, I try to be absent for as many of his visits as possible, but my wife and children seem to love him. I once heard my son say to his mother, 'Couldn't Uncle Adolf be our father and Papa be our uncle?'"

What an odd thing for a man to say in front of strangers. It betrayed either great loneliness or severe eccentricity, perhaps both. Siegfried laughed and giggled almost like a child who has said something naughty. Then he extended his hand to Hans.

"Hans Becker, how delighted I am to see you again. I have not forgotten you. Oh, no, you are unforgettable. I was going to send you a telegram next week, but prophetically, here you are." He took both of Hans' hands in his own like they were old friends, and his eyes twinkled merrily. There was a comforting sincerity about him. He next turned to Rolf. "And who is this strapping youth? Do you sing, too?"

"I'm afraid not," said Rolf, looking away slightly. "I don't do much of anything."

Without missing a beat, and taking Rolf's hand warmly, Siegfried replied, "But I'll bet you do it splendidly!" His smile was warm and welcoming to both young men. "Shall we go into the office? It's a bit less musty."

The office, too, was as Richard Wagner had left it, but less cluttered and more livable. There was a large, wood-inlaid desk with an impressive, oversized telephone on it. Nearby, rested a high stack of Wagner's musical scores, an inkstand and pens, and several ledgers. The inkstand was superfluous, as on a small table adjacent to the desk there was a modern typewriter and four or five expensive Montblanc fountain pens. Siegfried indicated that the young men should sit in two fine leather chairs facing the desk, while he himself moved behind it.

"First, I must ask you to excuse my wretched, exhausted condition. I have been conducting all over Europe, and with

Mother's advanced age, I have the entire festival on my shoulders as well. It's a tidal wave of responsibility, and I am doing my best to stick fingers in every dyke." He laughed at his own odd turn of phrase. "Oh, may I offer you something to drink? We have just about anything you might desire, right, Wolf?"

Wolf, the shadow boy had appeared in the doorway and nodded his floppy, black hair in agreement. Hans had become terribly anxious, Rolf just uneasy. "No, thank you, we're fine," they answered in unison like a vaudeville comedy team.

Siegfried shook his head and smacked his lips. "I could slap myself, honestly. Let's cut to the chase, shall we? You're dying to know the results of your audition. Well, the answer is a resounding, unanimous Yes! We want you to join our company for the 1930 season. Even grumpy, old Muck was bowled over by your voice and your manner. You will sing in the chorus and perhaps even be given a solo line or two."

Rolf could see that Siegfried was rather like Father Christmas delivering a special gift. He twinkled ever more brightly waiting for Hans' reaction. The young tenor did not disappoint. He rose from his chair and clapped his hand over his mouth. His dream was about to come true.

"You don't yet have the lower note strength and resonance you need to become a heldentenor, but we will work on that. And there is more!" Siegfried wagged a Father Christmas finger and laid it to the side of his nose. "Next season will be a season unlike any other. I am bringing in the great Arturo Toscanini from Italy to conduct. The National Socialist Workers party, of whom my wife is so inordinately fond, will have kittens because he is not German. Fur will fly!" He laughed merrily. "Schorr, a Jew, will sing Wotan, and Melchior, Tristan. I will mount brand new productions with modern set designs, and my 'Tannhäuser' will have a scandalous bacchanal unlike anything ever seen on the stage."

Wolf approached with a silver tray bearing three glasses of something blood red, and Siegfried slogged his down in one gulp. Rolf and Hans sipped cautiously. It was something with Campari. Siegfried moved around to the front of the desk and sat on the edge, crossing his legs at the ankle.

"All of this will tax me to the point of madness, and so, I thought rather than just coming for the three months of the festival rehearsals and performances, you might consider working here full-time as a staff assistant. The pay is crap, but we provide lodgings and meals and the artistic experience will be without equal." He held up both hands, palms toward his guests. "I should mention that the pay for the season is crap as well, almost non-existent, and that is for everyone, even the principals and the musicians. It was one of my father's stipulations that everything here be done only for art, not profit."

Hans had not sat down. He stood before the great man, son of the greater man, only hearing half of what he was saying. In his head, he was hearing Wagner's music, and in his mind's eye he saw Toscanini conducting it. And he, Hans Becker, would be singing it!

Later, literally collapsing in his lover's arms on the hillside below Wahnfried, Hans sobbed. "I made a total ass of myself."

"You were fine, you were wonderful. Especially when Siegfried asked you to sing for Cosima and Winifred."

Hans crumpled to his knees, clutching at Rolf's coat. "I sang for Cosima Wagner! He had me sing for them. Was it terribly bad?"

"I told you it was wonderful." Rolf knelt and took the

shaking young man in his arms. "Everyone except Wolf was most impressed. He was seething with jealously. Don't you remember that Winifred said you had a perfect German voice?"

"I don't remember anything. Not even what they looked like. You shall have to tell me all about it. Oh, Rolf, I am so glad you were there. I would be lost without you!" Hans clung to his lover and sobbed. The moon looked down upon them impassively. He had seen countless tenors come and go, and countless lovers come and go.

Still later in their hotel room. "I won't take it of course, the permanent position," Hans said, pushing aside a box of chocolates. "I'll come up just for the season, but I couldn't be away from you for more than a few months." It was one of those entrapment statements, spoken quite innocently by Hans.

"Of course you will take the permanent position. You must. We'll find ways to see each other. I'll come down to see you, or you can get a few days off to come up and see me in Berlin." Rolf was fiddling intently with nothing. "We always knew, Hans, that there would be times we would, by necessity, be apart for a bit. Besides I've got..." he never finished the sentence.

Yes, a part of Rolf wished Hans would sacrifice everything to be with him, partly because Rolf had nothing much other than Hans on which to hang. Now he shrugged. "And as the good book says, 'one of the thieves was saved.'"

Hans grabbed Rolf by the shoulder. "What is that supposed to mean?"

"Nothing. Nothing, my love, only that you have found your savior and I am still searching."

They had the remainder of the year to spend together before Hans had to report to Bayreuth and, as Rolf half-playfully taunted him, "Siggy's bed." Hans swore devotion to only Rolf over and over, kissing the golden ring on his finger, and the two young men decided to make the most of their time together.

That same August, the Nazi Party held a rally in Nuremberg, drawing well over one hundred thousand people!

CHAPTER 19

1930
    BERLIN, BAYREUTH
    PARTING

DECENT FOOD WAS hard to come by that Christmas, even for the wealthy and once wealthy, due to the incredible stock market crashes, first on Wall Street in America and then similarly in Berlin. The disastrous depression which followed was worse than anyone could have imagined. Stacks of almost useless money were required to buy a sausage or a loaf of bread. It would have been laughable had it not impacted people so horribly.

    In spite of that, Hans and Rolf had a lovely, quiet, simple Christmas, spending the actual holidays with their respective families. At Rolf's home, Helga refused to stint, insisting they could muddle through with things just as extravagant as always. Well, instead of turkey, they had duck, which everyone agreed they preferred. Professor Kainz remained unusually solitary and silent throughout the festivities.

Hans' family was welcoming and warm as always, so loving that Hans yearned to bring Rolf to meet them. Jacob did speak seriously to his son about them perhaps making plans to close up shop and leave Munich, which had become a hotbed of anti-Semitism. They would resettle someplace safe, like Paris.

"I've just gotten accepted at Bayreuth, Papa, I can't leave now. Besides, Siegfried Wagner staunchly defends his Jewish performers."

Jacob lovingly patted his son on the cheek. "Of course, of course, I understand. But eventually, you could make a grand career for yourself in Paris, London, or even America."

Hans smiled. "Papa, all of America has only two great opera houses, Berlin alone has a dozen. But let's take baby steps, Papa. If things get bad for you and mamma, you leave, and after I conquer Bayreuth, I'll come join you!"

Back together in Berlin, Hans noticed that a kind of permanent melancholy had settled over Rolf. He had lost much of his devil-may-care charm. Was it their impending separation or something more? They had worked out extensive plans for seeing each other with calendars marked in red and black, but the weight of the unknown future was heavy on them both. Once, when Hans kissed the golden ring from his lover, Rolf was reminded that in Wagner's "Ring" operas, to attain power and glory, one had to renounce love.

One cold, crisp January day, when the streets were glass and long daggers of icicles hung from eaves, Rolf, at his father's request, met the professor at a newly opened restaurant in Berlin Mitte, designed by Alexander Beer in the "New Objectivity" art style. It was in fact, formerly a Jewish girls' school, the "Jüdische Mädchenschule." The

Jews had been ousted to make way for the "new Berlin." Some crazy time to open a restaurant, when money was useless. And even at the restaurant's arrogantly extravagant prices, which required one to bring a suitcase filled with cash to dinner, a diner had to order off a limited menu of available foods.

Rolf noticed at once that his father looked worried and a bit haggard. He hadn't shaved closely, and his eyes were red. They made small talk for a bit, and Professor Kainz ordered pork and dumplings for both of them with beer to drink.

"I've asked you here today, Rolf, to share with you something about which I have not even spoken to your mother," he said in his usual formal style. He spread his hands. "The truth is, I don't know how to tell her."

"Oh, mein Gott, he wants a divorce!" were Rolf's first thoughts. In his young, over-active mind, he pictured his father recklessly consorting with a prostitute or dance-club girl. But that was not it.

"The unvarnished truth is, we have lost everything in the recent stock market crash. Everything!" The man's face took on a deathly pallor.

"Come, come, Papa, it can't be all that bad."

"I'm afraid it's worse. We shall lose the house and the car. Hilde will have to leave boarding school, and I shall no longer be able to foot your tuition. We shall have to dismiss our staff, which will kill your mother. My stubborn, single-minded stupidity has destroyed our family."

Rolf had never seen his father look so helpless, so pitiful. He wanted to erase the sight, but was helpless to do so. He reached across the table and took his father's hand. There is a point in every family when the children begin to do the parenting.

"We'll make do, Papa, and you mustn't blame yourself.

Thousands lost their fortunes in October. Some absconded with what money they could. Some committed suicide."

"Don't think I haven't considered both. If we move to our house in Switzerland, I can get a job teaching there. Not for the same salary as here, but the economy is much better there. Besides, the university here is no longer the free-thinking environment I once cherished."

The food arrived. Rolf tried to sound cheerful. "Don't worry about me, Papa. I'll stay in Berlin for now. I can get a job. And I'll visit you and Mother and Hilde often."

Peter Kainz nodded, his eyes filled with tears. "Selling the art work and some of the other things in the house should give us enough to settle comfortably in Geneva." He shook his head and removed his glasses to clean them with a handkerchief. "Our poor country." They ate in silence for a bit, picking at their food. "Will you come home with me, Son, to tell your mother?"

"Of course." How frail, fragile and unmasculine the distinguished professor now seemed. A man forced by circumstance to admit he was not all he thought he was.

Once, later during the mostly silent meal, Peter Kainz lifted his head to stare at the ceiling fans. "What will my friends who did not invest think of me?"

"They will love you just the same." But Rolf wondered, would they?

Hans traveled to Bayreuth to begin his work there, which thanks to Siegfried Wagner included daily vocal lessons with Herr Rüdel. Meanwhile, Rolf helped his father sell the house and goods and pack things for the move to Switzerland. Helga seemed in shock much of the time, but witnessing other prominent families in the same situation seemed to soften the blow. She immediately began to contact acquaintances for social introductions in Geneva.

There were depressing and regretful and bitter moments, but even with nothing, their nothing was considerably more than most people's everything.

Hans and Rolf kissed goodbye at the train station, promising to write every day or every few days, and reminding each other of their plans to soon meet. As he boarded the train, Hans turned back to see Rolf crying and waving madly. He seemed so vulnerable. On the afternoon that Hans left, Rolf drank heavily and spoke to no one. That evening, he made his way down a dark alley to a warehouse door with no number. One had to know the password to enter, which Rolf did. The club was called "Dekadenz."

Inside the smoky, main, low-ceilinged room, a negro band battered their instruments with hard jazz and bitter blues. The lights were dim, and the air was thick with forgetfulness. Nearly naked boys danced with groping customers who lived half their lives in secret. Rolf did not stop to dance nor to admire the dancers, but staggered through a beaded curtain and down a long, narrow hallway lit by shaded sconces that gave everything a green glow. Beyond a red doorway at the end of the passage was another large room, this one decorated in oriental fashion with tasseled pillows strewn about the floor and thick velvet drapes on the walls. Beaten tin lanterns hung from the ceiling giving everything the feel of a starry night. Here and there were low tables with mosaic surfaces bearing tall, ornate, brass hookahs.

In one corner, a skeletally thin, negro piano player pounded the keys to accompany the flicker of a film shown on a screen at the far end of the room. The film was a house specialty, featuring boys of questionable age getting sodomized by actors made up to resemble famous political leaders.

Rolf sank into an available pillow, and no sooner did so,

than a smooth-skinned, young man sidled up to him with a hookah and a dish of assorted drugs. Then, as Rolf, already drunk on liquor and loneliness, allowed himself to drift in this erotic wonderland, the boy's hand went to work.

Concern for Rolf was never far from Hans' mind and heart, but the excitement of moving to Bayreuth dominated his thoughts. He felt considerable anxiety and tension when he learned he was to report to Wolf, Siegfried Wagner's assistant. The lean and hungry, dark-haired boy greeted Hans in one of the rehearsal halls being temporarily used as a festival office. Wolf, wearing a thick, grey, cable-knit sweater and woolen trousers, brushed a hand through his mass of hair and looked Hans over as if giving him a military inspection.

"Ah, yes, Siegfried's new boy. We met at the festival. Herr Wagner is currently conducting in Europe, and so until his return, you will be working with Herr Rüdel, preparing the materials for the next festival. Herr Rüdel will also see to vocal lessons until Maestro Wagner returns and takes you in hand." There was slight sarcasm in his oily voice. Was he jealous of Hans? Everyone else was extremely kind and welcoming.

Hans spent the first week with a large rubber eraser, cleaning up the scores and librettos of pencil marks from the previous season. Over three hundred scores, and they had to be spotless. Maestro Toscanini would make his own cuts and changes with Wagner's approval of course. Rüdel was patient and nurturing with Hans during their vocal sessions. He worked with the young man to expand his lung capacity, something needed to sing the huge, taxing, Wagnerian roles. He helped develop the lower areas of the tenor voice, giving Hans baritone capabilities. One day, Winifred Wagner, some said the power behind the throne, wearing a filmy, grey dress that danced about her as she walked, stopped by to hear Hans' progress. She was polite and enthusiastic with her praise, but somewhat aloof. "I want to hear more of this young man," she told Rüdel. "Let's put him into some of our concert programs." She almost spoke about Hans as if he were not present, but then she turned to him. "How old are you?"

"Twenty-two, Ma'am." Hans felt like a stallion being sized up for breeding.

She turned back to Rüdel. "No wonder Siegfried likes him. Such potential." She allowed herself a small smile, turned and swooped out of the room. Even Rüdel relaxed when she was gone.

"She's a force with which to contend. Be careful with her," Rüdel warned. "There is a rift between her and her husband over several issues, the one I assume you have already perceived. Another is Frau Wagner's love for Adolf Hitler, which her husband does not share. There is controversy over how much of Richard Wagner's philosophy should be embraced and used by the Nazi Party. Siegfried is a strong believer that art and politics should remain separate. With your talent, either one of these two people could give you a magnificent career, but don't let them use you as a pawn between them." That was the most personal thing Rüdel ever said to Hans.

The months flew by, and other singers, musicians and technicians began to arrive. Hans made friendships with some, stayed polite and more formal with others. He was still feeling his way. Only Wolf remained somewhat recalcitrant. Hans gave Rolf detailed daily reports which he knew would only half-interest his lover, but it was a way to connect. Twice Rolf visited, and they made a little kingdom of the bed in Hans' small village room, where they formulated grand future plans for the two of them which might or might not materialize. At a certain age, reality rudely intrudes into the dreams of youth.

Rolf announced plans to help his parents get settled in Geneva, promising to return in a month. Hans joined him in Berlin to see him off and to pay a year's advance rent to keep their little apartment, a place that kept hope alive for their love. Always, they promised eternal devotion, and always, they meant it.

After seeing Rolf off, Hans met up with Fritz, who was doing quite well at the movie studio. Hans begged him to join him at Bayreuth. "They are dying for good pianists, and you'd kill them with your talent," he said over drinks. "Besides, I could use a good friend." Fritz promised to think it over. They had some laughs together and saw some operas and films, but Fritz sadly felt he was destined to comfort Hans whenever he felt the loss of Rolf, and never be anything more to him than just a good friend. Unrequited love is not an unusual thing used to cement a friendship, but it can be terribly painful.

Back in Bayreuth, Siegfried Wagner at last arrived, looking emotionally and physically drained. He had suffered a mild heart attack in Europe, and the artistic pressures on him would only get worse back home. He immediately plunged into every aspect of the new season. He looked upon Hans as a breath of fresh air and immediately took to him, much to the consternation of Wolf.

"Stay close to me, Hans, I have much for you to help me with. Your fresh, optimistic youth and your energy, not to mention your talent, give strength and lift me from my frequent depression." To say nothing of the fact that Hans was extremely easy on the eyes. Still, Siegfried behaved properly with the young man, at the most allowing himself a gentle caress or a pat here and there. Hans grew to admire him greatly.

One afternoon, as Hans worked in the Wahnfried office, where he found himself more and more frequently, Wolf came through the door.

He studied the young tenor, seated behind the great desk, sorting some letters.

"He likes his coffee cup placed so," Wolf said formally and efficiently. "And make sure there are plenty of sharpened, number two pencils in the cup. Clean up and re-sharpen the ones he throws when he is working."

Hans felt terribly sad for Wolf. "Look, I'm not trying to usurp your position here. I'm really not. I just appreciate the chance I have been given."

Wolf smiled enigmatically. There was a bit of sadness in his voice. "I understand. That's show business, isn't it? Beauty trumps loyalty, talent and intelligence. But beauty does not last. 'AND ONE WAS IN LOVE WITH ME, AND ALL WERE SLAIN.'"

Hans, quite flustered, tried to sound friendly. "Well, I hope I have some intelligence and talent. I'm sure you do."

Wolf nodded his head not unkindly. "Time will tell."

"I am besieged by the faults of others and my own mistakes. Like Wotan, I try to save Valhalla," Siegfried lamented one evening as he and Hans worked late. They often had a glass of something or other while they went over the work of the day. Siegfried had had explosive arguments with the scenic designers, the costumers, the lighting people. "I am trying to bring Wagner into the twentieth century!" He would shout over and over. Generally a kind, patient fellow, he became a tyrant when in the "creative mood." His arguments with the legendary Toscanini began as soon as the conductor arrived and turned into full-blown battles. "You are only the conductor," Siegfried would shout, paraphrasing his great father and waving about costume sketches and pages of notes for the singers.

"The conductor is everything!" the great maestro would shout back, his wild white hair snapping and twisting.

"Not here! Here Richard Wagner is everything, and everyone creates equally to serve him!"

Now, late at night, with only Hans present, Siegfried became less argumentative and more woebegone. "Today, Toscanini demanded that his name be on the program and posters. That has never happened in Bayreuth before. He also wants Lauritz Melchior fired. Says he will never learn the part, is a rotten actor, and wants unreasonable cuts. I shall have to tutor Melchior myself."

While it was true that Melchior, the internationally famous tenor, could be stiff on stage at times and was having trouble learning the roles, he was a kind man who worked hard and possessed one of the world's most beautiful voices. Siegfried stood by his singer. Toscanini, meanwhile, had fallen into his old habit of throwing musicians out of rehearsals.

"Get out. Go home and practice. You should be in a school orchestra!" Humiliation in front of the entire orchestra was one of Toscanini's tools.

To relax after a tense day of altercations, Siegfried often had Hans sing for him. He also participated in Hans' vocal lessons. "Your voice is maturing magnificently. Rüdel agrees. I would even consider you for a small featured role of one of the singing masters in our next 'Meistersinger.'"

Imagine, being told that by Siegfried Wagner!

It was at a concert in Munich with his parents when he was thirteen that Hans first heard "Isolde's Death" from the end of the third act of the over four-hour opera. The nerve-shattering spiritual and sexual orgasm of the music excited and terrified the boy like nothing he had ever felt. Wave after wave of mounting, breathless, sexual copulation, as the opera's lovers are united in death as they could not be in life, reaching the greatest musical climax in history, caused young Hans himself to have an uncontrollable orgasm right there in the concert hall. If his parents noticed the shaking, sobbing, wet mess of tears, and how could they not, they never mentioned it. But even now in his twenties, Hans could not listen to the piece without becoming painfully aroused, however, now it was by the opera's spiritual perfection as well as its erotic content.

He boldly discussed Richard Wagner's erotic power with Siegfried, who practically levitated at Hans' observations. "Yes, exactly, my dear, young friend. I knew you were special. What is the term for orgasm? 'A little death?' Papa made it a big, fat death! The biggest in all of music. It's the essence of 'Romeo and Juliet,' isn't it? Love is ultimately the only thing that matters, and love is more important than life and death. My father proved that, not through philosophical debate, but through music!"

While Melchior often lunched with several of the young ladies in the chorus and had beers with the boys, Hans sought out and became friends with Friedrich Schorr, who was a bit of a loner because he was a known Jew. Most of the cast were polite, but not overly friendly with him, in spite of the fact that he was hailed as "the greatest Wotan ever!" Hans did not reveal his own ethnic secret to his new friend, but spent many long hours chatting about art and playing chess with the singer.

One evening over a beer in the village, Hans asked him, "How do you deal with being a Jew in 1930 Germany?"

Schorr let out a hearty laugh. "What am I to do? I am

who and what I am. There are some opera houses that will not hire me, and I often think of moving elsewhere, but I'll tell you, there is no thrill like singing Wagner at Bayreuth!" He took a sip and reflected for a moment. Then he laughed again, a warm, merry, German laugh. "Hitler said he was physically sickened when he saw me sing 'the father of the gods' in 1924. I guess that's an achievement of sorts, eh? But Siegfried won't tolerate any political nonsense, so for now, I'm quite safe. And look how friendly you are, my blond young heldentenor. There are some good Germans after all, and bottom line, I consider myself German."

Hans was persistent, partly for selfish reasons. "But Herr Schorr, how do you justify loving Wagner when he wrote such terrible, damning things about the Jews?"

Schorr said that that discussion deserved another mug of beer each. He got them. "Flawed men can create art. Deeply flawed men can sometimes create great art. If we cancel the work of every great man who has made a legal or moral error, not only will there be no art left, but there will be no society left."

Siegfried's next battle was with Karl Muck, resident Bayreuth conductor who tried to out-Toscanini Toscanini! He demanded that Melchior be replaced as Tristan because the tenor complained the role was too long.

"Don't fret my boy," said Siegfried, hurrying from one screaming match to the next, "This is how it always is. Artists are a special breed. I'll pull it all together, and it will all work out in the end!"

And then, never getting to see his new production of "Tannhäuser,"

Siegfried Wagner had another heart attack and on August fourth, he died! Thus, opening the Bayreuth door to Winifred Wagner and Adolf Hitler…

CHAPTER 20

1930

BAYREUTH
CHANGES

"THE RIDE OF THE VALKYRIES" or "Walküren" blared loudly on a phonograph from another room in the usually quiet house. Since

Cosima Wagner had died in April at the age of ninety-two, and now with Siegfried dying in August, the atmosphere in the austere house had changed. The change began the morning after his death. The click and pause of the hard, high heels on wooden floor and oriental carpets combated the sound of one of the most famous pieces of music in the world. But this was music of glory and victory, not music of funereal grief. True, it was the music of female warrior goddesses carrying the dead bodies of fallen soldiers up to Valhalla, so it may have been appropriate after all.

Closing the heavy office door so that she might be alone,

and still dressed in her black mourning clothes, Winifred Wagner approached the grand desk from which the Bayreuth Festival empire was controlled. For the first time, instead of sitting in one of the chairs facing the desk, she moved around behind it. She stared down at the leather-bound document on the desk. What was written there would shake the Wagnerian world to its very foundation. Instead of Wieland, the eldest Wagner child inheriting, Siegfried had left the Bayreuth Festival and the Wagner fortune it controlled to her! Siegfried had left the power to his thirty-three-year old British wife. An outsider. And not even German! Cosima and Richard must have been spinning in their graves! Winifred, grew flushed and feverish with the realization of the responsibility and the might given to her. Heads would roll, doors would open and close, things would drastically change. The attractive, solidly-built woman brushed an errant strand of hair from her intelligent, if severe, face. She sat there soaking up the privacy and the power. She took a box of expensive cigars and exiled it to a bottom drawer in the desk. She pushed a button on the bottom of the desk lip, and a moment later Wolf entered the room.

"I'll need you by my side, Wolf, there is lots to do, and many changes are about to take place. We'll open my late-husband's production of 'Tannhäuser' as is, and finish out the season according to his wishes. He was a wise and creative man.

"The family will be up in arms against me for a while, but they will eventually settle down. More seriously, Muck will most likely resign at once. He can't stand the thought of a woman, Cosima excepted, of course, at the controls! Next season, we'll get rid of Melchior, he causes too many problems, and we'll bring in Max Lorenz, the Führer's favorite tenor.

Lorenz is as queer as they come, but Bayreuth is already crawling with homosexuals thanks to my late-husband, and Max sings like a dream. I'll try to work with Toscanini, but I'll have no tolerance for his crap. I also know he is no friend to the Nazi Party, and starting next season, we shall open our doors to them. Politics and art can walk hand in hand. I will bring in Furtwängler to conduct some of the operas. He knows how to kiss the hand that feeds him. Or the ass, when required. Schorr, the Jew, will probably have to go, although I have nothing against Juden myself, and a good Jew on the stage is worth a dozen bad ones in the banks. Even Adolf can excuse the odd Jew, if it serves his cause. Speaking of Uncle Adolf, as the children call him, we have another Wolf in our lives now. Wolf is the nickname we have for Herr Hitler. He visits us often in the evenings and puts the children to bed and reads to them. He calls me Winnie and I call him Wolf." There was a strange far away timbre to her voice when she said this, and her eyes became ever so slightly dreamy. "So, Herr Hitler will be Wolf One, and you will be Wolf Two. I hope you don't mind."

"It is an honor, Madame!" Wolf bowed his head, feeling privileged to be included in the inner circle. Dare he push?

She paused to take a long drink of ice-cold water from the glass and carafe Wolf had brought in. He cleared his throat, and she looked up at him with inquisitive eyes. "Ja?"

"What about your late-husband's new assistant, Hans Becker?"

"My husband is dead; he will need no new assistants or companions. You will assist me here as my secretary. However, Hans Becker has other talents... real talents that need to be encouraged and developed. We shall promote his singing career, and offer him a full-time position in our concert program, as well as a place in our company. He has potential as one of the great tenors of the future." Winifred was no naïve girl. She understood the art of business and the business of art.

Wolf was both elated and defeated; elated at his position with Winifred, and defeated at the news about Becker. Well, at least the "blond bombshell" would be out of his hair. But Wolf decided he would keep an eye on the young man, a scrutinizing eye.

One of Winifred's first and most important moves was to hire Heinz Tietjen as her general manager. Tietjen was already head of the Prussian State Theatre system and head of the Berlin State Opera. He was the most powerful man in the German opera world, and not a bad looking gentleman either. She could go for him, were her head and heart not totally filled with the glory and magic of the man who called her "Winnie."

In spite of the deaths, the dramas and the tragedies, the season was an enormous success. Rolf was there opening night, looking as splendidly handsome as ever, and stayed two weeks. He gave Hans a beautiful, Gruen, white gold wristwatch for an opening night gift.

"Rolf, you shouldn't have. I know you don't have much money now. How did you manage this?" He threw his arms around Rolf and kissed him.

"Without you there, you'd be surprised at the money I save. No new record albums, no pastries and candy, only dirty magazines." Hans put on the beautiful watch and studied it next to the gold ring from Rolf which he always wore. "You were the best one, you know," Rolf said.

"Rolf, there were fifty of us in the chorus."

"Still, I could hear you." The beautiful young man's face was quite sincere.

"Over an orchestra of over a hundred, you could pick out my voice?"

Rolf nodded solemnly. "I swear. Maybe it's just because I know your voice, or perhaps it is because I could always pick you out, even out of a crowd of a thousand." Hans shook his head and kissed his lover again.

"How could I ever be so lucky to have both you and music in my life?"

"It's because you are good, Hans, a genuinely good person. You make me a better person. I would do anything for you."

Rolf even got to meet Hans' parents when they attended the festival. They had dinner together once and drinks after the opera several times. Rolf found them to be charming, intelligent people with the same life-affirming energy he sensed in Hans. And they found him seductively charming, as everyone did. Fritz also came to visit and stayed a week. He actually spoke to and played for Rüdel, hoping to perhaps snag a position for the next summer. Hans dragged the pianist all over the festival grounds, showing him every nook and cranny from music to make-up rooms and introducing him to everyone.

"My God, is everyone here homosexual?" Fritz asked. "And knowing you, Opera Boy, you haven't climbed into bed with any of them."

Hans shook his head and said simply, "I love Rolf."

"I know! Sometimes, when you get everything you want, you realize you have nothing."

"Whatever do you mean by that, Fritz?"

Fritz shrugged and took a sip of his Campari and soda. They were at one of the inns near the hotel. "I work every day with more and more famous conductors. I play piano for the greatest film makers of our age and rub elbows with movie stars. I have all that I want. But do I?

You have achieved your dream of singing at Bayreuth, but is that what you really want? Would you trade it all in for a cottage on the Rhine with Rolf?"

Hans frowned. "Isn't it possible to have both?"

"To have it all, and then some? Look to your beloved operas for the answer, Hans. Only know this, I love you dearly and always will."

And for the very first time in his life, Hans would sometimes stand on the Bayreuth hillside late at night, studying the fat, full moon, and question what it was he really wanted. What if he had to make the hard choice? Love or power? Could he give up his career for Rolf? Sometimes, standing on the dark green wet grass, studying the moon, he thought he could. At other times, standing on stage before a full house, singing the most glorious music in the world...

The actual performing was quite different than Hans had imagined it would be. There was so much to think about that there was little time to bask in the glory of the music. Half the time he couldn't even hear it. He only heard the voices of the other chorus members. He was conducted by lights from the wings, green light sing faster, yellow light slow down. He had to dodge moving scenery getting on and off stage, as Bayreuth had no wing space and everything either flew or came down stage from the rear or up through the floor. It wasn't like the theater in Berlin at all. But it was still glorious. The singing load for the chorus in the Ring is mostly in the last opera, "Götterdämmerung," so many nights he could watch the performance from the rear of the auditorium. The chorus demands in "Tristan and Isolde" were minimal, as well. Hans got to play a sailor and a guard.

But in "Tannhäuser," it seemed he never stopped singing, and he was never happier.

On September second, 1930, Adolf Hitler became the supreme leader of the SA. In one of his first actions, he urged more force and thuggery in their activities. On September fourteenth of the same year, The National Socialist Party, in the Reichstag election, jumped from twelve seats to one hundred and seven, to become the second largest political party in Germany. Ernst Röhm, who had been out of the country for several years, partly due to scandals surrounding his open homosexuality, was called back to Germany and Berlin by Adolf Hitler to be appointed Chief of Staff of the SA. A few months later, he sent a message to Rolf Kainz to meet with him.

CHAPTER 21

1931
    BERLIN
    A DANGEROUS LITTLE MISSION

THIS TIME, the SA headquarters was even more festively festooned in red flags with huge, black swastikas and giant posters of politician Adolf Hitler, looking both humble and regal. On many of the more artistic posters, an "übermensch" Hitler was shown breaking the chains of the common man to free him, and these posters called him "Führer!"

There was actually furniture in the great hall this time, chairs and all, and music playing, which Rolf recognized as the overture from "Tannhäuser." It was all quite grand, with more young thugs than ever, dressed in brown uniforms, lurking in the shadows like a pack of hungry dogs waiting for the command to kill. In an odd way, it was far more decadent than any drag club Rolf had ever visited, and he could feel its kinky "dress up" attraction. All these lost boys, dressed up for Peter Pan!

The same spectacled, smooth fore-headed young man with the overly-efficient bearing waited on him. He had obviously not, as of yet, progressed up the corporate ladder. In the interim, though, he had acquired his own desk with an impressive oversized telephone. Rolf was amused to hear that the velvety smooth, youthful voice had been replaced by a sharp, nasal bark. There are many variations of the German language: high German, low German, soft poetic German, harsh militaristic German. This young man had cultivated the last. He fairly spit out his words, almost relishing the knife-edged sound he made; zero warmth, zero charm. But, oh, how that boy rolled his r's.

"Herr Röhm will see you in room 308."

Well, room 308 was considerably larger and more comfortable than room 215 had been. More spacious, with better art. The same basic furniture including the couch where Rolf had sold his soul to the devil for Hans' documents. There were new, modern floor lamps which cast a more sophisticated glow on proceedings, and the two chairs in front of the desk were better upholstered. The same desk, and behind it looking a bit more rotund, the same brown-shirted bully with an oversized cigar sticking obscenely out of his mouth. His manner though, had shifted. There was something humbler and almost effusive in his greeting. He pumped Rolf's hand vigorously and offered him a cigar and scotch. Rolf refused the first but accepted the second.

Rolf and Hans had spent a lovely fall and winter holiday season together. Although funds were limited, they dined, danced, made love, and did everything else just as they had always done. One evening, listening to Beethoven piano music on the phonograph, Rolf made an interesting observation. "You know Hans, as children, we are all encouraged to think that we are extraordinary. But the truth is that most of us are ordinary, some gifted, others exceptional, and only a very few rare ones truly extraordinary. In some ways, it does us a disservice to fill our heads with nonsense about how special we are.

You, my love, are extraordinary, but I, alas, am only gifted, at best."

"That's not entirely true, Rolf. Many of us have the potential to be extraordinary in one field or another, but time, circumstances, and sheer luck play a vital part. And some people find their strengths at different times in their lives."

"Still..." was Rolf's equivocation of an answer. And when Hans left again in the new year for Bayreuth, Rolf found himself drinking more and enjoying it less.

And so, he gladly accepted the very good scotch from Ernst Röhm.

"How was your trip abroad?" asked Rolf, knowing full well that it was made to avoid scandal and keep Röhm out of trouble.

"A fucking waste of time. Except for the Bolivian boys. You should see the maracas on some of them! The whole damned thing was orchestrated to shut me up about equal rights for homosexuals. According to some of the SA bigwigs, I am too outspoken. It's all right, as long as we keep it under our hats, eh? But now that Adolf is in charge and I have been promoted, things will change." He wiggled his eyebrows, and with the stupid cigar in his mouth, he looked like a cheap, music-hall comic, which in some ways, he was.

"But you know how it is. With everything good, there is a bad side. No more Eldorado Club for me, I'm afraid. The accusations against me are piling up, and I have to put on a 'respectable' front. Adolf says I've got to clean up my act!" The eyebrows danced and the moustache wiggled.

For some reason, Rolf felt in a position of some slight power, unusual for him. Röhm tapped ash into the crystal ashtray.

"There are a number of morality suits against me generated by intimate letters I wrote to this or that young gentleman. Adolf and some other friends will help me pull strings to fix those. But the thing is..." He paused to suck on his cigar and study Rolf. "The thing is, aside from Hitler, I don't know whom I can trust." The man's smile was now sickeningly sweet. "As I said, the nasty letters and slurs I can pretty much handle..."

"But?" Rolf interjected, enjoying his position more and more.

"But, there is the film!" Röhm drained his glass and uttered a big fat-man sigh. Then he burped. Rolf remained silent, this time with his eyebrows raised. "A film from a summer Hitler Youth Camp," Rohm continued. "A film of me misbehaving with a member of the Nazi Youth." He rose and crossed to the bar to fetch another scotch.

Rolf crossed his legs and held out his arm for more scotch as well. "How young?"

Röhm's cheeks puffed up like a balloon, and then he blew the air out, causing his moustache to flutter. "Young!" He gave Rolf his drink.

"And someone at the Eldorado Club has the film. I received a blackmail note written on an Eldorado Club napkin, that he would sell to the highest bidder!" He stared at a painting of naked, male angels. "It would ruin me, even with Hitler!" He returned to his desk, looking somehow smaller and older. "We'll shut the fucking club down, but not until I get that film."

"And that's where I come in?"

"That's where you come in, my friend."

The Master Singer

"I'm not your friend. You fucked me in the ass!"

Röhm bridled. "And you got the documents for your Jew boy!"

Mutual gratification. You know everyone at the club, and are thick as thieves with many of them. I need that film!"

Rolf was much less comfortable now, the sense of power had faded. "So, you are blackmailing me into helping you?"

Röhm shook his bowling ball of a head. "Don't think of it that way. It could be to your great advantage. We are walking on eggshells here. Aligning yourself with the SA could protect you and the ones… the one you love."

The scotch was warming Rolf and making even this scumbag and his disgusting offer a bit more palatable. "How about using some of your bully boys?"

Röhm raised both hands, palms outward, and shook them. "This has to be done outside the party; kept totally hush-hush. Get that film, by hook or crook. I'll support any necessary violence."

Rolf felt something he had not felt in years. The kind of crazy excitement he had felt as the "wild boy" at school, the popular bad boy everyone idolized. It made him feel good. There was almost a sexual excitement about it. "And this will help me, how?"

Röhm set his cigar in the ashtray, put down the scotch and with a sweeping, music-hall comedian gesture pointed at an adjoining door.

"Come. There is someone I want you to meet."

The man, who remained seated in a huge leather armchair was smaller than Rolf supposed he would be. Smaller and, in some ways, older, less firm. But those damned blue eyes looking up at him were at once hypnotizing. Extraordinary! They studied Rolf for a moment.

"This is my trusted friend, Rolf Kainz, about whom I

have been speaking to you," Röhm said, one hand on Rolf's shoulder.

When the little man in the leather chair spoke, his voice was soft and gentle, not a public speaking voice at all. Not like the voice of the "wannabe" attendant downstairs. The German here was simple and yet poetic.

"Do you like the movies? Do you go to the movies?"

Rolf nodded, rather stunned by the question. "Eh, ja, sir, I love the movies."

The little man in the big chair smiled. "Me, too. I like the new Hollywood musicals. Have you seen 'Whoopee' with Eddie Cantor?

It's splendid." One highly polished shoe extended itself and began to tap back and forth on the wooden floor. "Love me or leave me, or let me be lonely..." he sang gently. "Wouldn't it be wonderful if we could all sing and dance through life."

CHAPTER 22

1931
    BAYREUTH
    A DOOR OPENS

THERE WAS snow covering the ground at Bayreuth. The air was crisp and biting and the many leafless trees looked like skeletons dancing in the wind. Climbing the hill, Hans felt as if he were trekking on an alien landscape, perhaps the moon. The almost-deserted Festspielhaus looked cold and uninviting, more fortress-like than ever. Hans found the winter skeleton crew working there different too. They seemed guarded, on edge and ill at ease. Turnovers of this magnitude at Bayreuth were rare. There had only been Richard Wagner himself, then Cosima, then Siegfried... and now Winifred.

    Muck had resigned as predicted, and Rüdel was tense and tight-lipped. No one was certain of their futures or the future of the theater itself. Hans had not been notified of any changes in his position, so he showed up ready to work.

He spent a week sitting in the cold, drafty, rehearsal hall erasing marks in the myriad of scores from the previous season. It was tedious work but he could listen to music and chat with several other full-time employees. He had a vocal lesson from Rüdel, mostly just to warm up his voice and get the juices flowing after the Christmas break. When Hans asked the concert master what lay ahead, the slender man simply shrugged. "Give it time," were his only words.

The women in the costume department were a particularly good source of gossip, they seemed to have their fingers on the pulse of things. One could not, however, be sure which of the stories they shared were true and which were false. But they were colorful!

"She's going to fire everyone and start over from scratch!"

"She's going to restage every opera with a greater emphasis on German heritage!" As if that were possible.

"She's bringing in all of Hitler's favorite singers. Lauritz Melchior is out and Max Lorenz is in. No chorus boy is safe with Max Lorenz. They say he steals their underpants."

"She's going to get rid of any girl in the company prettier than she is. They'll be no one left, except for the fatty divas!"

"Everyone knows that the real father of her four children is Adolf Hitler."

"Because of funding problems, they are reducing the orchestra size to one hundred and the chorus to forty! How can Wagner be done that way?"

"They say Siegfried had his fatal heart attack while romping in bed with a young male member of the company! He was literally 'done' to death!" Did they look askance at Hans when they whispered this?

On the sixth day, he was called over to Wahnfried House. The snow crunched under his feet, and his breath

The Master Singer

made puffs in the air. He was understandably terrified. His future hung in the balance. After ringing the bell, he was made to wait five minutes in the cold before Wolf opened the door. While sucking on a tooth, he looked at Hans as if he were sizing him up, then stepped back and allowed him to enter.

The house inside was cold. Cold and dead. "Put your coat there," said Wolf, refusing to take it. Hans set his coat and cap on a hall chair and followed Wolf passed Richard Wagner's great grand piano and his velvet cap and conducting baton, not into the office, but into the library instead. Was this to be Hans' demise? Was he destined to go down in ice not fire in a room filled with books on history, philosophy and music?

She stood with her back to him, wearing a no-nonsense, dark blue dress with white collar and cuffs beneath a blue, winter, button-down sweater, studying the binding of a slim volume of poetry. Cold blue light poured in through a large window, but fortunately the orange glow from the fireplace gave the room at least some warmth. When she turned, he clicked his heels and bowed his head.

"Look at you," she said in a steely voice. "Stand up straight. If you want to sing the big roles, then you must never forget that wherever you stand is center stage!" He stiffened, trying to keep his legs from buckling. She was formidable, all right!

"My late husband was very fond of you. I hope not for all the wrong reasons."

Hans didn't know how to respond, or if he should. Was he expected to morally defend himself?

She watched him carefully, as one studies a still living butterfly pinned to a display board. "You are no longer needed here as a staff member!"

Hans' heart dropped into his boots. He looked down, realizing he had not wiped his feet thoroughly enough on the door mat. They now left a small puddle on the carpet. That puddle was all that remained of his dreams.

She watched to see if his shoulders fell, or if he would cry. When he did not, she smiled. "Beginning tomorrow, you will join a small but important group of singers studying here full-time at Bayreuth. You will begin training to become an elite Wagnerian Tenor! You will perform concerts to raise money and advertise our season. You will take lessons each day with Herr Rüdel and occasionally myself. You will learn how to walk and talk and breath differently! You will study how to analyze a role and how to interpret it on stage. You will learn to act..." She paused for at least some of this to sink in. Hans had stopped listening to the actual words a few sentences back.

"And when you are not singing or studying, I expect you to be here, reading every book in my father-in-law's library. Spend as much time here, soaking up knowledge, as you can. Come and go freely. You need not ring the bell. In ten years' time, you will sing Tristan at Bayreuth!"

He stood there, speechless, the room spinning around him. He must not embarrass himself by fainting or heaven forbid, wetting his pants. So, he stood there.

"Take the rest of the day off. You begin tomorrow. Now Go!" Was she amused at her power, or at his reaction? She was obviously amused. He stood there feeling that he had died and was resurrected in an instant. In silence, he turned and exited the library. He felt his chest swell as if it might explode. How foolish it now seemed to be intimidated by Wolf or anyone else in the world for that matter. He had been told he would sing Tristan. He would be Tristan.

"Ach!" he stopped in horror, one hand over his mouth.

He hadn't even thanked her, his savior, his goddess! He began to run back toward the library, sliding on the wooden floor, but skidded to a sudden stop and thought better of it. He turned and this time walked slowly toward the exit. He wanted to call Rolf. He needed to call Rolf. And his parents and Fritz, but mostly Rolf.

He smiled pleasantly at Wolf who guarded the front door. Hans put on his coat and cap. "Well, I guess we'll be seeing a great deal of each other. Don't bother with the door, I'll get it."

At King Arthur's Round Table there was one seat left vacant for the Knight of the Grail. The knight who would heal the land. It was a perilous seat, for the wrong person daring to sit there would die!

CHAPTER 23

1931

BERLIN

IN DEEPER

The streets were a slushy mess, and when the Duisenberg Model J backfired, an already jittery Rolf jumped, splattering dirty ice on the cuffs of his trousers. Fortunately, he wore rubbers on his highly polished shoes. The Eldorado Club still had its New Year's decorations up outside the building, even though it was February, but, with all the hard winter weather they had endured that year, the tinsel and lights now hung limp and lifeless. All of Berlin seemed tired, and its citizens were depressed by the depression.

Inside, the club valiantly maintained its gaiety. The band blared, and on stage two well-built male gymnasts dressed in nothing but thongs wrapped themselves around each other in ways that suggested another kind of sport altogether. The Countess, in something extravagantly beaded, floated her way across the purple haze of the dancefloor, twisting in and out of trysting couples, smiling, nodding and giving air kisses. Like many an old, savvy, drag queen, the Countess was a survivor. She knew the latest news before any of the newspapers and how to employ it to her advantage. In the last year, it had become a game of survival.

She halted at a table of schoolboys who had gained entrance through the influential father of one of them, no doubt to "see the queers." A few of the boys would return on their own again and again.

At the moment, they were pre-occupied hazing a junior member of their company by breaking eggs on his head and taunting him about how much the runny gunk was like sperm. The Countess put a stop to their shenanigans.

"Stop this at once, you dirty little pigs, or I'll throw you out. If you must bully the boy, find another way. Eggs are expensive and people are starving." She snapped a dishtowel from a waiter's arms and handed it to the beyoked lad who couldn't have been more than sixteen. "Is it really worth it?" she asked him gently. Then she turned her mascaraed eyes on the rest of the table. "I know how you got in here, but generally this place is verboten to children. And believe me you are childish, the lot of you. So, if you want to stay, sit quietly, enjoy the sights and play with yourselves!"

She stopped at another table to congratulate an elderly pair of gentlemen on their anniversary. The old gents wore too much powder and rouge, trying to stave off time, and each sported a huge, green carnation. The countess ordered free champagne for them and moved on. Next, she passed a few kind words with a pair of well-known lesbian authoresses. On the whole, lesbians seemed better able to navigate through scandal than male queers. The countess remembered that in the England of Queen Victoria, male homosexuals were imprisoned, while lesbians were forgiven, mainly because the Queen couldn't understand what sexual acts two females could perform. The members of her court were all too embarrassed to educate her.

Next, the Countess checked to make sure things were set up properly for a still vacant table reserved for a real-live Hollywood movie star, Edward Everett Horton. Fewer and fewer international celebrities visited the club in the last year. Times were hard.

At last, she greeted and air kissed Rolf, who had just checked his slouch hat, overcoat and rubbers. "Mon Petite Chou," she purred in incorrect French. "How are you, my darling, and how is our little blond nightingale?"

"He's studying at Bayreuth, a special program for gifted young singers. Doing quite well, actually."

The wily Countess picked up on something in Rolf's answer. "Everything good between you two?" she asked bluntly.

"Huh? Oh, ja! Perfect. It's just hard being separated so much." Rolf definitely looked anxious.

"Absence makes... darling, you two will be all right. You've been together forever. You're survivors."

Rolf always had friends at the club, and on this night, he went from table to table picking up gossip and fishing for anything that might take him closer to his quarry. At some point at each table, he brought up the subject of blue movies.

"With Hans gone, your poor hand is getting tired, eh, Rolf?" his friends teased. "How sad for someone as handsome as you to have to settle for one-handed, skin-flick films." Rolf realized his probes were getting him nowhere.

The band struck up "Makin' Whoopee," as Rolf worked his way through the room. Old pals and potential prospects flirted with him or brazenly hit on him. It was exhausting. And then, one of the schoolboys, a devilishly cute, snotty, little angel, took a shine to him. Trying to impress his pals, or perhaps as a joke, he almost flung himself at Rolf.

"I may be young, but I know what I'm doing," the sandy-haired teen slurred, his pomegranate lips parting to reveal beer breath.

"Well that's commendable," said Rolf. "Knowing what you are doing should earn you a merit badge." Rolf tried to push by the lad, but the kid was damned aggressive.

"Do you want to fuck?" the boy brazenly asked.

"No, thank you, I don't want to wrinkle my trousers."

The boy, who was trying so hard to be grown up, pouted. "Well then, let's dance." Rolf didn't want to humiliate the boy trying so hard to impress his mates who were watching with giddy erections, so he allowed the kid to drag him onto the dance floor.

Wouldn't you know it, "Makin Whoopee" segued into the romantic but melancholy "But Not for Me," and the schoolboy literally draped himself over Rolf, rubbing up against him like a dog in heat. The schoolmates applauded and whistled.

The kid seemed honestly smitten by Rolf, but there was a method to Rolf's madness. After the dance, he allowed himself to be pulled over to the student table, where after idle, meaningless chat filled with little boy naughtiness, Rolf asked them about sex films.

"Anybody here try to sell you guys any dirty films?" He asked casually, sipping the beer he had ordered. All of the boys answered in the negative, but then, the boy with egg on his head offered something useful.

"A guy asked me if I wanted to make some money by modeling for gay movies," he said.

"Christ, who'd want to look at you naked?" one of the other boys guffawed. The bullied boy slumped in his chair, but Rolf came to his rescue.

"I would, for one. I think he's damned handsome." That shut the bullies up. The bullied boy, whose name was Kurt, began to glow. Such a little thing can mean so much. To build Kurt's self-esteem even more, Rolf took the boy away from the table for a private conversation.

"Tell me, Kurt, can you point this guy out to me?"

Kurt, lost in Rolf's eyes shook his head. "He's not here anymore."

"Well, if he comes back, you let me know, all right? And do you know something else? You're too good to let those guys push you around. Find some better friends."

Next, Rolf approached the Countess. "There's a guy here trying to recruit boys for blue movies. Do you know anything about it?"

The Countess drew herself taller. "You insult me, Rolf. Of course not. Those boys don't belong here, but the father of one of them is big with the Weimar Republic. I run a decent, sleazy business, not a corrupt one. You know those bars where they show sex films? Well, some of them also make them."

Still later, while a lovely drag chanteuse was lulling a drunken clientele to "Falling in Love Again," Kurt came over to Rolf's table for two things. "The man is back, over there at the bar. The small weasel of a guy in the blue suit," and to hand Rolf a slip of paper with the kid's address and telephone number at school. Rolf smiled sweetly at the boy's instant teenage devotion. He kissed Kurt on the cheek. "You be careful, Kurt. Don't let anyone hurt you." Then Rolf wandered over to the art deco bar and ordered a martini. It was served, as it almost always was in those days, with a small glass and a personal shaker to keep the drink chilled. A tiny dish bearing two olives came along for the ride.

The Weasel in blue at first had his back to Rolf, but he soon felt eyes staring into the back of his head, so he turned. His face was a bit weasel-like, too, with a sharp nose, but he was not bad looking. He must have been in his mid-thirties. His hair was as black as Rolf's, but was slicked back and stiff with gel.

"Don't I know you from some place?" Rolf asked in his most charming manner.

The Weasel shook his head. 'I'm sure I'd remember."

"Maybe from here, or another club."

"Perhaps." He extended his hand. "Gunther."

"Rolf." They shook. Then they drank and chatted about nothing for ten minutes, the bar, the band, the boys. Finally, Gunther bit.

"You're an extremely good-looking, young man. Have you ever thought about doing any modeling work? There's good money in it. I'm a kind of talent agent." The man's lips became almost serpentine.

The sleaze was emerging.

Rolf could have played innocent or dumb, but he tried another approach. "Modeling? Is that a euphemism for making sex films?"

Gunther shrugged. "It doesn't have to be, but that's where the money is. And, the bluer the films, the more the money. In these hard times, it's a good way to make a living wage and more. I act in some myself from time to time. I find it fun."

Rolf leaned closer to his new friend. "And what if my sexual tastes are kinkier than most?"

"Even more money. We don't judge in my business. We

try to give the customers what they want. And of course, it's all very discreet."

Rofl didn't know how far to go in this setting. He was not sure what to do next. The thirty caliber Waffenfabrik Bern Model 1929 handgun that Ernst Röhm had given him for his protection was weighing heavy and bulky beneath his jacket. He knew very little about guns or how to use them, so the very thing designed to give him courage and clout actually intimidated him.

"What if my tastes lie in the direction of younger partners?"

Gunther's smile showed well-kept, white teeth. "The younger the partner, the more prized the film. My tastes lie in that direction as well, although I wouldn't toss you out of bed. But shall we go someplace more..." he looked around the busy club, "private to continue this chat? Do you know the club, 'Dekadenz?'"

When depressed, Rolf had spent a number of drug and drink-fueled nights at "Dekadenz" but this was the first time he reached the hall behind the orgy room which led to a private office. It was a typical, business office that might have belonged to a shipping company. Ledgers and document scattered across two desks. Bland white lights in the ceiling that washed any charm from the space. And a safe.

Rolf had absolutely no idea how to behave or what to do. Fortunately, Gunther the Weasel took the lead.

"I think we both know why you are really here, Rolf, if that is your name. You are not here to make sex films, but to procure one. I'm not one for wasting too much time talking bullshit. You are after a certain film mentioned on a note written on a napkin, correct? Well, I'm willing to negotiate on behalf of the man who shot the film. It's a doozy, believe me. I get lots of films across my desk, sometimes from nobodies, dull as goose-shit, but then I also get films that could, in the wrong hands, compromise prominent men and women. I don't want to see these prominent citizens hurt, so I offer a financial arrangement to settle the matter."

"How do you know which client I represent?" Rolf asked.

The Weasel chuckled. "Mr. Kainz, we are professionals. I keep an eye on the subjects of the films. You were seen entering and leaving the SA headquarters. You are also very popular at the Eldorado Club. Put two and two together." He poured two glasses of whiskey and handed one to Rolf. Then he sat on the edge of one of the desks. He did not invite Rolf to sit. "Let me explain something to you, my friend. Ernst Röhm is in the outhouse. True, Hitler protects him and has made him Chief of Staff, but it is young party members like Himmler and Goebbels who really influence "den Führer." They have convinced Hitler that Röhm's ideas of armed revolution and putsch are self-defeating, and that the way to win power is to do it legally and politically. Himmler is also forming a special political police force within the SA to be called the SS. They, not Röhm's people, will be Hitler's private army. My point being, that your friend Röhm hasn't a leg on which to stand, and he can't tolerate any more scandal. All of this must enter into our negotiations over the unfortunate film. Have you seen it? It is quite disgusting and also quite stimulating, if you like that kind of thing."

Rolf stood there trembling, in way over his head. This guy was no amateur. He slugged down the drink. "How do I know the film is in safe hands?"

"It's not in any hands. It's right there in my safe. The little Nazi who filmed it won't trouble Röhm anymore, so you only have to deal with me!"

Rolf, not knowing what else to do, pulled out the

handgun and pointed it at the Weasel. "Open the safe and give me the film!" He didn't even know how to fire such a gun. He lifted the gun to look for a safety. Gunther laughed, he actually laughed, at Rolf and shook his head, pitying the kid. "What have they gotten you into?"

Gunther was about to push a button on the desk to bring help, when a most fortuitous thing happened for Rolf. Suddenly, a piercing siren filled the building and the lights flickered.

"Scheisse, a fucking police raid. We've got to get out of here." Ignoring Rolf completely, Gunther crossed behind the desk and from a drawer produced stacks of money which he tossed into a leather satchel. Sounds of yelling and shouting and several gunshots came from beyond the walls. The police were firing warning shots to control the hysterical bar patrons. Oddly enough, the loud jazz music continued.

Gunther circled the desk and went to the office door and opened it. "There is another exit at the end of the hallway." As if to punctuate his remark, two nearly naked boys raced pass the open door and down the hall.

"Wait!" Rolf barked. "Open the safe! I want the film!"

"FUCK YOU!" The Weasel turned to leave the room, and in panic, Rolf pulled the trigger and, without even aiming, shot Gunther in the leg.

"You Bitch! You little, fucking bitch!" Gunther howled, grabbing his leg and going down onto one knee.

A trembling, hysterical Rolf waved the Waffenfabrik. "I'll do it again! I'll shoot you again. Open the safe!" More gunshots from beyond the walls, inside the club proper. More screaming and the crashing of furniture.

"You little cunt. You have no idea what you're doing. Oh,

Christ, my leg hurts. You shot me. You actually shot me!" The Weasel was wide-eyed, gripping his bleeding leg.

"I'll do it again! I swear, I'll do it again!" Gunther knew that the out of control, hysterical kid was more dangerous than a hired gun. He grabbed the bag of money and spun into the hall, where dripping blood, he limped for the rear door, leaving Rolf standing there waving the gun in panic.

The police whistles and battering sounds seemed nearer. Rolf didn't know what to do. Suddenly, he was a frightened weakling, not the man he wanted to be. "Got to think straight. Got to get my head together!" He turned and, pointing the gun at the safe, he fired again. The bullet went wide, ricocheted off the wall and smashed one of the ceiling lights. Rolf was shaking so badly, he had to hold the gun in both hands. He started to cry. He glanced at the open doorway and saw a black musician, embracing his bass fiddle like a lover, stumble down the hall. Somewhere in the building another door was battered down and there were more screams.

Rolf aimed at the safe door again and squeezed the trigger. "BLAM!" It blew the handle of the safe right off, and the door swung open. Now the ceiling and floor and walls seemed to thunder with the sound of running feet. Rolf threw open the door of the safe to reveal a stack of about a dozen eight millimeter films and piles of cash. He tossed it all into a canvas sack he found and headed toward the hallway. The wall sconces and ceiling bulbs were out, replaced by some kind of red, emergency lights, giving the whole scene a nightmarish, Faustian quality.

In the hall, someone bumped into Rolf and ran past him. He followed the escaping party-boy, as the door at the end of the hall behind him caved in and a voice yelled, "Police!

Berlin City Police! Halt where you are!" Of course, neither Rolf nor the hustler did. They made for the rear exit and found themselves in a Kreuzberg alley, leading to a maze of narrow, twisted, back-street slums. Bathhouses, where the poor went to wash once a week, slaughterhouses, and leaning, rickety tenements, horses attached to carts all night, and freezing, homeless vagrants wrapped in rags against the cold. An evening that had begun in slush, had frozen into slippery ice, and Rolf found himself on his ass more than once as he tried to escape from the police raid. Finally, he stopped long enough to catch his breath and toss the handgun into a garbage heap. When he had calmed down enough to think clearly, he caught a cab back to the apartment.

CHAPTER 24

1931

    BERLIN, BAYREUTH
    SEX STUFF AND SEPARATION

ROLF WAS SO SHAKEN by what had happened that he sat on the floor in a corner of the apartment bedroom trembling, with his arms wrapped around his knees. He hadn't even taken off his overcoat. Next to him was a canvas bag with a dozen illicit porno films and a million Reichsmarks, which considering the crippling depression wasn't the windfall it might seem to be, but still a very hefty chunk of money. He buried his head in his hands and sobbed, partly from fear, and partly from the adrenalin rush he felt. He'd actually shot someone, and the chances were that both the police and the gangster syndicate were now searching for him. The 8mm films in the bag might be worth fifty times the cash.

He cursed Ernst Röhm for getting him into this jam but, weirdly, he also felt the most alive he had felt in years. He rose, removed his coat, poured himself a huge glass of whiskey, sat back on the floor and opened the canvas sack. Röhm had said he would be protected, and Rolf now had to rely on that. He wanted to call Hans, but knew he could not in the middle of the night. He found a magnifying glass they used for map study when planning their trips, put a table lamp on the floor, removed the shade, and then began to go through the films, searching frame by frame for the one with Röhm.

What he saw shocked, disgusted and aroused him by turns. He recognized numerous socialites, business leaders and political and military personalities engaged in every conceivable sex act. Most were straight-forward, homosexual sex scenes, often involving these celebrities engaged with teenage boys. Some were revoltingly kinky for Rolf; those involving toilet games or animals. The worst and most sickening were the scenes with children involved. Four or five different scenes made up each reel of film. It was in the fourth canister that he came upon the Röhm film. It had obviously been shot in a cabin at one of the Nazi Youth Camps, and involved a fat, naked, cigar-smoking Röhm doing things with and to a beautiful, blond, pre-pubescent boy. Rolf poured and drank more whiskey. He set that reel aside and burned the rest.

"Why the fuck did I take the money?" he said out loud to himself. Now he had decisions to make. Should he lay low for a few days or get rid of the film to Röhm at once? The Weasel had said that he had been followed. Did they know where he lived? In a near panic, he packed a bag and decided to stay in a hotel for a while. He typed a quick letter to Hans, telling him that he was involved in a "political project" that might take some little time, but assuring the young man that he loved him more than life. He sealed, addressed and stamped the envelope and dropped it in the post box on the way out of the building. It was approaching morning, and light grey slashes of light ripped the night sky asunder. For now, light was Rolf's enemy. He had lost his slouch hat somewhere during his escape from the club, but had a cloth cap pulled down over his forehead as he hurried into a cab, suitcase in one hand and a leather satchel filled with stolen money in the other.

He checked into an old, highly-respected hotel in Charlottenburg, a place littered with antiques and stately charm. Rolf knew it because his father had sometimes put up visiting university-lecturers there. Suddenly, Rolf missed his parents terribly and vowed to visit them at the nearest opportunity. He took a long, hot bath, curled up naked in the luxurious bed and slept all day.

Around dinnertime, he telephoned Röhm at the SA headquarters. He was put through immediately. "I've got the item we spoke about."

"Good boy. Ja, I read about an incident in the newspapers. We should not say too much on the telephone, wire-tapping is the latest fad in Berlin."

"I can't come there. The headquarters is being watched. Meet me at the Dicke Wirten in Charlottenburg. I haven't eaten all day." The Dicke Wirten was a tavern restaurant that catered to artists, authors, actors and other bohemian types, fiercely defended and protected by Anna Stanscheck, fondly called "the fat lady." Rolf settled in and ordered the schnitzel which came larger than a phonograph record, accompanied by potato salad and a pickle salad. The beer and food helped to settle Rolf, and by the time a nondescript, black limo pulled up outside the front door, and a black trench coated Ernst Röhm barreled in, he was already on his third stein of beer.

When Röhm was anxious, the scar on his nose and cheek stood out, and today it was livid. His beady, little eyes bored into Rolf. "You've got it?" he asked without any prelude, like a child hungry for his Christmas gifts. He settled his big gut in the chair across from Rolf and raised his hand to be served. Rolf nodded in answer to Röhm's question but continued to eat. He liked seeing Röhm under his control for a change. Rolf sat there anxiously drinking and watching Rolf eat. Finally, the young man dabbed his mouth with the cloth napkin.

"You almost got me killed."

"You shot someone. That was not part of the plan. The gun was for your protection only."

Rolf turned red. "I was protecting myself. And I was protecting you. I'm not a military nut like you are. I only ever fired a weapon hunting."

Röhm snorted. "It's the same thing, only your target is human. You are the product of a weak and sissified society. You should be proud you shot scum like that."

Rolf raised his eyebrows. "And have half of Berlin searching for me?"

Röhm laughed. He actually laughed. "It's exciting, nicht wahr? Now you are a soldier. Last night, you may have saved Germany! Let me explain, my little puppy. There are four minds at work, trying to control Adolf Hitler and the future of Germany. Goebbels, the mouthpiece of the party, Himmler, whose sexual perversions make us look like choirboys, Göring, the one-time war hero, now a drug addicted socialite politician, and me. Himmler wants control of the SA and has started his own black-shirt police force inside of it, a special police force for Hitler alone. Goebbels has convinced Hitler that the route to success is not with the military but through legal, political control. Thanks to him, the party almost died in the 1928 election. Only the collapse of the economy saved us and kept us popular. But he has Adolf's ear. Göring lost his greatest asset, his wife, who really had all the connections, and now he, too, wants to start his own police force called the Gestapo! So, there are three military forces in the Nazi Party, the SA, the SS and the Gestapo. Himmler thinks he should control all three. A lot of infighting, and poor Ernst Röhm," he gestured to himself, "poor Ernst Röhm must tread lightly. Thank Gott, Hitler is still my friend. But that film would have ruined me." He held out his hand for the film.

Rolf handed the canister over to the fat man, who shoved it into his breast pocket. He then sighed a great sigh of relief and perhaps farted.

"'Blue Angel,' it's not!," Rolf said. "And the man who shot the film at the summer camp?" he asked.

Röhm smiled and reached for some of Rolf's bread. "I castrated him." Was his smile reassuring or threatening? "Talk is there was money taken from the safe as well." The moustache twitched.

Rolf shook his head. "I don't know about that. Must have happened after I ran out."

Röhm lit a cigar and folded his hands over his belly. Rolf ordered coffee.

"And now?" Rolf asked, perhaps a bit too casually.

"I PROMISED you that my boys would have your back. But believe me, you'd be safer inside our organization than out on your own. We are loyal to each other and protect our own."

"Well, I'm going to visit my parents for a bit. I'll think about it when I get back."

Röhm chuckled and smoke from the cigar enveloped his head. "Don't think too long or too hard. Thinking is dangerous in 1931 Berlin."

In Bayreuth, Hans was a bit distressed to hear that Rolf was going to Geneva for a month or two. It would be the first time since they fell in love that either of them missed a scheduled visit. Rolf promised he would make it up and, of course, Hans understood. But there were other things, evasions and small deceptions, that saddened him and gave him great concern.

Hans was kept busy. Not only vocal lessons and library reading, and the studying of scores. He was given breathing and posture exercises, diction and acting lessons, and more. When Winifred Wagner set her mind to something, she did not do it by half measures. He sang at various teas and luncheons, always with great success. Numerous high-ranking society Frauen and Fraülein offered to bed him, as well as numerous high-ranking husbands, and lots of single men. Even Winifred flirted from time to time to ensure his devotion, although it never came to more than that. He thought she held honest affection for him, but her ball-breaking severity made it difficult to tell. Wolf watched him like a wolf, and there, too, there was a certain almost erotic tension.

Once a month or so, a sleek, black limousine would pull up to Wahnfried House, and Hans would be ordered to stay away for a few days. Costume department chatter was the mysterious visitor was Adolf Hitler.

And so, while Rolf was getting a strong dose of reality, Hans was busy dealing with truth told through illusion. And then, two months into spring, Hans received two important letters. One from Rolf saying he was returning to Berlin and would see Hans as soon as possible. He said he loved him more than ever and missed him dreadfully. The second letter was from Hans' father:

Mine Zun: This is a letter I thought I would never have to write. First, know that your mother and I are as proud of you as can be. Everyone here brags about knowing you and your extraordinary creative gifts. But that being said, things have become intolerable here in Munich. I spoke to you before about our thoughts on selling the shop and leaving. Well, unfortunately, that time has come earlier than we would have wished.

Remember, my darling boy, the Nazi party began in Munich and it is still the center of their terror. Their anti-Semitic rhetoric has turned into daily, physical violence. Last week, our store windows were broken and some of our most valuable antiques and art work destroyed. Swastikas were painted on our doors and walls, and many beautiful items smashed. I reported it to the police who did absolutely nothing. They seem to condone such behavior.

And so, like my father and grandfather, once more we must emigrate to greener pastures. We have decided to settle in Paris and open a shop there. I have already shipped some of our more precious artworks, and we have friends there looking for a place for us to settle. I strongly suggest you consider joining us until the trouble here passes, which it is sure to do in a few years. You could have a splendid career in Paris and live a safe, happy life.

There is talk that all German banks may close, so people are withdrawing their money. I've left some money for you with Otto, the jeweler. The attacks at synagogues are increasing every week and have become more organized. I say with great love that you really must get your head out of the clouds and see the situation as it is.

I'll let you know when we are leaving. It will be from Berlin, so perhaps you might come down and meet us for a few days. Your mother and I long to kiss you goodbye, even if it is only for a while. We'll let you know the details.

Ich hobe dich lieb, Papa

CHAPTER 25

1931

   BERLIN
   HORROR

Rolf missed the 1931 season of the Bayreuth Festival. So did Hans' parents. It was a shame because the tenor was given his first solo lines to sing. He played the role of Balthasar Zorn, the pewterer in "Die Meistersinger." Hans had fulfilled his dream of singing opera at Bayreuth. It was terribly exciting, and Hans cried on opening night because Rolf, who was still in Geneva, was not there. The letters from Geneva were filled with love, and Rolf still pledged eternal devotion. He promised to return to Germany as soon as possible, but explained nothing. Winifred Wagner sent Hans a bottle of champagne, but the tenor celebrated and drank it alone. He wrote to Rolf: "There is a constant melody in my head, and the only melody is you!" This seems trite and stupid, I know, but Hans, the romantic, lived in a magic world of love, while things around him grew uglier. Friedrich Schorr had his make-up mirror smashed with the words "JEW PIG" written on it with lipstick. Hans spent more and more free time with the "greatest Wotan ever," but Schorr decided he would probably have to leave Germany.

As the season drew to a close, on the eve of the Jewish New Year, a large gang of Nazis attacked Jews on the Kurfürstendamm in Berlin, as they returned home from synagogue. There were many casualties. Once again, nothing was done about it. Hans received news that his parents would be leaving for Paris in three weeks from Berlin where they had to conduct some business and get their travel documents approved. At the same time, Hans received a letter from Rolf saying he was back in Berlin at last, and could his lover come up to visit him. Could he? Of course, he could! Hans read and re-read Rolf's letter and kissed it over and over.

He took his leave of Winifred Wagner, and promised to be back in six weeks to continue his studies. He packed programs from the operas for his parents and Rolf, and with two suitcases he boarded the train for Berlin. He sat in a compartment with two attractive young ladies, who flirted shamelessly and demanded that he sing for them.

In the city, brisk now with an early fall, Hans deposited his suitcases at the apartment, but Rolf was not yet there. Hans calculated that he thought about Rolf once an hour, but that may have been a low estimate. He hurried from his apartment to Alexanderplatz where he was to meet his parents at the railway station. He was early, so he went to a café for a coffee. Then, as he approached the main entrance of the station, he saw a commotion. About twenty SA Brownshirt Stormtroopers were roughing up some citizens.

Hans' blood turned to ice when he saw that the victims were his parents!

"We caught this Jew pig and his German-whore wife at the ticket counter. Come take a look at what is dragging our country into the gutter! They are polluting our pure German blood," a Nazi thug was shouting through a megaphone. Quite a crowd of citizens had gathered, Hans among them. Jacob and Gretchen stood at attention very still, their suitcases by their side, while hand printed signs were hung around their necks.

Her sign read:
"The biggest pig in town am I
It's only with Jews I choose to lie."

His sign read:
"As a man of the Jewish race,
I take only German girls to my place."

They both appeared rather stunned and confused. Then, the Nazis spit on them. Spit in their faces. Hans, watching the grotesque act of bullying, grew hysterical and lost all control. He made inarticulate sounds and tried to push his way through the crowd. His arms and legs wouldn't work, and he collapsed into the street, screaming.

"Here, are you all right?" a gentleman asked as he helped to pick the young man out of the gutter. A middle-aged woman also supported him. Hans tried to push gawking people aside to get to his parents, but when he caught his father's eye, Jacob shook his head fiercely. Some of the crowd were hurling slurs at the Jew and his wife, while others berated the Brownshirt thugs for their actions.

"Shame on you, leave them alone," an old man with a stick shouted. No physical damage was done to the humiliated couple, and eventually, the bullies, tired of this game and seeking another, wandered away. Hans' parents removed their signs and tossed them into the street. They wiped the trails of spittle from their faces.They took their suitcases and walked to Hans, who was in worse shape than they were.

"It's all right, Hans, it's over. We've got our documents and are leaving in an hour. Everything's all right." Both parents embraced their son, and they stood that way, clinging to each other, for a very long time. Then they went to have coffee and calm down. By the time their train left, Hans had promised he would visit them in Paris soon and at least consider moving there. Hans began to fantasize that perhaps he and Rolf could move to France and build a life there together.

It was a painful and tear-filled goodbye. Hans assured his parents that he was safe in Bayreuth. Jacob warned his son to keep a close eye on the quickly changing political climate. They gave Hans their address and telephone number in Paris and, with tears running down their cheeks, watched him grow smaller and smaller standing there on the station platform.

Hans was so shaken by the day's horrific events, he grabbed a cab and headed back to his apartment. He needed Rolf more than ever. He needed him at once! The apartment was still empty, and Hans sat on the floor in a corner and watched the autumn sunlight recede through the window. He drank but could not stop shaking. He found some of Rolf's cocaine and took a bit. Anything to forget the looks on his parents' faces as they stood with those ugly signs around their necks. The humiliation was overwhelming. At last, after hours of lonely torment, Hans heard the downstairs door slam and the clump of boots on the stairs. The boots took three stairs at a time, and Hans recognized Rolf's footfall. His heart leapt, he wiped the tears from his eyes, ran his fingers through his hair and grinned. The door opened.

And there stood Rolf Kainz in a brown SA uniform!

Hans screamed in horror, threw his hands over his eyes and curled up in a little ball. Rolf stood there in full boots and regalia, a bit stymied.

"Hans, sorry, I didn't have time to change after the meeting. Hans!"

Tears, snot and spittle ran from Hans' face. He lifted his head to look upon the end of his life. "Get out! Get out, do you hear me? I never want to see you again." Like a rabid dog he got to his hands and knees and spit at Rolf.

"Hans, listen to me. I can explain. I love you Hans. You are the only thing in life that I love! Let me…"

"I SAID GET OUT! I'LL SEND FRITZ WITH YOUR THINGS. YOU HAVE BETRAYED ME!" Rolf stepped in and squatted near Hans. He reached out a hand toward him, and Hans bit it. He swung his arms fiercely. "Get away. Don't touch me!"

"Hans, I love you so much. Let me explain. I got involved in a mess and this is for my protection. It can be for your protection, too. Please!" Rolf was crying now too.

"MY PROTECTION? THIS MORNING YOUR BROWNSHIRTS ABUSED AND HUMILIATED MY PARENTS. SPIT ON THEM! TO THINK YOU HAVE BECOME SUCH A LOATHSOME THING! I NEVER WANT TO SEE YOU AGAIN AS LONG AS I LIVE!" Hans screamed so loudly a neighbor thumped on the wall to warn them to keep the noise down. Then Hans curled up into a fetal position and sobbed. His breathing became ragged and labored.

"I'm… I'm sorry Hans, I have made some mistakes. Just let me explain. It will all work out…" Rolf was now hysterical as well. Hans grabbed the nearest thing to him which was a shoe and flung it at Rolf.

"I said get out. Go march with your bully boys and beat up some Jews! I SAID GET OUT!" Hans began to throw everything he could find at Rolf, records, books, bottles. Finally, a pleading, almost incoherent Rolf was driven from the room. He staggered, then fell down the stairs and, battered and bruised, stumbled into the street. His world had spun out of control.

Two lives were changed forever that day. Things would never go back to the way they were. But then, they never do, do they?

CHAPTER 26

1931-32
BERLIN, BAYREUTH
LIVING DEATH

As WEIMAR GERMANY teetered on the brink, a freezing, numbing winter once more settled on Berlin. It grew dark early and seemed grey and lifeless during the day. People wrapped themselves to bustle from here to there, and the "here" of home seemed most safe and comforting.

Hans literally lingered on the cusp of death for weeks, and probably would have died had not Fritz moved in to nurse him and call a doctor. In those first bleak hours after expelling Rolf from his life, Hans lay curled up on the floor until the room grew black with the blanket of night. Several times he awoke, only to slide once more beneath the comforting comforter of the unconscious.

Sometime, in the early hours of the morning, he crawled to the telephone to call Fritz. In Fritz's building the telephone was a shared one in the downstairs hall, and the sleepy landlady was none too pleased to have to fetch him at such a God-forsaken hour, especially when the voice demanding "Fritz, Fritz!" sounded so demented or drunk.

Fritz was there in an hour to find an empty bottle of Schnapps, an equally empty pill bottle, and Hans lying in a lake of vomit. Recovery did not come easily, if it ever entirely came at all. He slept most of the time, dreaming over and over that he was adrift at sea, like Wagner's "Flying Dutchman" who could not have peace until he found a faithful lover.

Sometimes as Fritz, who had moved in, bathed his feverish forehead or his sweaty body, Hans sang snatches of arias, alarmingly even "Pagliacci!" Often, he called out for Rolf over and over. In more coherent moments, he whispered to Fritz what had happened, and the pianist was appalled at what Hans had endured. Now and then, a repentant Hans begged Fritz to find Rolf and fetch him. The faithful friend did as he was bid with some loathing, but found no sign of Rolf at any of the usual Berlin spots.

And in this manner they approached Christmas. Hans existed mostly on soup and bread. Eventually, he was able to write to his parents who had settled safely in Paris and were planning to open a new gallery, and Hans was able to survive the day with a minimum number of crying jags. He stayed in bed except to use the toilet and had grown terribly thin and wan, a blond ghost of his former self.

Fritz actually telephoned Bayreuth, and was put through to Winifred Wagner herself to report that Hans was ill with fever and a stomach condition. Fortunately, 1932 at Bayreuth was what was called a "gap" or off year during which no festival was presented. These gap years allowed for the planning and development of new productions. Frau Wagner said that Hans was not absolutely required until late spring to resume lessons and perform in fund-raising concerts. With honest concern, she asked Fritz to give her frequent updates on Hans' recovery.

Hans slowly grew stronger but no less morose. On Christmas, Fritz forced Hans to go out to dinner. Walking the snowy streets, Hans was forever looking about for Rolf, longing for him and terrified he might actually see him. What if he saw him with another boy? Hans trembled and his legs grew weak at the thought, and Fritz had to support him. The cheerless dinner itself was something of a letdown. Hans picked at his food and spoke not at all.

The young men spent New Year's Eve together in the apartment wearing silly paper hats and sipping champagne. Once, near midnight, when he was certain he had spied Rolf from the window, Hans tore into the hall and down the stairs into the street. There was no one there except for the usual, homeless beggars.

At midnight, Hans and Fritz kissed a rather lingering kiss and embraced, as the clock dragged them into the future. And it was 1932, one year away from the end of the world.

Fritz was quite content playing piano at the movie studio during the days and coming home to Hans in the evenings. They would read Hasenclever, Wedekind, or Thomas Mann, chat about art, argue about Kandinsky, or listen to music. Often, as the latest recording Fritz had purchased played, Hans would get a far-off look in his eyes, and then he would stare dreamily at the phonograph and suck on the gold ring on his finger. Once, they almost made love.

Fritz had convinced Hans to dance with him to Maurice Chevalier singing "Isn't it Romantic?" And as they swayed in each other's arms, they kissed, the tall lanky pianist, tilting his head forward to meet the pale blond. They kissed again, a longer, deeper kiss. They clung to each other and fell back onto the bed where the kisses continued. On ears and necks and lips and eyes. Buttons became undone and the kisses traveled down slender chests onto stomachs. Fritz licked at the slim trail of hair that disappeared into Hans' trousers. And then, Hans pulled away, not forcefully or angrily, but gently and kindly.

"No, Fritz, I love you far too much to offer you a revenge fuck for Rolf!"

"I'll settle easily for that. I'll take it," replied Fritz, undoing Hans' trouser button and trailing spittle across Hans' stomach.

Hans was more resistant now, but no less gentle. "No, Fritz. Give it time, please. I would never want to jeopardize my love for you."

And so, as Maurice Chevalier rasped on about romance in the air, for the moment at least, they remained only friends. As someone once wrote:

"If you renounce love, you'll be rich,

if you renounce friends, you'll be famous."

Ernst Röhm was furious! He was being squeezed out by the power- hungry Himmler, Göring, and Goebbels. They had Hitler's trust. They held his future, while Röhm held only his past. He knew Hitler would never desert him, no, they were far too close for that, but he might sidetrack Rohm's influence and power. He had already appointed Baldur von Schirach as the new head of the Hitler Youth, robbing Röhm of that pleasure, although it may have been for his own good. And Himmler's damned SS was becoming more influential than Röhm's SA - not a good sign.

The up-coming election meant everything to the Nazis who were currently determined to win power through politics, not putsch. Part of Röhm hoped they would fail and come crawling for his more ruthless, brutal form of control. He was army trained and knew that sometimes words don't have the same clout as weapons. Still, the Nazi Party was making headway. They had just established the Faith Movement of German Christians with a religious push against German Protestants, Jews, Marxists, and Catholics. Adolf Hitler announced, "By warding off the Jews, I am fighting for the Lord's work!"

Hitler was busy making speeches to charm various German industrialists as well, and he was being given his full German citizenship, having held only Austrian papers before. Astonishing that he had gotten this far without it.

Röhm studied the boy in the corner on the floor polishing the man's high, brown boots. "Go away, Otto, come back and finish later," he said, ruffling the boy's hair and patting him on the cheek. The boy raised his arm in salute. "Heil Hitler!" he snapped and left. Röhm wanted to be alone, to smoke and have a drink and think. Thinking for Röhm was the hard part. He was dancing on the edge of a precipice, and he had to move most gingerly. He needed someone on the inside. Someone who would represent to Hitler the perfection and purity of German youth! The perfect German soldier. Someone Röhm could trust. Someone he owned. And he knew just the person!

Hans was singing again. He was terribly thin and still weak, and his voice was ragged and fragile, but he was singing again. The trouble was, there wasn't much conviction in his singing, as he seemed to have no purpose in life. He clung to Fritz, night and day, and didn't want to go anywhere without him. He even followed him to the film studio, and would turn pages for him while the pianist worked on film scores. He even got some small parts in movie musicals, singing in the background or in a chorus.

He spoke less and less of Rolf to Fritz, but seemed eternally melancholy. News of what was happening in Germany's art world didn't help. "The Rise and Fall of the City of Mahagonny," Brecht and Weill's jarring masterpiece follow-up to "Threepenny Opera," had been rejected and closed down several times as being too decadent. More and more composers, conductors and musicians were leaving the country.

In April, when incumbent Paul von Hindenburg defeated Hitler in the presidential election, things seemed to be looking up for those who didn't trust the now quite popular Nazi Party. Fritz and Hans celebrated by going out dancing. However, the Nazi movement was spreading beyond Germany. There was even talk of a branch starting in America called "Friends of New Germany."

The time had arrived for Hans to return to Bayreuth. He was terribly insecure, unsure of himself and unsure of his future, but like a faithful soldier of art, he kissed Fritz goodbye and boarded the train.

The town of Bayreuth had changed. Whereas before the shop windows were filled with Richard Wagner souvenirs - mugs, china, pictures, books, hats, figurines and posters - now, some of the shops displayed Adolf Hitler memorabilia - framed photos, his book, post cards, flags, and even china dishes. Hans also noticed Nazi flags flying from various businesses and private houses. It sent a chill through him. He settled into his room, putting a framed photo of himself and Rolf in a drawer rather than on the nightstand. He remained empty of all feeling inside. No, that was not entirely true.

He was soulless, not because he had lost the love of his life, although even that statement makes the love sound pitifully trivial which it certainly was not. No, he was soulless because, God help him, he felt horror at the fact that he still loved Rolf. He still kissed the ring every night before sleep, and he still dreamed of him every few nights. He dreamed not of the monster in the brown shirt that Rolf had by some satanic wizardry become. That was a Rolf Hans didn't know. He dreamed of the magnetic Rolf whose magic charm drew everyone to him, but who chose only Hans as his. Hans felt empty and soulless because in spite of all that had happened, he still loved him. How do you go on, when the thing you love kills you? You trudge up the hill to the festival theatre, longing for summer and for time to help you forget.

Winifred Wagner did not see him for several days. She wanted to hear him sing first. He was given his schedule by Wolf who greeted him with, "Well, well, well! You look as if a train hit you!" After three days of lessons, a silent Winifred stood in the back of the room to listen. Then, she requested him to visit her at Wahnfried. Again, it was Wolf who gloated and showed the young man this time, not to the library but to the business office. Frau Wagner was seated behind the huge desk, wearing a no-nonsense, long-sleeved, high collared, off-white dress, with her hair tied up severely in a bun. She offered him a seat and poured him a sherry.

"Tell, me, Hans, how are you? You are terribly thin and pale."

"Still recovering, Frau Wagner, but I get stronger each day."

"I hope so. I place great trust in you. Your voice is still pure, but your singing is now rather cold and lifeless. You need to mend that. I am setting up a series of vocal lessons for you with Heinz Tietjen, our new General Manager. He is the head of the Prussian State Theater System, and the most influential person in Germany when it comes to the performing arts. Take advantage of your time with him."

"I shall commit myself one hundred percent, Frau Wagner."

"And something else. A stroke of luck for you. Max Lorenz, our Tristan next season, will visit here for a month this summer when he returns from his engagement at the Metropolitan Opera in New York. He will be here to sign contracts and set up rehearsal schedules and so on, and I want you to sit in on some of the meetings. And I also want you to spend some time studying with him. He is one of the world's great tenors, and it is a once in a lifetime opportunity. So, beef yourself up and get in shape!" She had a small satisfied smile on her face. "He will teach you how to act when you sing and sing when you act, for they are inseparable. We've all seen too many good voices belonging to fat blobs who park and bark! Opera needs fresh, young, attractive talent that can act!"

Hans could not hold back the truth in front of such a wonderful woman. "Frau Wagner, I have lost everything in my life except opera."

She nodded and raised her sherry glass. "It is enough," she said. "It will suffice!"

Faithful Fritz wrote to him every day and planned to come visit soon. This cheered Hans considerably, and the hole in his stomach tightened and grew smaller. He plunged into his studies. He sang and sang and sang, but still had little or no heart in it, at least according to his new teacher. Heinz Tietjen was a severe, slender man in his fifties whom some said had had a long love affair with Winifred Wagner. Born in Morocco, he worked his way up through the opera houses of Germany and certainly knew his business. He was incredibly precise and demanding, asking Hans to justify every vocal decision with a legitimate emotional reason.

"But what is the character feeling here, and why? And

what is Hans Becker feeling when he sings this? You have such a splendid voice, Hans. What a shame you keep your feelings locked away in your heart."

Hans cursed himself. He had always been accused of wearing his heart on his sleeve, and now he had buried it down deep somewhere where it could not be touched. Sometimes he cursed Rolf and blamed him. Sometimes he blamed himself. Tietjen was a great listener, in fact, that may have been his greatest virtue. He had a broad forehead, with intense, trusting eyes that peered through rimless spectacles. When he listened, he seldom blinked. He gave himself over to the music and urged Hans to do so as well. With baby steps, Hans improved. He was able to put his pain and his need to love back into what he sang.

And then an event occurred that changed Hans' life forever. Max Lorenz arrived.

CHAPTER 27

1932
    BAYREUTH
    MAX

HE ARRIVED BY LIMO, a light-mustard-colored Maybach DS8 Zepellin Pullmann, stepping out of the back seat and holding the door for his new wife. His very presence caused a scandal. Everyone knew he was a flaming homosexual, and that his new wife was a Jew. He was dapper and handsome, in his early fifties, wearing a grey felt fedora at a jaunty angle, and dressed in an expensive, grey, hand-tailored suit. This was the international opera sensation Max Lorenz. Winifred Wagner, Heinz Tietjen and the entire staff lined up to greet him. Both he and his wife were given flowers and champagne, and Hans and others sang a song of greeting. It was all very Bavarian, and Max Lorenz seemed to eat it up.

    Like many famous opera singers, he was much pampered and a bit precious. He lived a rarified life, apart from the real world. But for all of that, he was a gentle, kind, intelligent man, quite friendly, warm and accessible. And he loved handsome, young men, so he and Hans at once got on famously. He agreed to work with the young tenor during his month at Bayreuth, and that was how they ended up in bed together. Well, it was not quite that simple, but almost.

Max could tell that Hans had great potential as a singer. He also sensed the young man's great despair. "There is no joy in your singing. There is no life," he said one day after lessons. They had taken to having dinner together in the village. "Frau Wagner tells me that it is as if the energy has drained out of you. Today, when I had you sing the piece from 'Die Meistersinger," Walther's aria, it had no love in it."

Hans stared down into his plate of sausage, ashamed. "I've had a very hard year, Herr Lorenz."

"Max. I am Max, and you are Hans. And when I am here next year to sing, we will become the best of friends. We all live many lives in one lifetime, Hans. Good times and bad. Both can be dangerous. But whatever you feel, put it into your music - don't let it be a barrier. Cast off the burden that weighs you down, so that you may fly free and put that into your song."

"My parents moved away to Paris last year, and... and..." he could not put it into words.

"And you twist the golden ring on your finger. So, you lost a lover. Death or a break-up?"

Hans found it easy for some reason to open up to this great singer. "A very ugly, nasty break-up." He twisted the ring and tears filled his eyes. "We were everything to each other, and then, well, then, politics got in the way." That was a gross over-simplification, of course.

Max's eyes filled with tears as well. This man had great compassion and empathy, which is perhaps why he was such a great singer. "I am deeply sorry you lost her... or him."

Hans studied the man seated across from him for a moment. Zither music played from another room, somehow carrying the moment. "Him. My lover was a him!"

Max reached across the table and patted Hans' hand. "I understand, that makes it more complicated. When we are young, love is like missing a bus. We can always catch the next one."

Hans shook his head. "Not with Rolf. It was much more serious and much more complex than that."

Max frowned and nodded. He became serious. "My wife and I have a very complex relationship. I genuinely love her as a person, and she understands my unconventional needs. She is my best friend, but always there is something else for which I am looking."

Hans wanted so to tell Max that he was a Jew. A homosexual Jew, but he couldn't quite go that far. Instead he did tell the opera singer about his former lover embracing the Nazi movement. "I just don't understand it."

"It obviously gives him something. Something he feels he needs. Which of us understands the secrets of the human heart? But it is your job, my new friend, to go on living. To pour all of that great feeling into your singing, not shut it away. Use it! Sing your pain and your grief, and soon you will also be singing new joy. Music is your special connection to life."

It was as if Max Lorenz had opened some door. Hans felt filled with light. The darkness he had lived with for so long didn't disappear entirely, but it was relegated to a distant corner of his soul.

"I think you may have saved my life, Herr Lorenz... Max."

Max waved a finger. 'It's not so simple. But it is a start. Trust music. It will never desert you."

Hans clapped his hands together. "I want to celebrate. What shall we do?"

"Well, we could have sex."

Hans thought for a moment and then smiled. "Yes, we could."

And so they did. It became a regular, late-afternoon pastime for them, following Hans' voice lessons. Lorenz was a gentle, caring lover, eager to please his partner. Hans was a vessel needing to be filled with love and care. And although they were not in love, they felt great love for each other. And when, at the end of the month, Max Lorenz and his understanding, Jewish wife climbed back into their limousine and drove away, it was with the knowledge that a new friendship had been formed and it would blossom the following opera season.

Hans' singing was much improved. He had a new freedom. His acting was more authentic, and Winifred Wagner suspected she knew the reason. She was delighted. He was ready for the "special event" she had in mind for him.

Hans, meantime, seriously considered asking Fritz to be his lover. He missed the pianist desperately and felt he might be ready to make the commitment. Was he getting over Rolf at last? Or was he just fooling himself? However, Fritz' planned visit had to be postponed because of some work he had done on the musical film "Sehnsucht," the debut of Miss Luise Reiner, which was to be released first in Austria. So, Hans hunkered down and threw himself even more into his music studies.

They left very early in the morning in four cars on the day of the mysterious event. No one except Winifred Wagner, Tietjen, and Wolf who rode in the first car knew the destination. Not even Frau Wagner's three other children in the second car, nor the pianist and members of the string trio in the third car, nor Hans Becker the tenor, Anna Gleb the soprano, nor Rudy Hoch, the baritone, in the fourth car. If the chauffeurs knew, they were not saying. Evening dress had been packed for the performers, so it was assumed this was to be some sort of fund-raiser. But why all the secrecy? Along with the Walther aria from "Die Meistersinger," Frau Wagner had asked a stunned Hans to prepare the terrifying "Tristan" aria.

"With all due respect, Madame, I am not qualified yet to sing such a piece in public," he protested, bowing his head formally.

She raised a silencing finger. "First, I say who sings what! Second, while you are correct, you voice is not yet ready for such a difficult aria on the big opera stage, this is an intimate concert, and the beauty of you voice will shine through. Tietjen will help prepare you." Hans was paralyzed with fear, but the famed conductor and impresario assured him he was ready. Hans was also scheduled to sing the hit song from Lehar's new operetta, "Land of Smiles," the same song, "You are My Heart's Delight," that he had sung for Rolf in Vienna years before.

The line of cars was soon speeding through the Bavarian woods which had turned a hundred shades of brown overnight with the onset of an early Autumn. No gold or red leaves, just every imaginable shade of brown, sometimes falling in their path as thick as rain. Then, as they climbed higher, the brown of the leaves was replaced with the emerald green of firs. Hans, who was quite friendly with his singer companions, guessed at their destination before they saw it, rising in its shimmering ivory whiteness above rushing Pöllat Gorge Waterfall and the fir-covered slopes.

The most fascinating toy castle in the world, Neuschwanstein!

The castle was an opulent mix of Gothic, Romanesque, and Byzantine architecture, its towers giving it the feeling of something out of the King Arthur legends. And indeed, those legends, mixed with a liberal dose of others, were Wagner's inspiration for much of his work, Kind Arthur becoming Amfortas in "Parsifal." This castle of the "mad" King Ludwig reminded Hans instantly of his sixteenth summer, of that summer of adventure and his fateful meeting with Rolf at "Hunding's Hut."

Higher and higher they climbed through the dense forest, and their excitement grew higher and higher as well. The castle became obscured by the trees, and then, a wide-open space that served as a kind of car-or carriage-park opened before them, and directly above them rising up and up and up stood this almost religious shrine to Wagner and the Bavarian King who loved him. Hans counted no less than twenty catering lorries, and a hundred workmen carrying boxes and trays of food up the footpath to the castle. Winifred Wagner, who could have driven right up to the castle, honored the tradition by dismounting from her limousine and leading her small band on foot up to the castle proper. Like something out of the Brothers Grimm, it enveloped and hovered over and around them. Legend had it that when the doctors and statesmen and military leaders made their way up the footpath to depose Ludwig and declare him insane, there was a terrible rain storm. Ludwig, looking down from the tower upon their open umbrellas, thought he was being attacked by giant spiders. They were worse than spiders, they were politicians come to make war upon a man of art and beauty.

Like a true daughter or daughter-in-law of her father or

father-in-law, Winifred Wagner climbed the first few step of the large, stone stairway leading into the castle's rooms and faced her little group. Or, perhaps, she was a bit like a tourist guide with her travelers. Nonetheless, the air bristled with excitement.

"Tonight, my friends, I urge you all to be at your very best. This will be by far the most important concert evening you will ever perform. I have chosen you personally to represent the 'New Blood' of Bayreuth - the artistic link between Germany's heroic past and its glorious future. Tonight's concert will be performed before none other than the great man who will usher Germany into that bright future, our beloved Führer, Adolf Hitler."

She stood there proudly, almost transfigured in her fox-fur-collared, cloth coat and smart hat with a half-veil over her face, and you could have heard a pin drop from the highest turret.

None of them knew what to say. None of them knew what to do. Then realizing what was at stake, Rudy Hoch, the baritone, snapped one arm in the air as he remembered seeing people in Berlin do, and shouted "Heil Hitler!" Everyone, even a bewildered Hans, followed suit. Winifred Wagner glowed. And an enthusiastic Wolf shot his arm highest of all.

They were ushered into a kind of anti-room, where they were served roast beef and ham sandwiches, tea, juice, and water. The performers were now so worked-up that nobody ate much. The event, they were told, would not take place in the opulent, lavishly-paneled Minstrel's Hall, but in the even more opulent Throne Room itself. And so, the "entertainment" hunkered down to wait the many hours until the performance. They would not be invited to the lavish banquet that preceded the concert, but would be served their own hot supper after. Anna went over and over her music with the ever-faithful pianist Klaus, the string ensemble played cards, and Rudy read. Hans took a risk and wandered out to see a bit of the castle, which, except for the caterers with food and workmen hauling chairs, seemed all but deserted. He passed the huge painted mural of a scene from "Tannhäuser," amused at how flagrantly erotic it was, and marveled at the many paintings there were illustrating key moments from "The Ring Cycle." Eventually, he found himself in King Ludwig II's jaw dropping bed chamber. It could be viewed as either a majestic masterpiece, or a garish, tasteless, bordello bedroom. Some said that Ludwig spent his own and the country's fortune on art because he refused to arm the military for impending war. Smart move, thought Hans. He basked in the grand, gaudy silence of the room. Then a familiar voice shattered the reverie.

"You didn't salute the Führer with much enthusiasm! You'd better do better tonight. It was Wolf, in evening dress, stepping out of the shadows like Mephistopheles approaching Faust.

Hans jumped. "Huh? Oh, I was taken by surprise."

"Perhaps it didn't suit you politically?" Wolf slunk toward Hans. His wild raven hair and his smirk made him look demonic.

Hans held his own. "Perhaps. My politics are a personal matter."

Wolf shook his slender, serpentine head and chuckled. "So many choices... so many decisions for the perfect, young, blond, Aryan warbler to make. How to climb the ladder, eh? Jawol, you are damned near perfect, but of course, there are certain flaws. The intimate friendship with the Jüdischen singer Friedrich Schorr, those late afternoons in your rooms with Max Lorenz."

Hans bristled. "They are friends with Frau Wagner as well!"

"But not in the same way. A Jew and a Queer. Interesting choices." Wolf moved so close to Hans that the tenor could smell the liquor on his breath. Hans put out a hand to keep him away.

"I do believe you have been spying on me!" Hans snapped. "Anything in particular you are keen to see?"

Wolf wrinkled up his nose and sneered. "You wish! But you've got me wrong, Herr Becker. Winifred Wagner has invested a great deal in you. You might say, I am protecting her investment. You want to be important and strong. Consider, strength lies in the determination of the will to make sacrifices."

Hans grew red in the face. "You know nothing of my sacrifices."

"No, but I know of your predilections!" He went to the door. "Be careful wandering around the castle, there are SS guards everywhere."

"You know, you're making it awfully hard to like you..." Hans shouted at the departing figure.

Wolf snickered. "But not to fear me."

Hans, with a bit more caution, continued his private tour of the castle. He even took a quick peek at the glorious throne room where the concert would be held. The performers would stand on the steps leading up to where Ludwig's throne was once stationed. Across a floor bearing a stone tapestry design of a circle decorated with elephants and boars and deer and so on, beneath a gigantic also circular golden chandelier of a hundred or more candles, sat an upholstered arm chair for the guest of honor, and twenty or so chairs of lesser elegance for lesser mortals. In the alcove surrounding the room, behind the pillars and golden ornamentation was where the elite SS guards of Adolf Hitler would stand, ready at all times to protect their leader.

A female voice behind Hans whispered, "It's magical, isn't it? Almost sacred." It was a smiling Winifred Wagner. Hans tensed, but she rested a hand on his shoulder to calm him down. But her words did the opposite. "This is a special day for you. A day you will remember all your life. You, Hans Becker, are going to sing for the greatest man in the world. Wait until you see him. He shimmers. He sparkles!"

"I am worried, Frau Wagner. Perhaps I should not sing the Lehar operetta song. I recently read that the Nazi party, if they win the next election, will put Richard Strauss in as Minister of Culture. He is already declaring all jazz and black music degenerate and all operetta useless and decadent waste. Perhaps it's not wise to…"

She raised a finger. "Politics and Art! I'll tell you a secret. My dear friend, Adolf Hitler, loves operetta. He especially adores Franz Lehar. I promise you, with your voice, your song will make him weep. Trust me, Hans. Sing that song and you will become his heart's desire."

They didn't perform until almost ten in the evening. First, a famous magician, whom Hans immediately recognized as Kalanag, their ambitious pal from the Eldorado club days, wowed Hitler and his friends. Winifred sat next to the Führer, and Tietjen. Next to Hitler, on the other side, sat the Wagner children. The boys, especially, gazed adoringly at the leader. The other guests were high-ranking members of the Party and socialite friends with money. Hans, sneaking a peak from one of the doors that flanked the throne steps, was amazed at the ease with which Kalanag moved among the Nazi big-wigs. He had Hitler himself choose a card for several tricks, and produced scarves from the ears and hair of the Wagner children.

Adolf Hitler, almost drowning in the huge, upholstered chair, giggled like a child and bounced up and down clapping his hands. His raven hair fell over those ice blue eyes of his that matched the blue of the Byzantine ceiling above, and Hans found it difficult to look at anyone else. Kalanag received thunderous applause from the laughing guests in the echoing room. He performed an encore in which a beautiful girl disappeared from a cabinet, to even more laughter and acclaim. How could mere singers compete? And then, it was their turn.

They filed out and took their places. The musicians played two pieces to begin with. The room settled down respectfully. Anna sang two arias, and then it was time for Hans to do the "Meistersinger" aria. It was a favorite of all Germans, and Hans saw listeners moving their lips along with the love song. Hitler, who had been polite, perked up at the sound of Hans' voice which rang with unusual clarity through the hall. Winifred smiled and nodded. Hans gained confidence, and suddenly, for the first time in ages, his singing took on new purpose. At the finish of his song, he was received ecstatically.

Rudy sang two numbers next, and then Anna again. Then, a piano solo. And then it was Hans' turn to sing "You are My Heart's Delight." He swallowed and blew out air to control his nervousness. He might well be booed off the stage by these Nazis, except of course there wasn't any stage. Upstairs in the gallery, amid a gaggle of husky, young SS guards, Wolf held his breath as well. Would this be the fall of Hans Becker?

The song went as well as ever, and while Hans sang, he remembered once again singing it for Rolf in Vienna. Tears filled his eyes, and he sang for Rolf once again. The Viennese accent he used for the song gave it a particularly smooth, silky sound, and he had never before put so much feeling into the words. When the number finished, the room was totally silent, except for the sound of the Führer weeping. The future terror of the world put a kerchief to his eyes. No one quite knew what to do. Then, Adolf Hitler stood and began to applaud. Everyone else then stood as well. Hitler approached the young singer and beckoned him down the steps. He stood inches from him, eye to eye. Then he leaned in and kissed Hans on both cheeks.

"You are the future of Germany!" he said. "Without art, there is no future. We must devote every minute of our struggle to beauty!" He took Hans' hand in his and pumped it. Those in the room cheered. Hans was dumbstruck. "An encore, please!" Hitler said and returned to his chair.

"What a fucking, clever woman Winifred Wagner is," thought Hans. "To save the 'Tristan' aria for last. The most powerful and the most difficult. To some, the greatest piece of music ever written." And so, Hans Becker prepared to climb the mountain or die trying.

In the gallery, the beauty of Hans' voice actually physically hurt Wolf. He had severe stomach cramps. And now, the fire of the tenor's Tristan fueled the flames of Wolf's hate. Adolf Hitler had taken Hans' hand, kissed him on the cheek! It was an outrage.

It was not Hans who sang, but Tristan himself, proving once again that love is stronger than life or death. And while he was Tristan, Hans believed it, too. When he finished this time, the silence in the room lasted for almost a minute. Hans feared he had failed. He scanned the stone faces in the audience for some sign. And then, pandemonium broke out. They cheered and threw their programs and waved their handkerchiefs. For a few moments, they forgot their social decorum and allowed themselves the ecstasy of elation. All except for the SS guards who stood frozen like statues. Well, two of them risked wiping tears from their eyes, and one had actually left the chamber during the number.

Adolf Hitler approached Hans again, this time bearing a glass of champagne for him. "You will sing Tristan for the Reich," he said in a gravelly voice thick with emotion. "You are the beautiful symbol of the Master Race!"

And then the performers filed out. Were Anna and Rudy jealous? If so, they never showed it. Perhaps they were as thunderstruck as Hans. They returned to the anti-room in a daze. And it wasn't until an out- of- breath Kalanag, his spectacles steamed up from running, threw himself at Hans, that the young man returned to earth. He thought his old acquaintance was there to congratulate him, but then he began to focus on the words.

"Did you see him? Ach, Gott, did you see him?"

"Hitler?" Hans asked.

"No, Rolf! Did you see Rolf. He's SS now. One of Hitler's black knights. Did you see him? Oh, mein Gott, when you sang, he left the hall with tears streaming down his cheeks. Rolf is here!" The owl eyes looked about to pop out of Kalanag's head.

Hans pushed passed Kalanag and tore out into the hallway. He had no idea which way to go or where to look. He ran mindlessly this way and that. Down stairways and through doorways. Where? Where was he? Everywhere there were soldiers in black uniforms. Twice, Hans grabbed the wrong person and had to apologize. Most people were still in the throne room, so the castle was relatively empty except for the guard, and the food staff clearing up. Hans became frantic, sliding several times on the polished floors.

He went up to an SS officer who looked approachably human.

"Excuse me. Do you know Rolf Kainz?" he asked breathlessly.

"Jawol. He just left on some errand, I guess." He gestured toward the main entrance and the long stone stairway to the courtyard. His heart pounding, and unable to breathe, Hans stumbled out into the dark night air, to see the taillight of a lone motorbike trailing off in the distance to be lost in the Bavarian forest. Hans let out a gut-wrenching sob and sank onto the stone steps. He had no way of knowing if it was even Rolf, but to the tortured young man on the cusp of stardom, Hell and Heaven were the same place!

CHAPTER 28

1932

BAYREUTH
NIGHTMARES

IT WAS five in the morning before Hans got back to the village of Bayreuth. He eschewed the company of others and made his way alone down the hill from the theater. Soon the sky would lighten for dawn, but for now it was dark and everything slept. Hans graciously accepted the praise he'd received, even a hug from Winifred Wagner who whispered to him, "Your future is assured." But inside, he felt a weight so great he could hardly walk.

The inn where he stayed was locked and dark, but there was a bell to pull, and a sleepy young boy who worked nights opened the door. Hans nodded to him and trudged to the stairs to his room.

"Oh, there was a message for you," the boy said, rubbing the sleep from his eyes. Hans froze with his back to the boy, who ran to the desk that served the hotel portion of the business. "Oh, sir, you should have seen him. He was magnificent. He was dressed in a beautiful, black uniform and arrived on a motorbike! I wanted to run off with him." He handed Hans a folded note which the tenor took with trembling hand. It was black inside the inn, but just as Hans grasped the note, a sliver of light from somewhere caught the gold ring on his finger. It was too much, and Hans broke down and began to cry again. He hung his head and his shoulders shook.

"Is everything all right, sir?" the boy asked, afraid that perhaps he had done something wrong himself. Hans waved him away with the hand holding the note, but then, fished into his trouser pocket with the other and gave the boy some coins. The boy chewed his lower lip, touched his forelock and back away into the darkness. Hans climbed the stairs. He switched on the room light, removed his jacket and sat on the edge of the bed, staring at the folded note. He heard what might have been a mouse, or perhaps just the timbers squeaking. Time once again stood still.

At last, Hans unfolded the note. What he read was short and simple.

"I was there tonight. Love, Rolf."

There was nothing to it. It left Hans numb. Why such a note? What did it portend? Hans let it float to the floor. He rose and slowly removed his clothing. He washed his face and hands at the washstand in the room, turned out the light, and climbed into the huge featherbed. Oddly enough, he was so exhausted, he had no trouble falling into a deep sleep.

He dreamed of that night when Rolf left. He dreamed of hearing his heavy boots on the stairs and the door flying open. And then it wasn't a dream! He was in the bed of the inn at Bayreuth, but the door was open, and some light from the hall lit Rolf from the back. Grey morning crept through the window, just enough for Hans to see his ex-lover in all of his glory. He wore black this time instead of brown, and there was something less awesome and even more fearsome about him. He walked toward the bed, as if he were stalking Hans, and the singer crawled up against the headboard, pulling the quilt with him.

"I suppose you're naked under there," Rolf slurred in a thick drunken voice. Hans raised his fingers to his mouth and shoved them in to stop himself from screaming.

Rolf's face was flushed and his eyes burned like hot coals. "You ruined my life, you know!" Not yet twenty-five and so bitter.

"As you ruined mine!" Hans rasped.

"Everything I did, I did for us. For you! To protect us!"

"Secrets. You kept secrets from me, and they ate you up from the inside. How? How could you join them, of all people?" Hans was spitting his words, hurling them at Rolf.

Rolf gulped air as if he might collapse. Hans could see tears running down his handsome face. Rolf lifted his head to the ceiling and searched for words that would not come. Finally, he looked at his former lover with a new, more gentle look on his face. A look of the old Rolf. When he spoke, his voice was soft and filled with love.

"It's awfully hard to be content when you can't achieve. You've never known that."

Hans replied, and his voice was not accusing, only trying to understand. "And you achieve through them?"

"Something, yes. Not everything, not enough, but something."

Hans shook his head to clear his own eyes. "Oh my, how I loved you!"

"How I still love you... but..." Rolf spread his arms, as if his uniform explained everything, and perhaps it did. He staggered to the door, went through it into the hall, then turned once more. "I shall never forget how you sang last night. It was like you were singing to me, in our bed."

"I was." Hans answered simply.

"I have to go. I mustn't be found here."

"No, not with a homosexual Jew."

And the next instant, the hallway beyond the door was empty. Hans did not move a muscle until he heard the sound of a motorcycle fading into the intruding day.

PART III

GÖTTERDÄMMERUNG

"Thus evil enters this house!"

Lohengrin

CHAPTER 29

1933
   BERLIN
   NEW OFFERS

   BERLIN, STAATSOPER November, 1932
   ERICH KLEIBER

   Dear Herr Becker:
   I hope this letter finds you well. It has been some time, hasn't it, since we last saw each other. I am delighted to inform you that your fame now precedes you, and there is much chatter in opera circles about the young tenor with whom I last worked on our concert tour several years ago. Your climb has been meteoric. Your praise well deserved. I can still recall your audition for "Wozzeck," and I lunch with our friend Fritz at least once a month.
   However, this letter is sent to you in my official capacity, to invite you to sing the wonderful role of

David, apprentice to Hans Sachs in a new production of "Die Meistersinger von Nürnberg" to be staged here in Berlin in spring. There are many here anxious to hear you sing a substantial role, and this is your opportunity.

I might add that a very prominent up-and-coming politician has requested, no, has demanded that you be given the role. While such requests are not unusual in the world of opera, such demands are!

As an old friend, let me quote the opera itself when it says, "Beware, evil tricks threaten us!" There is great speculation as to what will happen in the next election, and how that will affect the arts. Because of my feelings about both the recent politics of Berlin and the politics of the opera itself, it is likely I shall not be conducting. But here is your chance to cement your artistic career, and I extend the invitation to you to join us for this production. I need not tell you that the role of David is a superb chance to shine. And shine you will!

Please contact the Opera office at your earliest convenience for all the essential details. And when you next visit Berlin, let's please have lunch or dinner.

Yours, Erich Kleiber

HANS SPENT the holiday season in Berlin with Fritz. The two of them got along so well together that things were quite pleasant. They went to the Eldorado Club, which really hadn't changed much except that there were almost no SA members in the club anymore. There was some politically fueled graffiti against homosexuals painted on the walls outside the club, and the Countess warned the customers to be careful going home as there had been a spate of muggings recently.

Hans had given up the love nest he had shared with Rolf, and so he stayed with Fritz while he looked for a new apartment. The work on "Die Meistersinger" would last until May, when he would report back to Bayreuth. On New Years's Eve, Hans and Fritz made love, and it was one of the happiest nights of Fritz' life. They spent New Year's Day in bed, listening to all the latest recordings and bantering about which were the best. It was good to see that old light in Hans' eyes when he laughed. Fritz had a piano at his place, and they worked on the role of David in "Die Meistersinger."

"It's tricky, because it's a comedic role, but you also have some lovely, quite tender, moments," Fritz told Hans. "Don't ham it up, this is not operetta, although after the interminable gloom of 'Tristan and Isolde,' with its theme of love perfected by death, Wagner did want to give us something lighter and more hopeful." Hans was always amazed at the breadth of Fritz' knowledge. There truly could be no better way to spend a day or a week than sharing music with someone whose knowledge could match or exceed yours.

There were unwelcome intrusions, of course. Bad news from time to time. On January 30, 1933, a pressured President Paul von Hindenburg appointed Adolf Hitler the Chancellor of Germany! It was the beginning of the end. A pastoral letter from Austrian Bishop Gföllner of Linz stated that it was the duty of all Catholics to adopt a platform of "Anti-Semitism!"

And then in February, just as formal rehearsals for the opera began, flames consumed the Reichstag, the official seat of power in Belin. Adolf Hitler was quick to blame the communists and began to round up and arrest any active party members.

In early March, the Nazis won two hundred and eighty-eight of six hundred and forty-seven seats in the Reichstag election. Less than a week later, authorized SA attacks on Jews broke out all over the city.

"How was your day?" Fritz asked Hans, offering him a plate of cookies and a glass of schnapps.

"Shocking! Quite unbelievable. The rehearsal was stopped today by some SS officials who said that all Jews were to be dismissed from the opera company at once. Suddenly, in a moment, we lost half our orchestra and ten members of the cast." Hans downed the schnapps but ignored the cookies. He sat slumped in a chair, shaking his head. "Is this possible? How can this be possible? They have even turned our production into a celebration of Hitler and the election! There is to be a torchlight victory parade to the theater."

Fritz took Hans' face in his hands. "You have got to get out of Germany. Things will only get worse. Jews are being targeted in every profession. Please, Hans, join your parents in Paris. I'd even meet you there. We could build a musical future there."

Hans looked stunned. He frowned. "But, I'm to sing at Bayreuth this year. Solos, Fritz. I am to be a soloist at Bayreuth!"

Fritz kissed Hans on the forehead. "Is your art more important than your life?" But he already knew the answer.

On March twenty-first, the opera production opened. And there was indeed a huge torchlight parade. SA and SS formed a corridor down which Adolf Hitler, suitably late, strode. Every head in the audience turned from the stage to the royal box, as the Führer took his seat. Hans was appalled with himself for singing for this man, but that was the fact of the matter. He was singing for this man! He had been placed in this role by this man! And Adolf Hitler wept and laughed and applauded and cheered just like any normal, human being.

The most appalling event of the evening occurred when during Hans Sachs' magnificent anthem to Germany and Art at the end of the opera, the entire audience joined in singing, stood and turned to face the royal box! The singers on stage didn't know how to respond to this tidal wave of sound washing over the auditorium and all directed at Adolf Hitler.

Was the evening a victory? A defeat? A tremendous success? A disaster? Hans stood trembling in the receiving line as the new chancellor congratulated each singer with some acute musical observation. He knew his stuff, all right. And when at last he came, with blue eyes sparkling, to Hans, he took both of the tenor's hands in his.

"Such beauty! Such perfect, Aryan beauty," he whispered. His moustache twitched. "I cannot wait to hear you sing at Bayreuth. You know, they are turning the entire town and festival into a celebration of our great cause. A symbol of the New Germany." He squeezed the singer's hands and kissed his cheek. Then he moved on.

The other singers gazed upon Hans as if he had suddenly assumed sainthood, some with devotion and respect, some with a bit of loathing and disgust. Either way, they steered well clear of him. Kleiber and Fritz showered Hans with praise and wined and dined him through most of the night.

And then, on April first, Hitler announced the official boycott of Jewish businesses. Broken windows, boarded-up store fronts, and signs warning people not to shop in "Jewish establishments" filled the city.

Actually, this first attempt did not last long. It hurt the economy too much and had to be scaled back. But the purge had begun and only increased during the following months. SA troops were stationed outside Jewish businesses to take photographs of any non-Jews who shopped there. Badly beaten Jewish bodies lying in the street became an all-too-common sight.

Ernst Röhm was feeling quite pleased with himself. Things were looking up. He sat with his stockinged feet, crossed at the ankle, up on his desk, and sucked on a very good cigar. The young member of the Hitler Youth, who sat on the floor and polished his boots, snapped the rag back and forth on the brown leather to make it gleam. The shine on one's boots said much about a man. The boy was an angelic-looking lad whose duties, with Röhm's guidance, encompassed more than just boot polishing.

Next to Röhm's crossed feet on the desk lay plans for the assignments of SA troops to staff and maintain the new concentration camp at Dachau near Munich. This was only the first of fifty camps to be opened during the year, with many more to follow. The name "concentration camp" came from the British during the Boer War, but the German ones were designed to hold, and in many cases eliminate, communists, socialists, dissidents, and of course certain Jews - any enemies of the New Nazi State. At this early stage, the targets were mostly teachers, historians, political figures, and influential Jews. Röhm chuckled. "They never got their hands dirty in their lives. Incarcerate them, and then work 'em to death!" Röhm's bully boys would run the camps, although that worm Himmler wanted his elite SS to be in charge. Still, Rohm once again felt he was a big cheese.

He huffed and ordered the boy on the floor to fetch him his whiskey, which was already within arm's reach of the fat man. He enjoyed seeing the slim youth scramble for him. He admired the boy's pert ass in his uniform shorts and, in the SA, cute boys like this were a Reichspfennig a dozen.

Röhm seriously missed his evenings at the gay clubs like the Eldorado. He missed the openly licentious atmosphere and what one could pick up on a good night. But one had to make sacrifices for one's career, and Röhm had been warned in no uncertain terms to keep his extra-curricular activities under wraps. And this from Adolf, who had not been adverse toward turning a few tricks of his own during his poor student days.

Nowadays, Adolf would pontificate, "There is your public profile and your private profile. If your public profile remains untarnished, your private profile can tolerate a few stains. But the other way 'round' is verboten!" Such nonsense, thought Röhm, but then he was an old-time soldier, a head-basher, not a politician.

After taking his drink, Röhm allowed his hand to grope the boy's ass. The dedicated member of the Hitler Youth stopped all movement and stood perfectly still, almost at attention. Rohm set the wet glass down on a paper proposing to limit the number of Jews attending grammar schools and universities to under two-percent.

Jawol, by the end of the year, Ernst Röhm would once again be an extremely powerful and necessary part of the Nazi Party. And wasn't that what life was all about? To be necessary? And now, with Rolf Kainz as his reluctant agent in the SS, he had access to the temperament of Himmler, Göring, and the big, little man himself. Kainz had tried to quit numerous times, but Röhm needed only to remind him of a certain singing, Bavarian Jew to shut him up. Besides,

Kainz looked so dashing in the black uniform and did love strutting around in it.

Röhm remembered the second time he had taken Rolf to see Hitler. Rolf was already in his brownshirt SA uniform, and this time, the Führer was dressed in knee-high, grey stockings, lederhosen and a Bavarian blouse, and was learning Bavarian slap-dancing called Schuhplattler to the accompaniment of an accordion. A little, old, white-whiskered fellow squeezed and expanded his instrument, while a dance master put Hitler through his paces, slapping knees and heels and hands and chest. The master of the master race was not very good at it, he had one arm that seemed weak, and he huffed and puffed, but he was a game fellow and gave it all he had. Then, he wiped his forehead with a kerchief, took a huge slug of beer from a stein, and came over to Röhm and Kainz.

"I remember you," Hitler said, still catching his breath. "Ernst often speaks very highly of you. 'Potential' is the word he uses. You're a fine- looking fellow, no doubt, and you want to join the SS. Well, you do realize that the SS is my own personal guard, sworn to give their lives to protect their Führer and their country." He beamed when he said this.

"I am one hundred percent ready to do whatever is necessary both for you and Germany, mein Führer!" Rolf often wondered what he was doing in this dream landscape and how he had gotten there. He loathed almost everything about it.

Hitler wagged a finger. "Remember you said that. The day will come when I will hold you to it." He reached up and felt Rolf's bicep. "Beautiful Aryan stock, Ernst. Give his documentation to Himmler, and if everything checks out, have him put in my personal guard." He took Rolf's jaw in one hand. "What is your name?"

"Rolf Kainz, mein Führer."

Hitler smiled and nodded. His forelock had fallen quite far down onto his face. "Come dance with me, Rolf Heinz."

"Kainz," Rolf corrected, and Röhm frowned.

"Whatever..." Hitler said as he took the young man by the hand and led him deeper into the room. "Can you do this Schuhplattler thing? It's damned difficult." And together, for some time, they slapped their feet and knees and chests and often their hands together to the music of the accordion. It was one of the oddest afternoons of Rolf's life, and Röhm's as well. But it had gotten Rolf placed where Röhm wanted him... on the inside. And that was how Rolf ultimately ended up at Ludwig's castle on that fateful night when Hans sang for Hitler.

Yes, all in all, Ernst Röhm was quite pleased with the way things were going. He sipped his drink and sat in his desk chair, a smile on his chubby, scarred face. He wiggled a finger at the Hitler Youth attending on him and patted his ample lap. Then he reached out one hand to the boy. "Come here. Forget about the boots for now."

CHAPTER 30

1933-1934
    BAYREUTH, BERLIN
    A NEW GERMANY

AFTER THE OPERA production in Berlin closed, Hans had to return to Bayreuth almost at once. Fritz gave up his lucrative job at the movie studio to be able to join his emotionally fragile friend as a Festival rehearsal pianist. Hans depended more and more on the love and support of his loyal companion. Hans was welcomed with open arms by everyone in the company except of, course, for Wolf, who glowered and sulked at Winifred Wagner's attentions toward Hans. Even though the town was now festooned with Nazi flags and posters, Hans felt somehow strangely safe and protected in Bayreuth. The outside of the theater itself bore a huge portrait of Hitler, but nothing political was allowed inside, that sacred space devoted only to Richard Wagner.

    It was early May when Hans was having an outside meal of cheese, sausage, bread and beer on the terrace of the inn, when Fritz came running breathlessly up to him and slapped some newspapers down onto the wooden table.

"You should wear a scarf out here. It's still too cold. Have you read this?" Fritz was a worrier, especially when it came to Hans.

"I'm enjoying the sound of the spring birds. You tell me what it says, my dear Fritz. And have a beer."

"Dr. Hirschfeld's Institute for Sexual Research has been attacked by the SA. They burned thousands of books and photographs and arrested and beat the staff." A photograph on the front page of the newspaper showed a huge bonfire of books.

A stunned Hans set down his piece of cheese and took up the newspaper. "And Magnus Hirschfeld?" he asked.

"Fortunately, he was on a lecture tour in America. But he can never return to Germany, and his lover, who was left in charge, was quite seriously beaten. They say Hirschfeld is number one on Hitler's list of those to be eliminated. And that's not even the worst."

Hans looked into Fritz's eyes. "Tell me the worst."

Fritz opened his hands in frustration, as if not knowing where to begin. "Over thirty thousand books have been yanked from university libraries, banned and burned as decadent and degenerate. You can face arrest for reading Thomas Mann and many others."

"What are they doing? What good can come from this?" Hans scanned the articles.

"Control," Fritz said. "They are using trumped up moral issues to get control of people's minds and bodies." He took a swig of Hans' beer, and raised his fingers to the barmaid for two more. "All over Berlin, Jewish men are being publically stripped of their pants and shoes, sometimes stripped totally naked, and being made to wear large signs saying, 'I am a Jew, but I have no complaints about the Nazis.' Jewish women are forced to scrub the street pavement on hands and knees in only their underclothing."

Hans crumpled the paper in his hands. "And does no one stop this? Does no one stand up and protest?"

Fritz raised his eyebrows behind his spectacles. "Everyone is too frightened. Most of the Jewish composers and artists are fleeing the country. It is a nightmare, Hans, a nightmare," he reached across the table and gripped Hans' wrist. "And you have got to get out."

"Yes, yes, but after next year. I'm going to sing major roles at Bayreuth, Fritz. Only a little while longer, and I'll be singing really important roles."

Fritz let go of his grip on Hans, and almost spit, "Not if you're dead, you won't!"

Hans looked down, knowing he was being totally irrational. He let his fingertip trace the embroidered pattern on the triangular tablecloth. "This is Schorr's last season. He's moving to America."

"He sees the writing on the wall!" Their beers arrived. "Hans, I'll go with you. Wherever you go, I'll go with you. You'll never be alone again."

Hans shrugged. "I just need to sing here a little longer."

Max Lorenz arrived in Bayreuth and things brightened considerably. He seemed delighted that Hans and Fritz were a couple and accepted them both immediately as friends. He was so impressed with Fritz's piano skills, he jokingly threatened to steal him away from Hans. He ate with the two of them almost every day and always took care of the bill. He regaled them with hilarious opera stories. One story of a recent event in particular eased their worries slightly.

"Adolf Hitler, the amateur painter and politician, ordered Winifred Wagner to fire me because I am a homosexual. I swear this is true. It happened just a few weeks ago. She confided in me. Hitler said, 'Get rid of that faggot at once,' his little face all red and his blue eyes all beady and his moustache twitching with righteousness. And do you know what Winifred Wagner said? She who adores Hitler, as we adore sunlight? She said, 'Adolf, then shut down the entire Bayreuth Festival. Because without Max Lorenz there will be no more Wagner!'"

Hans and Fritz sat with their mouths hanging open. "She said that?" Hans asked in disbelief.

Max Lorenz held up his hand. "I swear! Perhaps because of her dead husband Siegfried having been homosexual, she protects 'the boys.' So, you kids are free to kanoodle all you like."

"I'm not so sure," cautioned Fritz, "we are not Max Lorenz!"

Lorenz, Tietjen and Frau Wagner all agreed that it was time for young Hans to shine, so he was given the small, but important solo role of the Shepherd/Sailor in Act Three of "Tristan and Isolde." He would get the chance to sing on stage with Max Lorenz. Max teased him. "You would get a solo curtain call, except of course at Bayreuth they don't do curtain calls."

"I already had a solo curtain call as David In 'Die Meistersinger' in Berlin." There certainly was a thrill in having the audience stand and cheer for you, but at the Festspielhaus, to preserve the worship of Wagner, there were no curtain calls. "Besides, it's only the music that matters."

And the music did matter. It carried him through that summer, in a Bavarian town now swathed in red swastika flags and tributes to the "Führer." And Satan himself arrived along with Goebbels in a blue 1933 Mercedes Benz 290 Pullman Limousine, flanked by SS on motorcycles. And the crowd at the opera house went wild, raising their hands and shouting "Heil!"

In deference to Richard Wagner and Winifred, Hitler issued the following statement to be put into the programs:

"At the explicit wish of the Reich Chancellor, it is requested that there should be no demonstrations made inside the Festspielhaus that do not pertain to the works of Richard Wagner."

However, during the intermissions, the Führer would appear in the window of the King Ludwig annex to be properly adored by his followers. And there, outside, during the interval, they could sing the national anthem.

The production was "Die Meistersinger" again, and Hans Becker replaced the scheduled tenor in the role of David. And at the reception with the cast after the performance, Adolf Hitler presented Hans with a rose. The room thundered with applause. The chancellor leaned in very close and whispered to him, "Soon, you will sing Tristan!" and Hans was euphoric, not with Hitler, but with the whole event. Always, always such mixed feelings. Elation and disgust, joy and fear.

That night, amid champagne and chocolates, Hans and Fritz made love three times, and in the morning, Max arrived bearing trays of breakfast, which they shared on rumpled bedsheets. Max's glory would arrive with the premiere of the new production of "Tristan and Isolde" featuring Hans in the role of "Shepherd/Sailor." At the reception for that production, Hitler shook Lorenz's hand and praised his singing, stating, "Without Max Lorenz, there is no Wagner," and Winifred coughed into her kerchief. The choir-master and four young men in the chorus, all with whom Max had been having sex, raised their glasses in a toast.

And at this very moment, hundreds of concentration camps were being constructed throughout Germany.

With the close of the 1933 season, Hans and Fritz moved back to Berlin for the winter holidays. Hans wrote to his parents frequently, but the letters were always carefully coded and very vague, as there were rumors that mail was being opened and read. Hans, not trusting the banks, had been storing away money, as had Fritz, so they were able to live fairly well. They even traveled a bit into the country and rented a cabin to celebrate Christmas and the new year. Celebrate, indeed! Rather, hope that the current political nightmare would pass. Hans still carried with him and treasured his books and letters from Thomas Mann who, rumor had it, had fled Germany.

And upon returning from the countryside to Berlin, Hans and Fritz decided to forget all the world's problems with a visit to the Eldorado Club, but they were shocked to find it closed and boarded up. The garish sign was gone, and the building looked like an abandoned factory. A huge, Nazi flag hung listlessly from a second-story windowsill. Ugly, anti-homosexual graffiti decorated for former club's façade. Hans and Fritz could not believe the sight. For the longest time, they stood across the street in stunned silence. Two burly SA men hung around what once was the front entrance to the club, as if to ward off any visitors, and their presence made an already cold, grey evening even more bleak.

Then, Hans noticed an angular-looking old man wrapped in an overcoat, woolen muffler and a floppy fedora, seated on a bench about half a block away. He recognized something in the posture of the sallow, unshaven fellow with wisps of white hair sneaking from beneath the hat, so he pulled Fritz in that direction. As they got nearer, the old man glanced at them for a moment, then looked straight ahead, staring at nothing.

"I come here sometimes to warn away the regulars, so they don't make a fuss and get themselves arrested. The Countess carefully tucked a wandering wisp of grey hair beneath his hat. He looked old, defeated and world-weary as a man. All the effervescence had fizzled. "We have to be careful. They're sending arrested homosexuals to camps now, you know." He looked away and then down, so little of the glamorous she left in the decrepit he. So ordinary. The one thing she fought her whole life to not be! Hans sat next to the old man.

"Careful, not too close. They're always watching the old, gay watering holes." The wasted body beneath the overcoat trembled. "They came one night, in their brown uniforms, with their billy-clubs and guns. At first, for a moment, I thought they were customers. They overturned the tables and smashed the chairs. They battered the men brutally, stripped the drag queens naked and beat them with belts. There was total chaos as people climbed over other people trying to escape. Some got out the back, others were not so lucky. They dragged Gus from his follow-spot perch near the ceiling, and when he fell, he broke his neck and died. Shots were fired, and bullets caught one band member in the side and another in the leg. Several of the naked drag queens were molested, and all were physically abused. They herded us into police wagons. I was one of the lucky ones. I got off with a beating, a stiff fine, and a night in jail. Some, married men with children even, who somehow had offended the Nazi Party in some other way, were transported to Dachau." He put a bone-thin hand with long slender fingers to his mouth, and Hans saw on the old wrist, creeping from beneath a frayed shirt cuff, a bracelet of jeweled bangles.

The countess chuckled. "I defy them in my own way." Then the other hand tucked the bracelet away. He let out a long, heavy sigh. "There is talk. One possible, proposed solution to the 'homosexual problem' would be forced castration. It's gaining popularity." He shook his head, almost in disbelief. "It was Röhm's SA boys you know. The very boys who drank and danced with us. You'd have thought that fat, faggot-fuck Röhm would have warned us. Jesus, our toilet door practically had his name engraved on it! Fittingly, they are going to turn the building into a new SA headquarters." And then, as an afterthought, he waved a hand. "No use looking, they've closed the other gay clubs as well." He became silent again for a long time. Then, "Do you have a cigarette?"

Fritz handed him the pack.

"Do you have money, Countess? Somewhere to go? Some way to live? We can give you some money."

But the old man shook his head. "No, no, I'm fine on that account. What I have lost forever is... the will to live."

That night in bed, Hans made a solemn promise to Fritz. "I swear that after this next season, I will leave Germany with you, and we will make a new life in Paris with my parents. One more summer of singing at Bayreuth is all I want."

Fritz kissed Hans on the cheek. "Ach, such a dreamer you are. You don't live in the real world at all."

"Why should I, when the real world is so ugly?"

"Herr Kleiber is fighting with the Nazi censors right now over the new Berg opera 'Lulu.' It was banned as degenerate. He will renounce his post and leave Germany for good. He is putting together a symphonic, concert version of the opera's score for his farewell performance." The two young men held hands and looked into each other's eyes... Fritz the realist, and Hans the dreamer. "Here's the thing Hans, Herr Kleiber assures us that if we pack up and get out, he can get us both plenty of opera work at La Scala, Covent Garden, and even in America."

Still, Hans resisted slightly. "Are Italy or England or America any better for Jews and homosexuals? I read of thousands attending a pro-Nazi rally at Madison Square Garden in New York, sponsored by the German American Bund. And congressman Louis T. McFadden delivered an openly anti-Semitic speech on the floor of the House of Representatives. As for Italy, Hitler has just met with Mussolini, and they're now best friends. I tell you, Fritz, the whole world has gone mad."

CHAPTER 31

1934

   MUNICH, BERLIN
   THE LONG KNIVES

THE MOTORCYCLES STOPPED FURTHER AWAY from the lake because of the way sound carried, especially at night, but the trucks slowly and almost silently pulled as close as they could. The back hatches on the trucks were lowered, and SS troops carrying MP34 submachine guns hopped down onto the wet grass and moved toward the large cabin. This was "Operation Hummingbird," and it was happening all over Germany on what would come to be called "Night of the Long Knives." The Führer himself and a large contingent of SS troops had flown into Munich that day. Gunther Koch was a young idealistic, SS soldier. His very name meant "warrior," and he was ready to prove it. That evening, he had actually seen the Führer in person. Now, in the dead of night, with the others, they moved up to surround the lake cabin. At the signal, a bird whistle, Gunther kicked in the wooden door. Ten SS troops poured into the dark space, swinging their submachine guns from left to right.

What they encountered were drunken, sleeping men. Young SA Brownshirts, minus their brown shirts and trousers. Naked, young men, snoring away, limbs wrapped around each other. The end of a typical SA homosexual bacchanal. When the order was snapped, Gunther and the others opened fire. Bedroom doors opened and blurry eyed young men in underwear or naked stumbled out to see what was happening. They were mowed down like summer grass. Bloody bodies piled up.

The officer in charge grabbed one shivering kid with close-cropped, blond hair by the ear and dragged his face close.

"Where is Ernst Röhm?" the officer demanded, holding a Luger to the young man's head.

The naked kid was so terrified he couldn't speak, so the officer backhanded him with the pistol a few times to loosen his tongue. With blood running from his nose and lips, the hysterical boy tried to focus enough to answer.

"I don't know exactly. I have done nothing wrong. Bitte, what is this all about? I am loyal to the Führer!" He tried to raise his trembling arm in a Nazi salute, but the officer knocked it aside.

"Where is Ernst Röhm? I will not ask you again." All around were the splayed limbs of slaughtered young men. The boy shook his head to clear it. "Up at the hotel, I guess. I'm not sure." He spit the blood from his mouth. "The hotel up at Bad Wiessee. I heard that Röhm and Heines took some boys up there."

The officer in charge raised his luger and shot the boy in the face. Gunther "the warrior" vomited violently on several dead bodies.

The next day, Reichsführer of the Schutzstaffel, Heinrich Luitpold Himmler, stared at two men across his highly polished, black desk. Two slender fingers reached out and spun a large silver globe. Himmler was a lizard of a man. A chameleon who could change colors instantly when required. With the boring face of an accountant, his small, weak chin, sharp nose, and long pointy tongue, he even looked like a lizard.

The two men standing before him were not at all certain why they were there. One was middle-aged, Hitler-loyalist Theodor Eicke, and the other was the young SS major, Rolf Kainz.

"Both Röhm and Edmund Heines were found in bed having sex with young boys. Röhm, being the Führer's longtime friend, was arrested rather than executed on the spot. In one night, we eradicated the licentious debauchery of the SA. Think of it as a palate cleanser before the main course." Himmler made a steeple of his fingers. "Of course, under the umbrella of 'moral cleansing,' we were also able to execute or arrest many other undesirables who were not really homosexual at all. But the dead can't defend themselves. The number of dead from last night, by the way, numbers in the hundreds." He spread his lizard fingers and indicated to the two visitors that they should be seated. "The number of arrested, even higher. I feel cleaner and healthier this morning already!" He allowed a tight-lipped slit of a smile to appear.

Like a little child, with his elbows on the desk, he leaned his face in on his balled fists and, behind his spectacles, his round lizard eyes studied the two nervous men. "And you are wondering what any of this has to do with you," he almost hissed.

"A test. A kind of test. Both of you have sworn loyalty to

the Führer. SS-Brigadeführer Eicke, you have proven it over and over, but young Kainz, you have yet to be tested. Ernst Röhm sits in a jail cell, an embarrassment to the Reich and all of our great goals. Adolf Hitler knows his former friend must be eliminated, but he wants his end to be dignified and humane."

Himmler zeroed in on Rolf. "You were recommended numerous times to both the Führer and myself by Röhm. You appeared to be Röhm's lap dog at times."

Rolf felt compelled to speak up. "I am loyal only to the Führer, sir!"

Himmler raised and wagged one finger. "That is what we shall see. Eicke, you will act as a kind of mentor and advisor in this task, but Kainz, the lapdog, will perform the actual duty at the special request of the Führer himself." Himmler slid open a silent desk drawer and removed a Browning pistol and a single bullet. Also, a manilla-colored envelope.

"Major Kainz, with Eicke at your side, you will visit Ernst Röhm in his cell, give him the pistol and the bullet, and implore him to take the decent way out. If he refuses, Major Kainz, you will assist him. The letter in this envelope states, 'The bearer of this document has full authority to do what must be done. Signed, Adolf Hitler.' It is hand written and officially stamped. You see, the Fuhrer has sentimental feelings for old friends like Rohm. Better a good former friend like you should do the deed. And naturally, the two of you will be amply rewarded by the Reich."

On their way out of Himmler's office, Eicke said to Rolf, "Röhm's problem was not his homosexuality, but his flaunting of it. And his greatest weakness was that he only knew how to influence others through brutal thuggery. If we make a good job of this, our futures could be secured."

A day later, Eicke and another big-wig, SS-Obersturmbannführer Michael Lippert, left Rolf alone with Röhm in his cell. Rolf knew damned well that by placing the act in his hands, the other two and Himmler were clearing themselves of the deed, should there be negative repercussions.

Röhm laughed and ripped off his shirt to face Rolf barechested. "Ha! So, they sent you of all people."

Rolf allowed himself a smile, even though he was incredibly shaken. "After today, I'll be free of you. Free of your blackmail and your control."

Röhm puffed out his huge naked chest and belly. "Don't be so sure. There are files and documents and documents and files. After today, you may be trapped forever. The masters may change, the but slaves stay the same."

Rolf set the Browning pistol and the bullet on the table. "The Führer wants you to do the decent thing."

Röhm barked another laugh, but his body glowed with the sweat of fear. "The decent thing? THE DECENT THING? Has there ever been anything decent about any of this? One day, Himmler will betray Adolf Hitler, mark my word. Of course, you won't be around to see it, not with the dangerous crowd who now control you. Before this is all over, you will betray everyone you know, even the ones you love."

Rolf blinked. He must not listen to Röhm's ramblings. 'I'll give you some time alone. Do the decent thing." That fucking phrase kept playing over and over in Rolf's head. He turned and left the cell to join Eicke and Lippert in the next room.

"Well?" Eicke asked.

"We'll see," answered Rolf. "I don't think he'll do it. I believe under all that bluster, he's a coward at heart."

Eicke raised an eyebrow. "Then, the two of you are not friends?"

Rolf shook his head. "Not friends. Do you know how many abused lapdogs long to bite the hand that feeds them?"

After twenty minutes, Rolf retuned to the cell and shot Ernst Röhm dead.

As a reward for his heroic actions, Theodor Eicke was made "Official Inspector" of the now growing number of concentration camps.

CHAPTER 32

1934
    BAYREUTH
    TRUTH AND FICTION

HANS WAS TAKING A BATH. He'd put plenty of coins in the hot water meter and filled the steamy room with his solos from "Tristan and Isolde," over and over. After all, he got to open Act Three. Often, the character of the Shepherd only gets to stick his head in a door or window, or he stands in shadows up on a platform, but that dear, dear Max Lorenz insisted that Hans be given a fully fleshed out persona and decent blocking in Tristan's sickroom. Winifred, who understood and appreciated Hans' abilities, had agreed.

"Kurvenal, Hey!

Say, Kurvenal!

Hear me, friend...

Has he not waked?"... and so on.

Now in his mid-twenties, Hans' body had become muscular and strong, but still smooth and shimmering in that mythic, Nordic way. He would make a grand Siegfried. His wet, blond hair hung over his eyes, and he stretched and twisted his torso in the large, iron tub. Fritz had gone out to get food for them. They would spend the evening listening to music.

The news in the papers was ugly. German President Paul von Hindenburg had died, and Hitler had declared himself "Führer of the German State, and Full Commander in Chief of Germany's armed forces." Austria was attempting to hold out against the Nazi regime, but the number of people now following the Nazis was staggering.

Hans heard the door open and close. "Fritzy?" he called playfully, climbing from the tub and intending to strip his friend and drag him into the water. Without grabbing a towel, and in a hurry for some foolish fun, Hans crossed from the bathroom into the bedroom to see not Fritz, but Wolf, standing with folded arms, leaning back against the door.

Wolf looked down at Hans' large circumcised penis and laughed out loud. "Well, Opera Boy, it's all out in the open now, isn't it? Our little homosexual tenor has another secret as well!" Hans had never seen Wolf so ecstatic. The dark young man actually applauded. "Well, I've got you now, haven't I? The Führer's little favorite is a Jew!"

"What are you doing here? Get out! GET OUT!" Hans screamed, covering his genitals with his hands.

"It's too late!" Wolf howled back. "The jig is up. The cat is out of the bag! Hitler championed you. He kissed your cheek in public, for Christ's sake! How will he live with the shame?" He cackled with glee and applauded again. The door slammed open, sending him tumbling into the room. Fritz stood in the doorway holding sacks of food and bottles of drink.

"What's wrong, Hans?" Fritz shouted. Steam from the bathroom circled and twisted around them, and they stood there frozen, warriors and the enemy in an alien landscape.

"What's wrong? What is wrong?" Wolf asked, regaining his balance and turning on Fritz. "You've been fucking a Jew, that's what is wrong! And I guess, nobody would much care how you dirty your dick, except for the fact that our Führer, Adolf Hitler, was made a fool of by this queer Juden more than once. This is a black stain on Frau Wagner and the whole festival." Then he spun on Hans. 'If I were you, 'Jew-boy,' I'd head for the hills!" He pushed passed Fritz and ran down the hall.

Hans stood there sobbing with his hands now pressed over his eyes. Fritz set the sacks of food on the floor and rushed to embrace him, just as the young tenor's legs gave out and he tumbled to the floor.

"It's over, Fritz, everything is over..." Hans wailed, as Fritz wrapped him in his arms.

"We don't know that. Wolf has no power, what can he do? I'd bet he's too scared to say anything to anyone. Why was he here?"

"I have no idea. I heard the door, and I thought it was you." Hans buried his face in Fritz's slender, bony shoulder and cried even more. Fritz rocked the man he loved, then hummed, then sang to him. They stayed that way for a very long time. Later, they played Mahler on the phonograph. During the night, in Fritz's arms, Hans dreamed several times of Rolf. The lines of an old British poem by a fellow named William Cowper rang in his head;

"We perish'd each alone:
But I beneath a rougher sea,
And whelm'd in deeper gulfs than he."

The following evening, Hans was to sing in "Tristan and Isolde."

He was packing his knapsack to go to the theater, where the long four and one-half hour performance was to begin at four-thirty in the afternoon, when there was a knock at the door of their room. Hans, froze, and Fritz went to answer it. It was another staff member, not Wolf, requesting that Hans meet with Winifred Wagner at once at Wahnfried. So, they climbed the hill to the Festival Theater together and crossed to the Wagner house.

"I'll be waiting right here," Fritz whispered, his long, thin, amazingly strong fingers gripping Hans by the arms. A female answered the door and showed Hans to the Wagner office. The house seemed cold, abandoned almost. The office itself was cast in deep shadows, unusual for a summer's day.

Winifred Wagner, dressed in something deep purple, stood behind the great desk, looking down at nothing as if it were of interest. One recalcitrant strand of hair from her tight bun had come loose and dangled provocatively over her face. She raised a hand and tucked it behind an ear. When she looked at Hans, there were tears in her eyes. If anything, her face was filled with sorrow and a bit of compassion, not anger.

"A Jew and a homosexual? How did you ever manage that?" she asked at last in a soft, gentle voice.

Hans shrugged. "Just lucky, I guess."

Her hands came together and twisted around each other. "It's dangerous for you, you know that. Not like Schorr or even Lorenz. I can protect them. It's dangerous for you because the Führer chose you. He championed you. He intended to use you as a symbol of the perfect German youth. He will not suffer the betrayal lightly."

Hans stood cap in hand. "Is it my fault? I only wanted to sing."

Winifred shook her head. "None of it is your fault. You are a victim of circumstance. Although I believe Adolf Hitler will bring Germany to the greatness it deserves, he and I do not agree on all issues. Homosexuality and issues of race being but two. I believe in art. The world must not be robbed of your art because of your heritage or your sexual inclinations." She fished a leather folder from the desk drawer, then came around the desk to Hans.

"You don't quite understand. Hitler and Himmler have shared their vision with me. They wish to purify the German race by exterminating any traces of foreign blood. Within a year, they will generate a program to eliminate all Jews."

Hans frowned. "Eliminate? You mean exile?"

She shook her head and that damned stray hair teasingly fell again. "No, not exile. Annihilate. Exterminate! There is no future for you and your kind in Germany."

Hans was confused. "But that is impossible. You cannot erase an entire people."

"You can try. I love Adolf Hitler. I love his love of art and children and his vision for a better Germany and a better world. He tells me that sometime, for political power, one needs to make the harsh, hard, ugly decisions. Hans, he believed in you. He honored you in public. Newspapers printed photos. Your very being now will horribly embarrass him. He will hunt you down and kill you." Tears, which seldom flowed down the cheeks of this outwardly stern, self-contained woman, now had free reign. She drew the young man into her arms and held him.

"I so wanted to hear you one day sing Tristan. But you have to go. Wolf, that sniveling coward, has reported you to

Berlin. I have already ignored two telephone calls from the Führer, to ignore a third would be disastrous. After today's performance, you must disappear. In this folder are new identity papers, train tickets, letters of recommendation and lots of cash. If you are in danger of being caught, please, dispose of them." She forced the folder into his trembling hands.

"All I ever wanted," he said, "was to sing."

She shook her head again. "A bird in a cage sings differently than a free bird. Sing free, Hans. Today you sing for the last time at Bayreuth, tomorrow, you sing free." She kissed him on the forehead.

Hans' heart was so heavy as he left Wahnfried for the last time, he found it difficult to walk. "The dream is ended, Fritz."

"So, we build a new dream. One man lives many lives in one lifetime. In the new dream, we will live and work together, perhaps with Herr Kleiber. You will sing leading roles in the great opera houses of the world. You go to the theater, Hans, I'll return to our rooms to pack."

But Hans stopped him. "No, it's not safe for you. You can still come and go as you please. It's better if we travel separately and meet at my parents' home in Paris. I'll leave right after today's performance."

"My God, I love you, Hans, you know that." Fritz said, wrapping his long arms around the trembling tenor. Then, the lanky pianist loped off down the hill to fetch a few necessary items for Hans.

Chewing his lower lip with shame, Hans felt he had to confess his predicament to Max Lorenz. Max gave that gentle smile of his and put his hand to Hans' cheek. "We must all survive however we can. I shall miss you. I shall struggle on here a bit longer, but my magic charm will only hold power for so long. Eventually, my Jewish wife and my homosexual self will meet you again, perhaps in New York, in America. But for today, with the mountain ahead of us to climb, we must think only of Wagner and of singing."

The crowd arrived, the trumpets blared, and the opera began. There were any number of German officers and their spouses dotting the audience. After singing the beautiful off stage role of the sailor at the start of the opera, Hans had three hours to wait until his entrance as the shepherd. Two hours in, during the second interval, Fritz came tearing backstage.

"Hans, there are SS swarming the hillside. Frau Wagner is not sure, but she thinks they are searching for you. Wolf is with them, which is a pretty good indication. She will not allow them in the Festspielhaus during the performance. If you cut through the back woods it can take you to the railway tracks. Don't board at Bayreuth. You need to leave now! Not a moment to waste!"

But Hans shook his head. "I have to sing first. "

Fritz grabbed him by the shoulders and shook him. "Are you insane? ARE YOU CRAZY?"

Poor Hans looked totally lost. "I cannot let Max and the others down. It's too late for an understudy. I can't let Wagner down."

"Gott damn you, Hans, this will be the end of you!"

"I'll leave the moment I finish, I promise. I'll see you in Paris. But I must sing. You understand that."

Fritz kissed Hans a dozen times, and then ran off into backstage darkness, fighting back his tears. Max, made-up as the wounded Tristan, took Hans aside. "There are soldiers everywhere. After you finish your part, do not wait, but leave by the stage exit. I have pulled my car up to load some make-up and costume supplies. Climb into the boot of my car. No one would dare touch it. I'll drive you to a station down the line. But for now, concentrate only on the singing! If you don't sing divinely, I swear, I'll turn you in myself!"

Hans sang his small solos at the very start of the opera, and then in Act Three, perfectly. His voice was clear and strong and beautiful. Knowing it might be his last time on the Bayreuth stage, he sang his heart out. And then, during Isolde's final scene with Tristan, Hans quickly changed clothes and made his way to the loading dock at the very rear of the theater. Because Bayreuth has no wing-space, everything must be brought on from the rear, or from above or below. The loading dock area was cluttered with scenic pieces, but deserted of people.

As onstage, Isolde launched into her final aria, which after four-and one-half hours finally, musically resolves all of its haunting themes, and climaxes in an orgasm unique in all of opera, Hans opened the small exit next to the huge, loading-dock doors. He saw no soldiers at first, but he did notice the moving beams of flashlights in the distance. During the performance, a beautiful, summer evening had settled on Bayreuth. Hans moved silently toward Max's mustard-colored Maybach. A huge spare tired lashed to the rear of the auto helped to hide the car's boot which was really more of a large, traveling trunk. Hans halted when he saw six SS soldiers standing about a dozen feet away, smoking and chatting, glancing now and then at the rear of the theater.

Hans stood there, flustered, when a small compact figure moved out of the darkness toward him. "Just put that in the boot, will you?" said Max Lorenz's wife, loudly and clearly enough for the soldiers to hear. "Max will be out in a few minutes, after that interminable last aria of Isolde's. Honestly, I don't know how he can lie still for so long."

The Master Singer

Hans moved in and opened the boot. He deposited his knapsack. The soldiers gave them a look and then went back to their chat. Lotte Lorenz quickly and silently gestured for Hans to climb into the boot. It was a tight, uncomfortable fit, but they had provided a blanket and a water bottle for him. "Thank you, young man," she said toward the door to the theater, while she slammed and locked the trunk. Then, she brazenly called to the SS soldiers, "Excuse me, my husband is Max Lorenz. I wonder if one of you would be so kind as to pull our automobile around to the stage door entrance? He doesn't like to be swamped with fans after an exhausting performance. I'll ride along, if you don't mind."

A strapping, young SS Unterfeldwebel, eager to get behind the wheel of such a car for even a few moments, jumped forward. She handed him the keys. Some of his cohorts shouted humorous encouragement.

"Just pull around right up to the stage door. Right about here. That's perfect. Leave the keys in the ignition, so we can make a quick getaway from the screaming fans. Thank you so much, young man," she said in a flirtatious way.

He climbed from the Maybach and saluted. "Heil Hitler."

Seated inside, she raised one hand slightly. "Heil Hitler."

The young man rather cockily strode back to his friends, eager to describe the automobile, and how the opera singer's wife threw herself at him.

Thirty minutes later, with fans swarming around from the front of the theater, Max Lorenz exited the stage door, smiled a gleaming smile, waved broadly, got into his car, kissed his wife, and drove Hans Becker out of Bayreuth.

CHAPTER 33

1934
BAVARIA
AT THE BORDER

Hans could not bear to put Max Lorenz and Lotte in danger, so, forty miles outside of Bayreuth he bade them a tearful farewell, and with his knapsack on his shoulder, he disappeared into the woods. Homosexual international opera star Lorenz and his Jewish wife returned to Bayreuth to continue to walk the tightrope.

Hans zigzagged back and forth across the countryside, over fields and through woodlands, for the next two weeks. It was a beautifully warm September, and Hans sometimes slept out in the open air. Other times, he sought out a barn or stayed at a small inn. He purchased new clothing at market fairs, and let his sparse blond beard and moustache grow out. It was actually a peaceful time for the young man, and although he did encounter groups of SS and SA soldiers in every village, none of them seemed to be hunting

The Master Singer

for him. Perhaps Adolf Hitler and his "boys" had bigger fish to fry and greater things about which to fret.

He decided to cross the border into Switzerland and take the train to Paris from there. Finally, at a shabby, simple, station platform with an open-air toilet and a large, swiss clock with roman numerals, adjacent to a one-street village, he boarded the train that would take him to Bern. He buried himself amid some overly-zealous, young sports enthusiasts and, amid their shouts and laughter, he fell into a deep sleep. He dreamed of Rolf and once again of that summer he met him in the Bavarian forest. The last ten years had been like a lifetime for Hans. He awoke to find himself twisting the gold ring on his finger to the sound of singing. A group of teenage girls had joined the boys and they were having some kind of song-fest while they ate lunch. It was so innocent and so charming that Hans could not help but join in the song. The young people were delighted with his voice, although he was careful to not use his opera sound, nor to sing anything solo. The time passed pleasantly until they reached the German-Swiss Border.

As expected, German officials walked through the cars, checking the documents of the passengers. Hans had destroyed all of his Hans Becker papers and was now traveling as Karl Rotter, a music teacher. The papers provided by Winifred Wagner seemed to be in order. Two men in plain clothes, one extremely tall with a tall hat, and the other short and stout with a small, round hat, making them look like something out of the music hall, moved quickly through the car, giving mostly cursory glances at the papers.

The short fellow handled Hans' documents for only a moment and then gave them back. "So, you are a music teacher? Are you visiting Switzerland for a holiday or on business?" the small man asked almost jovially.

Hans smiled. "A little bit of both." He fished out the letters of recommendation, which he need not have shown. Although they referred to Hans as "the bearer of this letter" and not by any name, one of the recommendations was stamped "Bayreuth," and this seemed to raise a red flag. Hans realized his mistake at once, and could have kicked himself. The smiling, short man called to his tall compatriot who was on the other side of the car, and the two of them conferred for a few moments. Then Hans was politely requested to come with them.

"What is this? Is there some problem, gentlemen?"

The tall agent waved a hand dismissively. "No, no, nothing serious. Just a formality." They led him from the train into the station office, where he was requested to take a seat. The place had dull brown tiled walls, a stone floor and smelled slightly of tobacco and urine.

"May we have a look at your bag, bitte?" Hans handed over his knapsack, mentally going over the contents. Nothing too incriminating, he hoped.

"Ah, said the short man, almost with glee as he pulled the signed copy of "Death in Venice" by Thomas Mann from the bag. "This book is forbidden." He said, waving the slim volume.

"Just a memento from my school days," Hans replied, his forehead breaking out in sweat.

"Ja, ja, I get it." he continued to fish in the bag to finally produce some sheets of music. The shepherd's solo from "Tristan and Isolde."

He held this up and raised his eyebrows.

Hans protested, "I am a music teacher. Look, is there some mistake?"

He was offered a cup of coffee while they checked with Munich and perhaps even Berlin. Still, all smiles. The train hissed and coughed and pulled out, leaving Hans stranded with the enemy. Even without the Adolf Hitler hunt, he was on shaky ground with false papers and no thorough back-story prepared. Nervously, Hans kept glancing at the wrist-watch Rolf had given him so long ago.

"That's a very expensive watch..." Shorty exclaimed, almost hungrily. Was he looking for a bribe? Dare Hans try it?

"Ja. It was a gift. Soon, I'll have to sell it for bread and cheese." Hans laughed artificially, and both agents joined him, equally artificially.

Klaus Rotter was eventually matched to a Bayreuth picture of Hans Becker, and that was that. So simple, yet it took a day-and-a-half. He was never really questioned, and his own insistent questions remained unanswered. The official charge was "Enemy of the State." What that meant exactly was never explained to him. He was a political prisoner.

"But what are the exact charges?" he screamed, unable to contain anger and frustration any longer. "What have I done?" For his outburst, he was beaten unconscious. He learned quickly that such demonstrations were frowned upon.

Shorty leaned over him and wiped the blood from his mouth and nose with a paper napkin from the coffee pot. "Apparently, you have somehow offended some of the wrong people." He glanced at a piece of paper in his hand and wiggled those raised eyebrows. "Some very important people. It says here you are a possible homosexual. Homosexuality is now against the law and punishable by a long prison sentence."

"But what proof is there that I am homosexual?" Hans

twisted his head around looking at the four or five men standing over him.

The tall agent looked very severe. "Proof? It's proof enough that some gentlemen very high up in the Reich say you are. You don't have to suck our dicks to prove it."

It was ironic then, that without a hearing or a trial, he was condemned, not for anything he actually did or even was, but for what was speculated about him based on Hitler's animosity. Vindictive little shit! Hans was certain Wolf must have been consulted as well.

The hours of waiting, of nothing happening, went on. Now and then, one of the men gave Hans a strange, almost sympathetic, look. Was he secretly one of the boys? Hans occupied his time, thinking of trivial things. He pondered over some items he had left at Bayreuth that he wished he might have brought with him... not that he would be allowed to keep any of them. His newly sprouting whiskers itched, and he wished he had shaved. He longed for something to read. He tried to switch on the music in his head but had difficulty.

Less than a week later, he was imprisoned for an indefinite term, at Dachau!

CHAPTER 34

1935
BERLIN, DACHAU NEAR MUNICH
MISSING PERSONS

"Any word of him?" Erich Kleiber looked up over his eyeglasses, as he pulled another stack of scores from the bookshelf in his office. Fritz, looking ever so thin and wan, shook his head. He dropped into a chair and buried his head in his hands.

"He simply disappeared. He never reached Paris. Herr Kleiber, I am dying here of worry. What can I do? There was never an arrest notice, never a court case."

Kleiber harrumphed. "Those are things of the past. Today, people are yanked off the street and they disappear." Kleiber shook a finger at Fritz. "You were lucky to get out of Bayreuth without further trouble yourself."

"Wolf had no solid proof that Hans and I were anything more than roommates. Frau Wagner fired him the following day. She officially forbade politics from interfering with the festival. I left before the Führer himself arrived to see the operas, but I gather it all went splendidly. Hans Becker simply never existed." The lanky young man rubbed his eyes. "What can I do?"

"You can come with me! It is impossible to work in such a place! After they cancelled the production of 'Lulu,' Berg said to me that if I tried, I could work within the new system. Bah!" He tossed some scores into a box on the floor for disposal. "How can one conduct half an orchestra? If you kick out all the creative Jews, there is no one left!" He removed his glasses and cleaned them furiously. "Berg says to me, 'You can negotiate, Erich. There is some leeway for negotiation.' Do you know what I answered that poor, befuddled, talented man? I told him, 'Let Furtwängler kiss the Nazi asses and turn in his Jewish musicians, I am out of here!" And with an uncharacteristic burst of anger, he swept a pile of opera scores from the table to the floor. Fritz went to a sideboard and poured Kleiber a brandy. That seemed to help a bit. Kleiber took Fritz's hand.

"Come with us, Fritz. I'll find work for you. And when we find Hans, I'll find good work for him as well. You are both talented, young men. Your best years are ahead of you. You promised Hans you would go to Paris, and that you must do. We must think now only of music and art. That will be our salvation."

It was music that kept Hans alive from the moment he entered the concentration camp. Music he played in his head. Operas he sang in his head, while men were beaten and burned and tortured and killed around him. More than ever, he had to live in his dream world in order to survive.

He was still in shock when he was herded with a group

of half a hundred other dissidents through the gates of the camp, beneath a large sign that proclaimed "WORK WILL SET YOU FREE." No one spoke, it was all too surreal, and besides, speaking out of turn could get you beaten or shot. Perhaps as a kind of lesson on behavior in the camp, the SS officer in charge, a skeletal, specter of a man named Kurt Zeller, who welcomed them, raised his luger and for no reason at all, shot one of the group in the face. The young man dropped like a sack of potatoes, blood everywhere. He didn't die instantly, but lay there twitching for thirty seconds or so. The rest of the prisoners were then ordered to strip naked. Their clothing was collected and carted off. Hans held his hands over his genitals. The entire thing was disgusting and humiliating. They were then instructed to toss all jewelry into a basket on a small wooden table. Almost without thinking, Hans removed the wrist watch, but stuck his finger in his mouth and swallowed the gold ring. He would not part with it so easily.

One could smell the terror, and some men pissed themselves. They were of all ages, old men and teenage boys, all naked and shivering before their captors. There were other smells as well, disinfectant and feces. At this point, Dachau was not yet an official extermination camp, still, somedays, hundreds of deaths occurred. One of the first things Hans noticed was the stench from a bonfire of human corpses. Another lesson. Breathe through your mouth.

"Stand at attention. Hands on your heads. You will now be assigned to the appropriate barracks and work details. Your heads will be shaved for hygiene purposes, and you will be hosed down and given your prison uniforms." Officer Kurt Zeller had an unfortunate, high, nasal, sibilant voice, and he spit when he shouted. Hans would never forget watching that spray of spittle his first day at the camp. By focusing your mind on tiny insignificant things, you can blur the greater horror. No one in his group looked down at the body of their faceless, former comrade. Who was he? What was he? Communist, queer, gypsy, politician? Nothing, now. Not even a face.

When Hans was forced to put his hands on his head, his circumcised penis caught immediate attention, as did the penises of several other men and boys. There was still no official program for imprisoning Jews just for being Jews, that was still in the works, but the Jews in the camps were singled out for "special treatment." Zeller seemed fascinated that such a blond Nordic type would be circumcised. He ordered Hans to step forward. The SS Officer reached out with his riding crop and tapped the tip of Hans' penis.

"Well, here is an interesting specimen. Perhaps your contribution to the camp can be to help us out with our research on pure, Aryan blood- types." Hans ran a piece of music through his head to stop himself from screaming. He must be strong. He must not fall apart so easily. Zeller placed the crop under Hans' scrotum and lifted it. "Jew or German? We'll have to find out."

A thin, young, teenage boy collapsed, and Zeller had him dragged off by two guards. Hans and the others stood there for an eternity, naked with hands on head. Then, they were put into two lines to face prisoner/barbers who shaved their heads. Hans' glorious, golden locks floated into the dirt along with most of his identity. The men were then hosed down with cold water and allowed to scrub themselves with some kind of harsh stone soap.

The uniform Hans was handed was striped, as was the striped, thin, winter coat. No underwear. He was issued a pair of well-worn, third-hand boots, and carrying these, he was marched to the barracks, which were deceptively cheerful, white buildings on patches of lawn. Looking closer one could see rows of barbed wire and narrow alleys of filth between the barracks buildings. Inside, Hans wandered the rows of triple-stacked, raw, wooden bunk beds, looking for the number assigned to him.

"Ignore the numbers, you can always switch. Try to get a bunk bed on the top. It's much safer, in case the sleepers above you have diarrhea or bladder problems." The voice belonged to a shrunken, older man with frizzy, white hair. He pointed. "Up there would be good. That fellow just died." Hans set his prison uniform on the top bunk and then began to slowly dress.

"It's difficult at first, it all seems so unreal," the old man said. He waved a boney hand. "But don't worry, it only gets worse." He held out the dirty hand. "My name is Hermann. Hermann Hirshman." Hans struggled over which name to give but finally decided it didn't matter anymore.

"Hans Becker." The little old man had watery eyes and his handshake was limp.

"I'm glad you caught me still alive. I probably haven't long to go. The food and recreation here leave something to be desired." He smiled. His teeth were few and rotting. "I'd laugh, but I don't think that's allowed. Only our keepers may laugh. Roll up your winter coat and use that for a pillow. We'll try to find you a blanket somewhere."

"Can we get letters out to family and loved ones?" Hans inquired.

Hermann did laugh then, laughed so hard he had a coughing fit. "Letters? Get letters out? Are you meshuga? Don't you understand, we are dead. We are living dead." Suddenly, a shadow clouded the old man's face and he sat on a lower bunk until his breathing returned to normal.

"Don't listen to me. Find something, anything, in your head, to keep you going. Just keep going. Who knows, God willing, the Third Reich may fall apart any day now. I mean, how much longer can such insanity go on?"

After holding it in for so long, Hans needed to talk. Wanted to share with someone else his grief. "My mother is German, my father a Jew," he said.

"Congratulations, you qualify! But I suspect that is not why you are here. I was the highly respected, Jewish principal of a primary school. But I spoke out against racism. To be fair to the bastards, I was warned, but I couldn't keep my big mouth shut. So, they trumped up charges that I molested little Christian boys, and here I am."

Hans felt emboldened. "I'm a homosexual." It felt so strange, so freeing, to say that. Had he ever actually announced it before?

Like a crazed scientist making a new discovery, Hermann raised one finger high in the air. "Aha... now there is a charge they can get you on. Never mind if you are or not, truth doesn't matter. But they can imprison you for being a queer if someone accuses you, and that's enough."

"There was never a trial, never any formal charges…"

"Aha, have you ever read Kafka? Somebody in a cushy, leather chair doesn't like you. Wants to erase you." Hermann rose with some difficulty and studied Hans for a long time. "You're a good-looking boy. Strong. Do everything in your power to stay strong. A year ago, they released a whole passle of prisoners as a publicity stunt. Obviously, I was not one of the 'chosen ones.' Oh, and every now and then, they send inspectors through to make certain we are being treated well. During that time, the torture and the killings don't stop entirely but decrease for a bit." He yanked on Hans' sleeve to encourage him to sit on the bunk opposite. "He won't mind. He won't mind, he's out digging ditches. Listen, while we are on the subject of torture and killings, a bit of advice. Stay as far away as possible from Sturmbannführer Kurt Zeller. The man is a sick, twisted, perverted piece of filth, and those are his good qualities. Also, steer clear of Oberfeldwebel Heinz and his pet dogs. He enjoys watching them eat prisoners. You'll learn. A couple of the guards will give you cigarettes now and then. Or a piece of chocolate. If you get a job working in the canteen, life is cushy." Hans trembled with fear and confusion. Hermann put a hand on the young man's arm. He leaned in very close to stare into his eyes. Hans smelled death.

"Most important. Most important of all to survive. What do you love?"

Hans frowned. "Well there were two people that..."

Hermann slapped Hans' arm. "No, not who do you love? That will only make you lonely and depressed. What do you love?"

"Music. I love music. I'm an opera singer."

Hermann nodded. "Good. Very good. In life, you were an opera singer. Beautiful. So now, do not think for yourself any more. Do not question. Do as you are told, and simply crawl into your head and listen to music. It will help you endure."

And it did.

Back in Berlin, Fritz went to the movie studio to say goodbye. He loved walking through the lot amid pieces of gigantic, moving scenery, everything from palm trees to alien planets. Workmen pushed and jostled these huge set pieces past chariots, steam locomotives, pens with camels and horses, a Chinese pagoda, and an entire, old-time, Bavarian village. There was realism and surrealism, and it was all magic to Frtiz. He hated to say goodbye, but he had accepted Erich Kleiber's offer to travel with the conductor and his wife, and then to settle in Paris.

He slid open one of the massive, sound stage doors and entered the dark, cool world of the movies. He paused for a few moments to watch the filming of a musical production number with showgirls dancing down one hundred white steps. As they descended, each step lit up. He headed toward the rear of the sound stage, where the costume and production tables were set up. He needed to bid farewell to his dearest movie-world friend, Margot Thanger, a savvy, sophisticated, independent production assistant. Margo was a smart cookie all right. She had learned how to navigate through an industry of male "Berlin bullies." She somehow always managed to have silk stockings and an extensive, fashionable wardrobe some say was lifted from the studio costume department.

On this day, Fräulein Thanger wore a tailored, burgundy dress with a high collar and a hem that teasingly played about her gorgeous gams. A pencil or two was shoved into her piled-up, auburn hair. Yes, sir, she would be a real catch for any man, but she looked upon most of them as either competition or carnivores. She adored Fritz. She threw her arms around him and kissed his cheeks over and over, leaving marks from her blood-red lipstick. Then with a cloth from a table of dress samples, she carefully wiped his face clean. He stood there, rather embarrassed, but nonetheless delighted.

"Hey, Toots, how's tricks?" he asked, looking at how wonderfully put together she was.

"You missed all the excitement, Fritzy. So much has happened while you were hiding away, licking your wounds." Fritz kept few secrets from Margot, and had given her a safely edited account of events at Bayreuth. She had met Hans on numerous occasions. She giggled and slapped her hands together. "All hell broke loose here!" She held up a hand to increase the suspense while she got two cups of coffee and dumped some liquor or other into them. "Bitte, setzen Sie sich," she flirted teasingly, batting her big, brown eyelashes.

"One day, the awesome and all-powerful Heinrich Himmler himself appeared at our doorstep. His intention? To revamp completely the German film industry. He swept through the studio with a squadron of big, black swans, and all work halted at once. He is a man who makes the egos of actors seem inconsequential. Be careful, the coffee is hot.

"He called for a meeting of all studio-heads and producers and directors." She raised one perfectly plucked and drawn eyebrow. "That took some doing. My presence, of course, was required as well. I filled two notebooks and wore out five pencils that day."

Fritz laughed. "And the upshot is?"

"The upshot is that the German film industry has been conscripted to serve the 'glorious' new Nazi Government. We are to put our best faces forward, and our best feet forward, and our best everythings forward, in fact, to show the Reich in only the very best light." She began to roll a joint.

Fritz shook his head and clicked his teeth. "So, they are going to take over film production." It was not a question.

She raised one bangled wrist and wiggled it. "Well, it is somewhat understandable, considering the Olympics next year and the good impression the Nazis must make on the world. To quote Herr Himmler, 'We must all show our best sides,' which if I am to believe some of the SS officers in attendance, included my ass."

She lit the joint, inhaled and passed it to Fritz. "I've been assigned as production assistant on a new version of 'Merchant of Venice,' to be followed by 'The Jew of Malta!'"

"Will you be all right?" Fritz asked her seriously.

"Oh, you know me. I'll muddle through, by hook or crook." She crossed one elegantly stockinged leg over the other. "I'll pay the rent, and to hell with art."

Some kid stopped by and dumped a stack of reels of film onto her work table. She paused long enough to label each reel and record the data in a log book.

"But that's not the big news!" She framed her beautiful face with her hands like a movie musical starlet. "The big, big news is that Fritz Lang and Herr Himmler had a blowout in front of everyone. Lang openly accused the Nazis of being racist and anti-Semitic... as if that is news to anyone. But, my dear, to say this to Himmler's pinched, red face in front of everyone was shocking. I think some of the SS wet their pants."

Fritz whistled. "I'd have thought he would have been arrested on the spot."

Margot laughed merrily. "It seems that Fritz Lang is too big, too popular, too important to arrest. He's a film director. Bigger than all the Nazis. Everyone knows that people in the movies are bigger than life. Well, it turns out that Himmler banned Lang's new film, "The Testament of Dr. Mabuse, so in retaliation, Lang is packing up and heading to Hollywood!"

She batted her lashes again. "Who knows, maybe I'll go with him." Then, after a moment gazing off somewhere, she switched her look to sincere. "You, know, Fritz, I'm only half kidding about leaving." She wandered over to an upright piano. "Play something for me, Fritz. Something light and gay. I long to feel alive again."

On his second day at Dachau, Hans crawled into the

narrow alley between two of the barracks, squatted and shat out the ring. He washed it under a hose, polished it with his shirt, and hid it between two loose pieces of wood on his bunk. Each night, he took the ring from its hiding place and clutched it in his hand while he slept.

CHAPTER 35

1935-36
DACHAU
NOT EVEN NUMBERS

Two months passed, and Hans had settled into the unsettled daily horrors of Dachau. There were too many prisoners now, and really not enough labor for them, so they were exercised relentlessly "for their health." Several times a day, they were rounded up and put through their paces, and those who dropped from exhaustion were simply shot. Those assigned to work on the construction of new barracks for the ever-expanding camp were no better off. Like Nibelung slaves, they dug holes, sank beams into the earth, carried concrete blocks, and hauled timber for the glory of the Reich. When they fell, they were often dumped into the very holes they had dug.

Those not assigned specific tasks spent their days aimlessly wandering the grounds, searching for stray bits of food or perhaps some discarded cigarette butts. A man might trade away a button for a cigarette butt with something left to it. The daily meals consisted mainly of a watery, vegetable soup and some stale bread.

Right from the start of their friendship, Hermann insisted that Hans eat some of the old man's portion of food, much to the envy of other hollow, eager eyes. "You're young. You need to stay fit as long as you can. Who cares if my old bones poke through my tissue-paper skin?" Hans tried to refuse, but the former school principal was adamant. "This is something I can do for you. To help you stay alive."

And in return, in the evenings, Hans would tell Hermann the stories of the great operas. He spoke. He did not sing. In the camp, Hans would not sing a note. He only sang in his own head. He sang in his head to endure. At night, in his bunk, holding the ring to his lips, Hans sang all the great opera roles in his head, starting with Tristan, of course, but eventually even singing Butterfly and Tosca and Don Giovanni. In his head, he could sing them all effortlessly, and he could master the most difficult arias. He was truly a "Meistersinger."

It was in the third month that he was summoned to the officers' quarters. This was at once terrifying because, as Hermann had so often reminded Hans, the secret to enduring in the camp was to become invisible.

"You thought I had forgotten you. No such thing. But the trains bring in more each day than we can handle." Kurt Zeller leaned back in his wooden chair with his boots up and crossed at the ankle on the wooden worktable before him. Five other officers were occupied with various trivial tasks: polishing their belts, cleaning their guns, flipping through magazines or even reading approved poetry. In the corner of the room, a young, junior officer with headphones sat at a large, bulky radio receiver. By contrast, a small radio sat on a nearby stand, cranking out American jazz, including Louis Armstrong who was officially banned but not removed because of overwhelming popularity. There seemed to be no consistency to the Reich's policies.

"So…" purred Zeller, tapping the toe of his boot with a riding crop, which was ludicrous since the only horses in the camp were those out in the fields outside the fences, used to haul cut-down timber. "So…" he said again, using the tip of the crop to flip open a file on his desk. "Find Hans Becker! Someone in Belin is interested in what happened to Hans Becker. An irritating and impossible task. So many prisoners arrive each day, they no longer have names. They no longer even have numbers. Their crimes tumble and melt one into another." He pointed the crop at Hans. "You are Hans Becker, accused dissident and homosexual, trying to escape Germany under a false identity." He had a very slight speech defect that accentuated the sibilant sounds. Middle-aged, reed-thin, and leathery, he had worked hard to get wherever it was he got. He was not officially in charge of the camp. That distinction belonged to Theodor Eicke. But Eicke was seldom, if ever, around, and so the day-to-day running of the place fell to Zeller, a job he relished.

He flipped his feet to the floor and leaned on the desk, staring at Hans who stood trembling at attention. Zeller opened a slim volume on the table, which turned out to be a child's school book.

"It says in this primary school text, and I quote:

'THE DEVIL IS THE FATHER OF THE JEW.
WHEN GOD CREATED THE WORLD,
HE INVENTED THE RACES:
THE INDIANS, THE NEGROES, THE
   CHINESE,

AND ALSO THE WICKED CREATURE CALLED THE JEW!'

So, homosexual, circumcised Hans Becker, the question is, are you also a Jew?"

There was no point denying it anymore. "My mother was pure-blood German. My father was a Jew."

Zeller chuckled, which came out as more of a hissing snort. "So, your mother was a German whore then. She craved greasy, Juden cock. And although you look like a perfect child of the Master Race, you are in fact, the degenerate, pathetic offspring of the bestial coupling of a whore and a swine."

In learning to navigate the Bosch-like landscape of the camp, Hans had learned to quell any inclination to strike back at these monsters. For some reason, he was playing Rossini in his head. The music helped control the pain, but not the shame. And it was shame upon which Zeller thrived.

"Strip!" he ordered. And the other men in the room suddenly took interest. Zeller was known for his fun and games.

Hans instantly kicked off his boots, stripped off his shirt and dropped his striped trousers to the floor. He now stood naked before Zeller and the others. The young radio operator removed his headphones and took interest as well. Louis Armstrong had been replaced by some awful, generic, German polka music.

Hans had already lost twenty pounds and his body was now lean and angular. Zeller studied him with something of the look of a hunter and his captured prey. He turned again to the folder on the desk.

"We have an obligation to Berlin, to keep some kind of records of the inmates that we use for our medical experiments." He paused to let the dreaded words sink in. "Nothing too extreme. Measurements and so on, to determine in what ways a Jew differs from others. And also, perhaps, to explore what makes a homosexual. We can't erase the filth without understanding its source. You may be of great assistance in these endeavors. Hans Becker, are you a filthy homosexual? Are you a dirty, filthy cocksucker?"

Hans lifted his head, trying to retain a modicum of pride. "I am a homosexual." But there could be no pride for prisoners.

"So, then, you are a cocksucker. Well, then, since there are seven of us officers of the Reich here in this room, Cocksucker, you had better get started. Begin with young Schmidt, our radio operator. I think he's still a virgin." That was how it started!

The actions themselves became mechanical. After a week or two, Hans knew exactly which piece of music to play in his head to escape. But there were other games, games designed to destroy any humanity left in him. Particularly degrading were the "Judentests." They would strip him and then take "measurments" of different parts of his body and record these in his file for Berlin. Using a caliper and various tape measures, they would measure the size of his head. He would stand at attention or sit stiffly on a wooden chair while they recorded the width of his head, the circumference of his head, the distance from his forehead to his chin and so on. Zeller measured the size of his ears, and the length of his nose to see if it had any jüdische qualities. They made him stick out his tongue and measured that.

They measured his hands and feet, fingers and toes. his waist and chest, as if he were being fitted for a fine suit. All of this went into the record, studying if Jews had certain discernable, physical characteristics. Even a blond, Nordic-looking half-Jew. It was a game. A fucking, sadistic, ridiculous game.

They took special delight in measuring his penis, length and thickness, soft and hard, and discussing it with each other. And when Hans couldn't get an erection due to his terror, they threatened to shoot him on the spot.

"If you can't follow orders on the spot, you are of no use to us. Now get it hard!" Zeller, half drunk on this occasion, barked, waving his Luger about. Hans pumped frantically. They measured him hard. Then they measured and weighed his testicles.

Hans became more and more frantic. He was having trouble finding the music. He couldn't crawl away. His mind raced through archives of music, searching for something to help.

"Good. Now we need a sample of jüdischen sperm. Please masturbate for us like a good, little, homosexual Jew pig."

It took some time, but Hans eventually spent to "Die Walküre" in his head. They didn't even bother to collect the sample.

"Lick it up."

The months dragged on into a year, then more. Hans grew thinner and weaker. His blond hair turned to a dull ash color. His nose and cheekbones looked more prominent because of his sunken cheeks and eyes. Hermann did his best to help. He cradled the young man, promising that Zeller would soon tire of him and move on to another prisoner for his games. But he wasn't certain at all what would happen to Hans then. Hermann himself grew weaker and weaker, and rather than waste good food on a dying man, they cut his rations in half.

Hans was placed on construction detail, and although that lessened the frequency of Zeller's games, it did not cancel them all together.

One evening, Hans was summoned. Zombie-like, and working to make his mind a blank, he trudged over to the officers' quarters. For some reason, the music in his head kept returning to Berg's disturbing "Wozzeck." Hans understood. He had become Wozzeck. He was surprised when he entered the building to find a group of over a dozen SS and even some SA soldiers having a kind of party. His blood froze. Would he have to orally satisfy all of them? And then he saw Zeller standing with a small, frail, young, teenage, boy prisoner.

"Look, Hans, we found a new friend for you. This is Jacob. He's a Jew, too. A Jew for you!" The boy trembled head to foot and his legs almost gave out. His big, dark eyes were wide with horror. It was as if he had seen Satan, but in his heart, Hans knew the boy had experienced nothing yet. Zeller actually had his arm around the teenager, giving him a squeeze every now and then. Then, he pushed the boy towards Hans.

"Well, what are the two of you waiting for? Strip down!"

Hans, so used to following orders, shucked his clothing at once. The boy was too petrified to comply, so Zeller literally ripped the clothes from him. The poor kid held his hands over his genitals as Hans had done on his first day at the camp.

"Ja, Jacob is new here. Just arrived. So, we want the two of you to become special friends. Hans, show us how a jüdischer homosexual fucks his new friend up the ass!"

That was it. The music stopped playing in Hans' head.

End of the recording. There was no way out and nowhere to go.

"I won't do it," he said simply, his raspy, raw voice producing very little sound at all. "Go ahead and kill me, I won't do it."

The hysterical boy had fallen to the floor and curled up into a little ball. He lay there, his still growing teenage limbs jerking and twitching, wrapped around himself. The room was silent. But Zeller, who had played this game before, was way ahead of Hans.

"You won't do it? Very well. Don't worry, I won't kill you. I'll just kill the boy. And you'll be responsible for cutting his life short. You will be responsible for his death. I'll make it slow, first putting a bullet into each kneecap. Then a bullet into each shoulder. And last, a bullet in his head. So, what's it to be. Which do you think this sweet boy would choose? Shall we ask him? A cock up the ass or a bullet in the head?"

The boy chose life, and Hans descended yet one circle lower in Hell.

CHAPTER 36

1937
   DACHAU
   THE VISIT

"Two Jews are carrying a load. So, I shoot one of the two Jews. An old rabbi asks me, 'Why did you shoot one of those two Jews carrying that load?' I tell him, "For a load that size, one Jew is enough!"

Kurt Zeller had just told this very clever joke to one of his officers, when the Mercedes-Benz W31, with the gloss-grey body and the gloss- black fenders and running-board pulled through the Dachau gate on a wet spring morning in 1937. There were only eleven such motor cars in existence, created for the highest echelon of the Nazi Party. Kurt Zeller's breakfast nosh was interrupted by the unannounced arrival of some big-wig from Berlin.

"Hurry and clean up this pig sty," Zeller snapped at his subordinates, grabbing his uniform jacket from the peg where it hung. He felt conflicted. His personal life here at the camp was easy enough, even though the number of arrivals increased each month. He had his underlings to manage day-to-day camp affairs. And, he had the freedom to indulge in the kind of sick, perverted entertainments that suited him. For a man like Zeller, authority was eros! All of that was most satisfactory, but the question loomed whether Zeller's career was on an upward trajectory. Would he forever be second or third in command at this or that post? Would he never taste the finer wine of being number one? Certainly, not Number One as in Adolf Hitler, but perhaps number one as in charge of a region or a large, dignified command post.

He tugged at his uniform jacket and placed his cap upon his head. Another visit from a Berlin hot-shot meant another day or two of obsequious bowing and scraping. One of the underlings adjusted the row of medals on Zeller's chest.

"It's probably about our bookkeeping again." Berlin was always bitching about sloppy bookkeeping. They had no idea how difficult it was to keep accurate records with so many bodies in and so many out each day. The solution to overcrowding, of course, was to keep the number of corpses equal to or in excess of the number of new prisoners arriving each day. Some days, they couldn't strip the bodies of the dead quickly enough to provide uniforms for the new arrivals.

Zeller handed his dirty coffee cup to someone who would rinse it, and let out a great sigh. There was also the matter of life in the camp being so deadly dull. One can only spend so many hours a day kicking dogs before one tires of the game. The recreation respites in Munich were not nearly long enough nor frequent enough to compensate. Was it any wonder one's sadistic tendencies emerged?

Zeller had considered becoming a family man, but the very thought of being burdened by a wife and child exhausted him. And he did enjoy the "other thing" far too much to ever give that up. And a wife and child were really only useful to parade out every now and then to show the world what an upstanding moral citizen one was. Ha! He was old and wise enough to know that all "good" men harbor sick secrets.

There would be war soon. Everyone seemed pretty certain of that, although the rest of Europe and America were conveniently closing their eyes to the knowledge. Adolf Hitler had rebuilt Germany's military might right under their noses. And the new, young warriors with their new-fangled machines of death seemed almost possessed by the gods themselves. At the recent political rally at Nuremberg, Hitler had announced that his Third Reich would last a thousand years. Who knows? Perhaps it would. Where and how did Kurt Zeller fit into all of this?

He pulled back a curtain to watch the SS motorcar pull up outside the officers' headquarters. The visitor from Berlin was driving himself, most odd. No doubt, a calculated display of humility amid the gaudy grandeur of the automobile. Was Zeller in some kind of real trouble? Was Dachau suddenly to be placed in competition with the efficiency and glamor of the newly opened Buchenwald, the current "darling of the camps." Zeller snorted. It was always something.

The door to the office opened, and in stepped SS-Oberführer Rolf Kainz.

"Heil Hitler!"

"Heil Hitler!"

He was young, so young, and so arrogant. Just thirty years old and already so important. He must have been kissing the right asses! Still, Himmler and Goebbels were only in their twenties when they began their meteoric journeys to power. Perhaps Zeller hadn't been ambitious enough. It was probably his mother's fault.

Kainz set down the large suitcase he carried, peeled off his driving gloves and tossed them, along with his cap, onto the work table. He unbuttoned his long, black, leather trench coat. "So, Zeller, the good work goes on, eh?" He completely ignored the four other officers and the young radio operator who stood at attention.

"He knows who I am…" thought Zeller as he clicked his heels and responded. "The good work, ja, Oberführer." Was knowing his name a good thing or a bad? Should Zeller be elated or apprehensive? Was this unannounced visit about Zeller?

Kainz tossed his coat over a chair and threw himself into another. "Please, Herr Kainz is sufficient. So difficult to keep track of everyone and everything these days, eh?" He pointed at the coffee pot on the hot plate, and three officers leapt into action.

"We do our best, Ober… eh…Herr Kainz."

Kainz smiled and waved a languid hand. "Oh, it's not easy, I grant you. So many deaths to deal with each day, even the latest IBM tabulating machines in Berlin can't keep up. A tragic necessity is it not?"

Zeller relaxed just a bit. "Nobody ever asks how many lives it took to build the pyramids."

Cups were filled with coffee, and the atmosphere relaxed even more. Kainz made trivial passing comments on the spring weather.

Then…

"Speaking of keeping accurate records, Karl Koch and his lovely and talented wife, Ilsa, over at Buchenwald are thus far doing a splendid job of inmate registration. I dare say, you could find a homo in a haystack over there." Kainz had an almost ridiculous laugh.

"Ja, but that IBM Hollerith machine is not available to us. We have to do everything manually."

Kainz held up a well-manicured hand. 'I am not criticizing, merely commenting. It does make it inconvenient, however, when we have to search for certain, specific prisoners."

Zeller nodded enthusiastically. "Sometimes almost impossible."

The smile on Kainz' face froze. "But, I hope not really impossible."

He reached into a pocket on the outside of the large suitcase and produced a dozen or so files which he tossed on the table. "Berlin has asked me to locate these men. I shall spend today and tomorrow doing so."

Zeller looked down at the files and began to calculate how to blame the impending fuck-up on certain of his men. "This... eh... will not be easy. We record when they come in, but not always when they go out."

The drop of fear-sweat on his nose betrayed his ingratiating smile.

Kainz froze again, the coffee cup midway between the table and his lips. He paused that way, silent. Like the silence between when a grenade is tossed and when it explodes. Then, very calmly, he said, "Well, let's hope, these particular men have not 'gone out.'" He tapped the top file.

HANS BECKER.

Zeller blinked and blinked again. He ran his finger over the identification number that followed Becker's name. He had absolutely no idea whether Becker was still alive or not. He doubted it. They had fucked him up pretty badly before

Zeller had moved on to someone younger and fresher. He glanced at the other folders. The names and numbers meant nothing to him.

"I'll want to interview these men, starting with Becker, and perhaps even take one or two of them back to Berlin."

Zeller bridled. "Oh, but that's impossible. No one leaves the camp without..."

Kainz cut him off, producing a document from inside his jacket and slapping it on the table. "Tread lightly, Herr Zeller. You could be cleaning latrines at Hitler Youth Camps tomorrow!" Then he smiled again. "Speaking of cleaning, could you have one of your boys give my Mercedes a wash?"

Zeller looked down at the letter spread open on the table before him. It was officially stamped. The handwritten message was short and simple.

"The bearer of this document has full authority

to do what must be done."

Adolf Hitler

Zeller gulped and extended one finger to touch the signature, but Kainz snatched it away. He presented Zeller with a calling card instead. "Your direct administrative superior is SS-Brigadeführer Theodor Eicke, a personal friend of mine. Here is his private number. Telephone him if you have any questions or complaints."

Never! Never in a million years would Zeller telephone Eicke. He withdrew his hand, so Kainz would not see it shake, and ordered one of the officers to attend to the Mercedes.

"Your coffee is lousy," Kainz said pleasantly.

Zeller signaled one of his officers. "Camp conditions. Perhaps you'd like a little something in it?" The officer produced a bottle.

"Well, it's a little early in the day for me, but, since I'm going to be stuck drinking this sludge, perhaps just drop or two." Kainz whipped out a cigarette from a gold case and four SS proffered flaming lighters.

Kainz puffed. "I'll need this office until tonight, perhaps even tomorrow. I trust your staff will not be too inconvenienced." The eagerly compliant Zeller shook his head so hard his teeth rattled.

"Good," Kainz continued. "You, Herr Zeller, will not be inconvenienced at all, because you will not be here. I am entrusting you to deliver this packet of classified documents and private papers to Munich. You will leave at once and travel alone. While you are there and waiting for a reply, take advantage of some of Munich's pleasures. Enjoy yourself for an evening or even two. There is a most entertaining art exhibit opening officially in July, but drop my name and you'll get a preview. It is called, 'Degenerate Art' and consists of over six-hundred and fifty banned paintings, sculpture pieces, photographs and books. It's lots of fun. You deserve to enjoy yourself a bit." He slid a stack of currency across the table.

"But, Oberführer, I wouldn't think…"

"Good. You're probably at your best that way. Now, everyone hop to it. Start with locating Herr Becker. If I find what I want, I may be out of your hair by this afternoon. If not," his bright tone darkened, "who knows?" Kainz raised one arm to stretch, twisted his wrist around and pointed at the young radio operator. "You will remain to assist me."

The young soldier snapped to attention. Kainz frowned at Zeller. "Are you still here?"

Zeller cleared his throat. "The, uh, the papers you want me to deliver to Munich?"

Kainz threw back his handsome head and laughed. "Ah, yes, silly me. Some days my head is screwed on backwards."

He slid the packet across the table. "If they fall into the wrong hands, I will personally castrate you. Deliver these to Major Strummer at SS Headquarters in Munich. Find yourself a nice hotel while you wait for the reply. Now, off you go! Pack a bag."

The room cleared except for the radio operator, salutes and "Seig Heils" all around.

CHAPTER 37

1937
DACHAU
"LIEBESTOD"

IT WAS the longest and most torturous hour of Rolf's life. And time was of the essence. Everything hinged on getting Hans safely out of the camp by early afternoon. Twice, Rolf opened the green office door to have the radio operator snap to attention. Twice Rolf asked, "Why the delay?" In his heart of hearts, Rolf feared Hans might already be dead. For the past year and a half, he had been working out this escape plan, collecting documents and papers, finding where Hans had been imprisoned, and then, using the horribly humiliating photos from Zeller's "Dachau Jew File," to forge passport photos. Rolf had sobbed when he first looked at the disgusting pictures of Hans being "measured" for Jewish traits. And all the while, the Nazi noose tightened around Germany.

Rolf paced the claustrophobic office, switched on the

radio to listen to a few seconds of "Heil Hitler Dir" which was being played endlessly, everywhere, in honor of Hitler's approaching forty-eighth birthday, switched channels to hear a bit of the American tune, "The Way You Look Tonight," and then turned the thing off. He had a knot in his stomach that was driving him crazy. This was the day. The day in which his entire life either made sense or proved useless. He'd considered suicide many times over the last few years, but dreaming of this day had kept him going, given him a reason to live.

The door opened, and Hans Becker stumbled in. Or rather the ghost of Hans Becker. Skeletally thin, his head almost a skull, overly-large eyes staring vacantly from deep, dark sockets, skin stretched perilously thin over prominent cheekbones, the lower face sunken and lax.

He shuffled more than walked into the room, his bone-thin hand automatically doffed the striped prison hat he had acquired from somewhere, revealing a patchy stubble of ashen hair.

Rolf gasped and covered his mouth with his hands. After a few seconds of internal struggle to orient himself, Hans squinted his eyes, blinked, and recognized Rolf. The bug eyes grew even larger. He made a croaking sound and promptly collapsed unconscious onto the wooden floor.

The radio operator who had ushered the prisoner in didn't know what to do. Should he kick him? Or tend to him? Or get help? He stood looking helplessly down at the body on the floor.

Rolf dove down onto one knee and scooped the frail form up into his arms. "Water! Get some water," he screamed at the radio operator. Hans groaned. The smell of death from the camp was everywhere on Hans, on his clothes, on his skin, in his hair, on his breath. Rolf cradled the skull in his lap and put the glass of water to his purple lips. "Sip the water, Hans, slowly." After a few seconds, with the water pooling on Hans' lips, he began to come around. The thick, music-less, vacuum-like silence in which he had been enduring for months began to clear slightly. He heard, not music, but breathing. His own and Rolf's. Was it Rolf? Was it really Rolf and not another illusion? The real Rolf? When they had gang-raped him, he had so often shut it out of his mind by pretending it was Rolf making beautiful love to him.

Rolf snapped at the radio operator,"Go outside and guard the door. I must question this prisoner. Let no on in, on peril of your life." The young soldier, who knew all too well what Nazi interrogation often entailed, was only too happy to return to his post outside.

The darkness in Hans' head cleared a bit more. His mind, like his body, worked infinitely more slowly these days. The big eyes blinked and blinked again.

"Hans, it's me, Rolf. It's really me. I've come to get you out of here. I've been hunting for you for a year and a half." Tears dripped from Rolf's eyes down onto the sunken features he cradled in his lap. "Everything is going to be fine, Hans, but we've got to move fast."

Hans' mind seemed to finally catch up with the moment, and seeing Rolf staring down at him, he made a terrible effort to wrench himself away. He rolled his frail body out of Rolf's arms and curled up on the floor in a fetal position. Then, in a voice that sounded like sandpaper on wood, he cried. "No! Don't look at me, Rolf. I'm too ashamed!" He buried his face in his boney hands. "I've become so ugly!"

Rolf crawled across the floor after him and covered Hans' body with his own. "No, Hans, you're beautiful. You are always beautiful! You are my Hans. My beautiful Hans.

In my whole life, I have loved only you. Only you. I'm going to get you out of here... to Paris!"

For almost thirty minutes they lay that way together, with Rolf on and wrapped around Hans. Once, there was a gentle rap at the door, and Rolf screamed, "Go away!" Then, slowly, he helped Hans into a chair. He poured him a cup of coffee. There was some cake and some fruit which Hans wolfed down like a starving animal.

"They, they stopped feeding some of us who looked like we were dying anyway..." he said by apology, scraping up the crumbs from the tabletop. "We have to survive on what we can find." He studied Rolf with his bug-eyes. He shook his head violently. "You... you should not be here. It's too dangerous. Go, Rolf, while there is still time!"

Rolf took Hans' hands. "Listen to me, Hans. I've come to get you out. I've got a plan. I'm powerful now. I'm going to drive us right out of this camp!"

Hans mouth opened and closed several times. He shook his head again. "No, no, Rolf. Sweet, naïve Rolf. No one gets out of here alive."

"You do, Hans, you do. I've been planning this for months and months. I've got clothes for you in the suitcase. I've got papers..."

Hans half choked something that almost sounded like a laugh. "That's what they said last time. That's what Winifred said. They stopped me at the border. They arrested me at the border. I can't go through that again. I'd sooner die. I'd sooner die, anyway." His look began to drift off somewhere distant. Rolf grabbed his face!

"Not this time. No one will stop you this time. You will travel as "Wilhelm Frick, personal diplomat from Adolf Hitler. You'll go to France. Paris. You'll join your family."

Hans took a deep ragged breath. "And Fritz? In Paris... Fritz?"

Rolf's eyes seemed heavy with sadness. "Yes, and Fritz. He'll take care of you."

Hans nodded like a little child. "Fritz took care of me, last time.

When you..." The words died on Hans' lips with the thought. "I'm frightened, Rolf. I'm so frightened!"

Rolf took the emaciated face in his hands, leaned in and kissed him long and deep on the lips. It was like their first kiss. Like their thousands of kisses after that. And like the dream kisses since they were apart.

"Oh, my poor, poor Hans. I'm getting you out! But you must be strong for me. Stronger than you have ever been in your life! Promise me you will do this. Do this for me!" The kisses did something. Took Hans someplace. Someplace good. Someplace where hope, battered and bruised and almost destroyed, still lived. He raised his eyebrows, what was left of them.

"Will you come, too, Rolf? Will you come, too?"

"I'll try. But first we must get you out. By tomorrow, you'll be in France. But you must hurry. Here, a shaving kit, with soap and toothpaste and shampoo. Go into the washroom and shower and shave." While he spoke, he urged Hans onto his feet and gently steered him toward the washroom.

Hans took a few hesitant steps, then stopped and turned back to Rolf. "I... I have to go back to the barracks."

Rolf became frantic. "No! Hans, please listen. We are leaving the camp. I am getting you out. Don't you understand?" Tears rolled down his face.

Hans reached up and wiped away Rolf's tears. "Ja, ja, I understand. You are my Walküre, come to carry me away on your big, grey stallion. But I must return to the barracks for a moment first, to fetch something." There was solemn resolve in his shaky words.

"Ach, mein Gott! Bitte, Hans. Nothing can be that important."

The skull smiled, showing yellowed and blackened teeth. "Oh, it is, dearest Rolf. Believe me, it is. And I won't go without it!"

"Hans, listen. Whatever this game is you are playing could cost us both our lives."

Still with that unearthly smile on his ravaged face, Hans put down the shaving kit, crossed to Rolf and placed his hands on his chest. When he spoke, it was in a whisper. "This is no game, believe me, Love. Back to the barracks, quick as Loki, and back here with the treasure. I must do this, or I can't go!" He was so sincere, and his eyes so huge and pleading that Rolf could not protest.

"Is it safe to walk through the camp?"

"Never. But I know the way."

He did, too. He moved quickly and silently from shadow to shadow, as he had learned over the past year. He traveled the narrow alleys between the barracks buildings. Twice, his mind clouded over and he stopped and stood perfectly still, lost in some dream for a few moments, but then he returned again from that dream to this one. It must all be a dream, right? To see Rolf again. To kiss him. These were often part of his every-night dreams, but to escape from Dachau with Rolf, this was something new.

An SA guard passed very close to him, and Hans melted even further into the shadow of a building. He'd huddled in these protecting shadows before to watch innocent men being slaughtered, put in cages, buried in the earth up to their necks, hung from crosses, and more. When the guard had passed, he moved on. He froze again for a moment when he heard dogs barking. Dogs that ate of the men who were treated worse than dogs. Barking and growling and chomping somewhere. He paused again at the sound of gunshots. They were often still curious but no longer startling. Who'd been shot this time? Where? Nobody, not even the soldiers, much minded gunshots anymore.

It had rained recently. A lovely spring rain, so there was the light scent of rebirth in the barracks that helped quell the stench of death and urine and feces. Except for some rattling near-corpses who hadn't risen for work today, and would probably be dead by evening, the barracks was empty and silent. Somewhere in the rafters a bird twittered, and on an ordinary day, that would have been an event. But not on this day. Not on the Day of Rolf!

Hermann was one of those near death, hanging on by just a thread. Prattling on about perhaps seeing his family again, which, of course, he never would. He talked on and on, in garbled words, in great detail, of making love to his wife. He spoke to the empty bunk above him of when he and his wife had first met, of their first shy kisses, and their first frantic love-making. There was a senseless poetic beauty to it, and whenever he could, Hans listened. Hermann's tales slipped from German to Yiddish and back again.

Hans and Hermann had become close friends, and it was Hermann who taught Hans much about what it meant to be a Jew. They had kept each other alive, and sometimes slept with their bodies wrapped around each other. Now Hermann was dying, and who knows, perhaps Hans was dying, too. He could not believe that the escape would work, but he would go through with it for dear Rolf, who had risked everything for him. He approached Hermann's bunk across from his own.

"Hermann. Hermann, meine zeeskeit," Hans whispered sitting on the old man's bunk.

The washed-out eyes opened, and the sunken face brightened. "Shefele... is it evening already? You just left. Did you find some food? You eat it, I'm not so very hungry today." He lay bent and broken on his bunk, his limbs no thicker than broom handles.

"Listen, Hermann. I have news. Rolf has come for me. He's going to try to get me out. It won't work of course, but I'll go through the motions for his sake. I'll probably die."

The old man's dry voice rattled with a chuckle. 'I'll race you to the grave."

"Imagine, Rolf risking everything for me." It was magical, mystical.

Hermann's throat rattled harder. Hans found that he had a bit of saliva in his mouth from the fruit he had eaten, so he passed it down into Hermann's mouth. The old man smacked his thin blue lips together and sank into a peaceful half-slumber. Hans crossed the narrow aisle and climbed up to his own top bunk. The climb had become more difficult in recent months. Top bunks were for strong men who were still alive. He carefully slid aside the loose piece of wood and removed the gold ring which he kept wrapped in a bit of cloth. He looked at it lovingly for a moment, kissed it, and slid it on his finger. Of course, it was far too big for that boney digit, so he ended up putting it on his next finger like a wedding ring. Even there, it was a bit too large.

He was climbing down from the bunk when a harsh, sibilant voice cut through the rattles of death and the birdsong. "What the fuck are you doing? There is something nasty going on here!" It was Zeller, pointing his luger at Hans. "I knew something was not right about all of this. Now, speak! Tell me, faggot, or I'll blow your head off."

In the dark of the building, in his black uniform, only the silver of his buckles and his medals shone. And his eyes. Red, fiery eyes of a wolf.

Hans tucked his fingers with the ring into his fist, but otherwise froze. To move when a Nazi spoke to you could mean instant death. No provocation was required. It was a shame that Zeller would kill him now. Hans wanted badly to see how this latest dream with Rolf would end.

"Why does Oberführer Kainz want to see you, of all people?" The gun shook, making it even more dangerous. "Does it have something to do with me?" The voice was more than strident, it was shrill! Hans realized that Zeller was as much a prisoner of this distorted world as he was.

Hans shook his head. "Don't be so vain. It has nothing to do with you. You are not part of our world."

Zeller laughed, but it was a strained, painful laugh. "Your world? You forget what I forced you to do. I made you copulate with dogs! You dirty, Jew bitch!" But as he squeezed the trigger of the luger, a filthy, half-naked old man rose up before him specter-like and heaved himself at the Nazi. Zeller tripped sideways and fell to the floor. Hermann, who could no longer control his movements, lay atop him, flapping his spindly arms and legs.

"GET OFF ME, YOU FILTHY, STINKING PIECE OF..." Somehow, Herman's flailing hand had gotten hold of the luger, which he now shoved into Zeller's open mouth. There was a muffled "thud" and the bullet ricocheted around in the Nazi's skull. Silence again. The singing bird seemed to approve.

Hans stared down. "Mein Gott, we killed him. What will happen now?" They waited to see if anyone would respond to the gunshot. No one did.

Hermann could hardly move but managed to roll off the

dead body. He looked up at Hans with an almost ecstatic smile on his withered face. "We'll stuff him down the shithole," he said with a simple certainty. "They won't find him for months."

There were rows of wooden planks with holes cut in them that served as toilets. They were so filthy that most inmates just squatted and shat outside. Beneath the wooden planks were deep pits. When the pits became too clogged with waste, they were filled in and new pits were dug. The latrine pit would deservedly be Zeller's final resting place. After disposing of the Nazi, Hans dragged Hermann back to his bunk.

"Go, Hans, hurry, meine khaver. Go, follow your dream!"

"I'm sorry. I'm sorry to leave you."

The withered hand waved, and then pointed one finger. "Don't be sorry. I dumped a Nazi down a pit of shit. Who could ask for anything more?"

Hans stumbled back into the officers' building looking a bit crazed, but somehow more full of life.

"Jesus, I thought I'd never see you again," cried Rolf, hugging the frail, Jewish former Bayreuth opera tenor. Hans actually glowed. The pale, almost translucent skin seemed to light from within.

"Look!" he rasped. He held up the golden ring. "They never got it. No one ever got it. You were with me all this time."

"You mad dreamer. You crazy, wonderful, mad dreamer." They stood enveloped in each other's arms for a moment. Rolf urged Hans toward the washroom. Hans got to the doorway, then turned. "Oh ja, we killed Zeller. We shot him in the face and tossed him down the shithole."

"Now we really must hurry. Please, wash and shave, my darling."

CHAPTER 38

1937

    DACHAU, THE BAVARIAN WOODS
    "LIEBESTOD" PART TWO

HANS WAS TOO weak to do much by himself, so Rolf washed and shaved him. The soap and shampoo had a wonderful smell, and Hans could have stayed there all day. Once, looking in the mirror, he mentally drifted away, and Rolf feared he had lost him.

"Hans. Hans!" Rolf prompted with no results. His lover simply stood transfixed by the stranger in the mirror. "Please, Hans!" In desperation, Rolf began to sing;

> "You are my heart's delight
> And where you are I long to be.
> You make my darkness bright
> When star-like you shine on me."

Slowly, Hans returned to the present. He looked at Rolf in the mirror and whispered, "Vienna."

Showered, shampooed and shaved, with freshly brushed teeth, Hans did indeed look like a new man. Still ghastly thin, the clothes hung on him like a marionette's costume. He stood there, stupidly awkward, the baggy pants synched at the waist by a belt in which Rolf had made extra holes, the shirt cuffs over his fingers.

"It'll be fine. Under the trench coat, it'll be fine. You'll be singing again in no time. You'll be the star of Paris." He handed Hans a bit of chocolate. He had to be careful how much he allowed him to eat. Too much food too soon, could kill him. Minute by minute, Hans seemed to improve.

"You think I'll sing again?" he asked like a child as Rolf tied his necktie.

"Of course, you'll sing again. Better than ever. There, you look like a new man. As I said, the trench coat will hide a lot."

"There's not a lot to hide."

Rolf stared into the big, nervously twitching eyes. "Hey, was that a joke? Did you just make a joke, Opera Boy?" He kissed Hans tenderly, all the while more frightened than he had ever been in his life. Frightened of the plan and also frightened of Hans' fragility.

They packed up carefully, and Rolf called for his car. He messed with the radio and telephone connections just enough to confuse anyone trying to use them, but not enough to draw obvious attention.

He led Hans, bundled in trench coat and slouch hat, and wearing handcuffs, out to the grey Mercedes. He helped Hans into the rear seat. "I'm taking this man to Berlin. He may be innocent. We've made a terrible mistake arresting him."

"You'll need a guard," the radio operator said. "There is an SS training camp at the other end of the compound. We can get you an escort from there."

"He's been guarded enough for sixteen months," snapped Rolf. "Sometimes even the Reich makes mistakes." And then to restore calm, "Could you dash over to the canteen and make up a small but nice picnic lunch for us?"

"Shouldn't we go?" Hans whispered, slouching in his slouch hat and coat, trying to hide his face.

"It is important we show calm and control in front of them. We'll be through those gates before you know it."

Once again, some officer insisted that Rolf have an armed guard accompany him, and once again, Rolf flashed the handwritten letter from Adolf Hitler. "Call him! Call the Führer! Or call Eicke! I insist."

Shortly after noon, the big, grey stallion designed especially for the Nazi elite pulled through the camp gates with Hans Becker seated in the rear like a highly respected German diplomat, and Obeführer Rolf Kainz driving. As a departing gift for them, the Nazi's at the camp had packed a lovely, picnic lunch of bread, sausage, cheese, olives, fruit and wine. Rolf did not drive toward Berlin or Munich. He drove through the woods, up into the mountains. A short way from Dachau, he moved Hans up into the front seat next to him and removed the handcuffs. Hans only took his eyes from Rolf long enough to take in the majestic scenery he'd thought he would never see again. Fields and streams, mountains and forests, such green, breathtaking beauty.

"You'll catch the evening train for Paris from an out of the way station. I've booked a private compartment for you as befits a diplomat."

Hans removed his hat and opened his trench coat in which he was drowning from heat. "It won't work, Rolf.

Let's just park the motorcar by the side of the road in the forest and sit together for a while. That will make me happy."

Rolf shook his head. "Dream bigger, Opera Boy. You are going to Paris. You're an emissary for Adolf Hitler and your papers are in order. No one dares challenge you."

"We'll see."

They did stop for thirty minutes to picnic. They sat in the spring sunlight and soaked up each other, accompanied by joyous bird song. They even spotted the rare blue-winged teal.

"Your watch?" Rolf asked.

"They took it the first day."

Rolf removed his own Rolex and put it around Hans' wrist. "You'll grow into it," he said with a smile. "Oh, by the way, there is a shitload of cash in the briefcase. Best transfer it to your breast pocket. I know you only like first-class accommodations."

Hans looked wistful. "Like our little apartment in Berlin."

Rolf nodded, his eyes filled with tears. "The finest apartment in the whole world." He stroked Hans' face. "Do you remember how we lived in bed?"

"It was those memories that kept me alive. I must have bored you, singing to you all the time."

"No, no, on the contrary, never enough. You are my own personal Meistersinger. You sang with such genius, even then."

Hans pondered for a moment. "If there was any genius in my singing, it was because as Mozart said, 'Love is the soul of genius!'"

And for a few moments, time kindly stood still for them.

They drove into the dusk and then the into the blessed

night. Between shifting gears, Rolf never let go of Hans' hand, and his fingers never ceased caressing and stroking.

Hans had considered asking Rolf who and what he had become in the Nazi Party, and how he could live with it, but he decided not to. Instead, he concentrated on Rolf being there, with him. And he began to speak Tristan's words in the great Act Two love scene, perhaps the greatest love scene ever written, with the possible exception of "Romeo and Juliet."

> "Oh, now we are night consecrated.!
> Malevolent day filled with envy,
> Though it parted us through fraud,
> Can trick us no more with its lies."

He was silent for a few moments, staring at Rolf. Then,

> "Holy night, where forever
> Solely true,
> Love and rapture awaits."

"It won't be long now. The station is only a few minutes ahead."

Hans tightened his grip. "I won't go without you, you know. I'd just as soon die."

"'I must be gone and live, or stay and die!' Don't be silly, Hans.

This is a journey you must make alone, at least for now. Look at us. As far apart as two people can be, and yet forever closer than most. It's our destinies, Hans. That's why you must sing again. To give my life meaning."

There were lights up ahead. A small railway station nestled in the mountains, its only distinction a large, Swiss clock with Roman numerals. Rolf pulled his car into the parking area, and the few passengers waiting for the train stepped back in awe of the automobile. Out of nowhere, two SS officers stepped up to the Mercedes.

"Here goes nothing, my love! Be strong, and remember always, I love you more than life!" Rolf stepped from the car, and the two SS saluted.

"Heil Hitler. May we assist you, Oberführer?"

"No, thank you. I am just conducting a German diplomat to the train." He moved around to open Hans' door for him.

"If we can help you in any way, let us know." They clicked their heels.

The evening was quiet and beautiful. A radio in the station played Bavarian music. People on the platform chatted quietly among themselves. Clutching his briefcase, Hans sat on a bench with Rolf next to him. "The train will be along any minute now. Just remain calm."

"I didn't kiss you goodbye. I should have kissed you more in the car. I don't want to go." Hans almost reached for Rolf, but held back.

"You prefer Dachau?"

"Honestly, Rolf, I don't think I can do this."

"You can. You must. Remember your Greek plays, Hans. Remember your Euripides. "Nothing has more strength than dire necessity!"

Strange, to long for a train to arrive and to fear its arrival almost as much. The sound, so faint at first, like something in your imagination. Then, like the buzzing of a bee in your ear, then growing into the infernal repetition of the wheels clacking on the tracks and the heaving of the engine. The light growing brighter and brighter. The dozen or so passengers moving together on the platform. The stationmaster holding them back, as steam clouds the light. The train had arrived.

They stood, looking awkwardly at each other. Rolf put his hand on Hans' arm. "We'll shake hands here. Walk ahead of me to the train and board. Do not look back. And remember, every time you sing, my love, think of me."

He would sing again, he told himself, walking stiffly toward the steam and whistles. He would not look back. Like Orpheus, it might damn him forever. Someday, Rolf would join him. They were meant to be together. He was the last to mount the steps of his train car. He felt the rattle and heard the hiss. He must look back, if only to see him one last time. He could not resist. And so, as the train moved, as the engine at the front already disappeared into the dark night, and the regular clacking of the wheels created an eerie musical soundtrack, Hans decided to turn, to look back. To wave one last time or perhaps even blow a kiss. He knew from his experiences that something so little can mean everything. He turned. The platform was empty. Rolf had gone.

He removed his hat and coat and set them neatly on the seat across form him in his private compartment. He sat very still, with his hands pressed between his knees, waiting to be arrested. Waiting to be taken off the train. But that did not happen.

When the attendant came around, Hans allowed himself a cup of coffee and a pastry. Just one, more would have made him sick. By the third bite, his sense of taste, which had been mostly absent until then, began to return. And his sense of smell. Things no longer smelled quite so much of death. These senses didn't return completely, of course, that would take time, but enough to alert him to the fact that he was not dead. The pastry made him feel full, fat even, and for some reason that seemed terribly funny. He thought of Rolf's hand, holding his tightly in the car, and he looked down at the ring which shone brightly.

At the border, they never even entered his compartment, but stood respectfully outside. He handed over certain documents. "The bearer of this document has full authority to do what must be done." Adolf Hitler

Outside the train compartment window, the morning sun lit up the French countryside. It caused Hans to think of Rolf. Not the black-uniformed SS Rolf, but the free-spirited, wild, young Rolf who had kissed him in the rain one early morning outside the Eldorado Club. Of the Rolf who slept all night with his lips pressed against Hans and his strong, young body forged against him. Of a Rolf who, like Hans, had been kidnapped by love and held ransom for life.

The click and clack of the train wheels played the last moments of "Tristan and Isolde" and Hans once again heard music in his head. Hans would sing again. He knew that now. He did not know where or when, but he would sing again. And he would sing the truths he now understood about love. That love is stronger than life and death. That love is eternal!

THE END

AUTHOR'S NOTES

Author's Notes

The people, places and events of my novel are for the most part real. The restaurants, nightclubs, theaters, inns and offices, with a few exceptions, all existed. The two young men and their families at the heart of the book are creations of my imagination, although based on the stories I discovered of a number of real people. I labored to keep historical events in their proper place and time, but did take a few important liberties. Dedicated Wagnerites will search in vain for details of a 1929 Bayreuth season because there was none. It was one of their "dark" years. I created it to keep events in my story moving along. I also took liberties with which of Wagner's operas were presented during which season, to allow me to explore the works and the festival and to allow my characters to act within them. While Kurt Zeller never existed, I found, to my horror during my research, many like him. Too many like him. In our own country, today, we must ask how ordinary men turn into monsters, and how does a good society grant them the power?

The rest of the major Nazi characters were real people, as were the inhabitants of the Bayreuth world with the exception of Wolf. A concert performance for Hitler did actually take place at Neuschwanstein Castle, although I moved the date forward just a bit. Hunding's Hut in the Bavarian forest was demolished in the 1940's, but sketches and drawings still exist. The notorious Eldorado Club was indeed raided and closed by the SA, many who had previously been customers, and the staff and patrons beaten and arrested. Some were black-mailed by members of the SA. Erich Kleiber moved his family to Buenos Aires and continued to conduct all over the world. Max Lorenz faced difficulties with the Nazis as their anti-Jewish and anti-homosexual programs expanded. At one point, while he was away, Nazis raided his home, and his Jewish wife and mother-in-law were arrested. Lotte Lorenz bravely informed the arresting soldiers that they were under the personal protection of Winifred Wagner and Adolf Hitler, and the Nazis backed off. Max went on to have a stellar opera career around the globe. As the war approached, and the Nazi policy toward the Jews turned to one of mass extermination, Dachau became an even greater nightmare than the place described in my novel. The distinction between the artist and the art is a delicate issue. There are many today who hunt for the flaws in the lives of artists and then wish to cancel the art they created. If we were to cancel the art of all terribly flawed artists, we would have to abandon the Mona Lisa, the ceiling of the Sistine Chapel, and the works of Cellini, Caravaggio, Botticelli, Mozart, Tchaikovsky, Pound, Gide, Byron, Wilde, Wagner and countless others. In fact, almost no great art would exist at all. Flaws are part of the human condition and are a part of all of us. Some of us are more flawed than others but, like diamonds we all have many facets. Extremely flawed people can create wonderful things, and we are, all of us, both Jekyll and Hyde.

I wish to thank my dear, old friends Sandy, Jimmy, Patrick, Piya, Marilyn, Bobby, David, Larry, Mike and my editorial Goddess, and my new friends, too, including Paul, for stimulating my interest in life and what makes us who we are. Remember there is no difference between someone who does not read and someone who cannot read!

ABOUT THE AUTHOR

D.H. Gutzman is a novelist, playwright, and theater director. He was twice named "Director of the Year" by Theatre Week Magazine. He was appointed Associate Director of the Odessa Russian Drama Theater in Odessa, Ukraine. He has written for "The Sondheim Review." For ten years, he worked in Thailand, directing theater works for the Royal Family and the Bangkok Symphony Orchestra. He has also written a multi-media piece performed by Neil Diamond. Several of his original plays have been performed around the world. His novels are an attempt to bring to popular culture a greater awareness of the contribution of important gay artists in history.